"Sweet Tea

Le Doux Mysteries #4
By Abigail Lynn Thornton

SWEET TEA AND MURDER

First edition. February 8, 2022.

Copyright © 2022 Abigail Lynn Thornton.

ISBN: 979-8201399580

Written by Abigail Lynn Thornton.

DEDICATION

To my little Beta Reader.
May all your book dreams come true.

ACKNOWLEDGEMENTS

No author works alone. Thank you, Cathy.
Your cover work is beautiful!
And to Laura, for your timely and thorough editing!

NEWSLETTER

Stay up to date on all my new releases by joining my newsletter!
You can find it and other exciting news at
abigailthorntonbooks.com

CHAPTER 1

Sweat poured down Wynona's neck and soaked the edge of her T-shirt, but still, she forced herself to keep going.

Don't give up now! Violet cried, her voice almost ruining Wynona's concentration.

"I'm trying," Wynona said through gritted teeth. Her hand was outstretched, the fingers wide as she attempted to lift her Vespa from one end of the yard to the other.

For any other adult witch, this would be simple. But for Wynona, whose powers had been bound until just recently, she was having to start from scratch. Gaining her familiar, a purple mouse named Violet, had gone a long way in helping Wynona learn to reach her burgeoning powers, but controlling them was another matter.

The scooter wobbled and Wynona heard Prim, her best friend, gasp in concern. Wynona shook her head, ignoring the pain behind her eyelids, and tried to maintain the steady flow of magic. Too much would send the Vespa careening across the yard, breaking the line of trees in the Grove of Secrets. Too little would have it crashing to the ground, more than likely giving the gathered audience a nice bonfire and ruining Wynona's only mode of transportation.

No pressure.

Her hand began to shake and Wynona finally closed her eyes, doing her best to conserve energy. Using magic was like any other muscle. Paranormals had smaller amounts when they were children and with repeated use, those muscles grew, accommodating greater amounts of magic as they grew up. However, if someone got their powers most at the same time and in the amount of an ultra powerful witch...there seemed to be complications. Such as exploding objects, broken pottery and endangering friends.

Just a little farther...

Wynona's entire body was now shaking. The amount of sweat soaking her shirt was the least of her worries if her knees buckled. Working with her magic was like trying to control a waterfall. She couldn't throw the whole amount at the object, but holding back the power to slightly more than a trickle was beyond difficult.

"I can't," Wynona bit out.

Don't you dare stop! Violet scolded.

"I'm going to drop it!" Panic laced Wynona's voice and she felt her body respond. She stumbled slightly and her eyes popped open, seeing the Vespa drop a few inches.

Wynona Angelique Le Doux! Get your head together!

Wynona closed her eyes again, ducking her head and refocusing all of her powers. She could do this. She *could* do this. Le Douxs did hard things. Especially her.

Now ease it down, Violet purred, a smirky type of satisfaction in her voice, as if she had been the one to perform the magical act instead of Wynona.

The Vespa finally hit the ground, a little harder than Wynona had intended, but softly enough she was reasonably sure there was no actual damage.

"Whoo hoo!" Prim shouted, raising her fists in the air. "You rock!"

Wynona could barely get her eyes open and when her knees shifted, she allowed herself to crumple to the ground, gasping in large quantities of air. A light breeze began to caress her face and Wynona cracked an eyelid to see a large bush fanning her. Her open eye found Prim's satisfied smile and Wynona gave a weak one in return.

The ground vibrated ever so slightly as heavy footsteps came toward her. Wynona didn't bother to look up. She knew exactly who had stopped by her side. "Hey, pretty lady," came Rascal's concerned voice. "Are you doing okay?"

"Well, I'm drenched in my own sweat, I can't lift any of my limbs, my head is about to explode and I'm being fanned by a plant. All in all, I think it's a pretty good day."

He chuckled, the sound deep and rumbling. It sent a thrill through Wynona and she wished she had enough energy to ask for a kiss.

She never would have guessed when she escaped from her parents' castle that befriending a wingless fairy, getting her magic, finding out a purple mouse was her familiar and dating a werewolf was in her future, but Wynona knew she would never want to change the direction her life had gone either.

Even though that direction included her helping solve several murders alongside the police, which is where she had met Rascal. He was the Deputy Chief of the Hex Haven Police, second only to Chief Ligurio, a grumpy vampire who had an on-again, off-again friendship with Wynona.

"Want me to carry you inside?" he asked, using the back of his fingers to lightly trace her cheek bone.

A new kind of shiver ran through Wynona and she finally pried her eyes fully open. Rascal's glorious golden orbs were smiling at her, and Wynona, tired as she was, smiled back. "Thank you, but I can do it." She started to push her body to rise, but when her arms shook like a newborn fawn's, she collapsed back down. "Just give me a minute to catch my breath." She sighed in disgust with herself, then jolted. "Oh!"

"I've got ya," Rascal said, holding her close to his chest.

Wynona wanted to protest, but the words died on her lips. Really, this wasn't too bad. Strong arms, warm chest, and a contented rumbling sound were enough to have her burrowing in for the long haul.

"Let me get that," Prim called from behind them.

Frowning, Wynona glanced at her friend, then at her house to see a vine reach out and open the doorknob so Rascal could walk inside. Ah...so that's what Prim was referring to. Wynona gave her fairy friend a little wave, then settled her head back on Rascal's shoulder.

After walking through the small house into the family room, Rascal eased Wynona onto the couch. "Hang on," he said. Reaching over to one of the armchairs, he grabbed an afghan, then settled it over her lap. "Better?"

Wynona grabbed his hand and gave a squeeze. "Thank you," she said softly.

Rascal winked, one of his favorite flirtation tactics, and straightened, looking to the other side of the room. "Prim? You want to make her some tea?"

"On it." Prim's pink hair came darting back into the room. "What kind, Nona?"

Wynona closed her eyes and focused for a moment. "Green tea and lemon verbena," she said thoughtfully. This was a magic that Wynona could do in her sleep. In fact, her ability to know what tea people needed most was something she had been doing before her magic had been freed. Her wide, dark eyes popped open. "With a hint of jasmine!" she called out.

"Okay," Prim called as she ducked into the kitchen.

Rascal chuckled as they heard the fairy mumbling something about the order being oddly specific, but Wynona didn't change her mind. She didn't trust herself not to drop her Vespa, but in this, Wynona was sure. She would feel a lot better after sipping the healing brew.

Rascal seated himself next to her. "You're making progress," he encouraged.

Wynona blew out a breath and let her head rest on the back of the couch. "It doesn't feel like it." She pouted. "Moving a scooter like that should be child's play."

Rascal snorted. "Only a crazy strong child, and still. The fact that you didn't blow it up or drop it says your control is growing." He tucked a piece of hair behind her ear.

Wynona's black curls sometimes grew a little unruly, and with the workout she had just endured, she could only imagine what she must look like. A tiny shiver ran up her spine from Rascal's touch. He always seemed to have that effect on her. The simplest touch was enough to leave her weak in the knees and yet, Wynona could never quite get enough of him.

Perhaps it had something to do with the fact that he was her first real boyfriend, but she sincerely hoped not. Growing up as the dirty little secret of the presidential Le Doux family had been a lonely existence, but Wynona liked to think she was a little more mature than a teenage girl who fell for the first boy to smile at her.

"Thanks," she said breathlessly, in response to Rascal's compliment. "But I couldn't do this alone." She frowned momentarily and looked around. "Where did Violet go?"

"Said she was starving," Rascal replied with a grin. "She went to get something to eat."

Wynona pinched her lips between her teeth, trying to puzzle some things out in her brain. "You really can communicate with her?"

Rascal shrugged and turned so his back was against the couch, not facing Wynona head on. "Most of the time." His eyes glanced at her. "It's gotten a lot clearer since you two connected your magic."

Wynona sat in stunned silence. Once upon a time she had thought she knew a lot about magic, but now that her curse was fading and her own magic emerging, she was discovering a large difference between textbooks and real life.

It had never occurred to Wynona that Violet was her familiar until Rascal had pointed it out. And while it might just be an outsider's perspective, it had made Wynona feel inadequate. She didn't blame Rascal. She mostly blamed her family, who kept Wynona in the dark, both literally and figuratively, about everything having to do with the magical community at large.

If they had had their way, she never would have stepped foot outside the castle, but Granny Saffron, bless her soul, had somehow known it was her time to pass on and had set Wynona up to escape her family on the Spring Equinox, the very night Granny died.

In order to honor the only relative who had shown Wynona any love, Wynona had named her tea shop after her grandmother and used the herbal skills that she had been taught in order to serve custom teas to happy customers.

Friends like Primrose, Rascal, Violet and a few others were just icing on the cake of a simple but happy life.

"I *might* have filled the cup a little too full," Prim said with a sheepish grin as she handed the cup and saucer to Wynona.

Wynona laughed softly and took the offering. "Thanks," she replied. Being extremely careful, she brought the brew up and took a long inhale. "Ahhh..." Prim had put just a touch too much jasmine in it, but it would be alright. Even from the smell, Wynona could feel the healing properties begin to hum in her system. She dared a sip, but pulled back when it scalded her tongue.

Eager, are we?

Wynona turned to see Violet looking smug by the fireplace. Ever since the tiny creature linked with Wynona and could be heard in the witch's mind, Violet had taken to sharing every sarcastic thought she had. Evidently, being a mouse had held the animal back from a job in stand up comedy. "Wouldn't you be?" Wynona asked out loud, earning her a weird look from Prim. "It took everything I had not to crush my scooter. I think I earned this cup."

Violet rolled her eyes as if Wynona were the prima donna, which was not the case. The purple mouse sniffed and rubbed at her nose. *You're getting better, I'll admit,* she reluctantly admitted. *But we still have a long way to go.*

"Don't I know it," Wynona mumbled into her teacup, daring another sip. It was still slightly too hot, but it felt good going down Wynona's throat. Now that she knew what to look for, Wynona could feel the subtle hint of magic tingling through her body. She closed her eyes and let herself just feel for a moment.

Rascal chuckled, shaking the couch slightly. "Feel better?"

Wynona cracked an eye open and gave him a playful glare. "Maybe."

He reached over and wrapped his fingers over hers, slowly pulling the cup toward him. His eyes never left Wynona's and she felt an electric charge hit her when they began to glow. It was a dead giveaway that his wolf was close to the surface. Once the cup was at his mouth, Rascal took a sip, then jerked back and made a face, his nose crinkling as his tongue scraped against his teeth.

Wynona and Prim burst out laughing. Even Violet snickered from her place across the room.

"That's what you get for trying to be *sexy*," Prim said through her laughter.

"Keep laughing," Rascal argued. He pointed to the tea. "But you're the one who made that poison."

Wynona took another sip while she smiled. "This wasn't meant for you," she said in a teasing tone.

Rascal stopped trying to get the taste out of his mouth and cocked his head to the side. "Are you saying tea tastes bad if the wrong person drinks it?"

Wynona shrugged. "A custom tea probably does." She frowned slightly. "Are you feeling under the weather? Do you need a pick me up?" She felt his forehead. As a shifter, his skin always ran hot, but how hot was too hot?

Rascal grabbed her hand and brought it down, kissing her palm. "I'm fine. You just seemed to be enjoying yourself so much, I thought I'd give it a try." He made a face. "Apparently, that was the wrong thing to do."

Wynona took another sip, her left hand still in Rascal's grip. "Sorry. I could make you something," she offered.

He shook his head. "Nope." Dropping her hand, he slapped his thighs. "I actually need to get to work." Standing, Rascal waved at everyone in the room. "I'll see you all later."

Wynona tilted up her face as he leaned down for a quick goodbye kiss. "Dinner tonight?" she asked, allowing herself to get lost in his golden orbs.

"Will there be dessert?" His lips twitched.

"I'm sure I can get Gnuq and Kyoz to—" Rascal cut her off with another kiss.

He straightened and winked. "See you at seven."

Wynona's eyes were glued to his back as he sauntered out of the small home.

"You do realize he wasn't talking about tea pastries?" Prim said wryly.

Wynona forced her eyes over to her best friend. "Hm?"

Prim rolled her eyes. "You're so far gone you can't even come up for air," she said dramatically.

Wynona laughed softly and played with her teacup. "Sorry. I'll try to tone it down."

"Don't you dare," Prim scolded. "I have to live vicariously through someone."

Wynona just smiled and sipped at her tea some more. "Your time will come."

Prim rolled her eyes again. "We'll see." She sniffed. "If I can find a guy who can handle my Venus Fly Trap, then we'll start taking things seriously."

Giggles from the two women bounced around the room as they settled in for a break and a nice chat. It was Wynona's favorite type of morning. Good tea, good friends and good conversation. What more could she ask for?

CHAPTER 2

"Green tea with orange peel for you," Wynona said as she set a cup and saucer in front of a young fairy. "And jasmine with a hint of rose petal for you," Wynona said, setting another cup in front of the fairy's mother. "Enjoy!"

"It smells wonderful," the mother said, leaning down to catch a whiff.

Wynona paused to smile her thanks. "We do our best. Thank you so much for your patronage." The mother and teenage daughter team had been in several times before, though their appearances weren't regularly scheduled.

She had noticed because the two seemed close and it made Wynona slightly envious. How she wished her mother had taken the time to share tea time with her growing up.

But Granny did.

Wynona always ended up pushing the thoughts away. Granny Saffron had done all she could and that had included many tea times over the years. Wynona knew it was time to be grateful for what she did have, rather than dwelling on what she wished had been.

"It's no wonder you've opened a second location," the mother continued. "It's always so busy in here, I can imagine that your business is growing by leaps and bounds."

Wynona's black eyebrows shot up. "A second location?"

The teenager's bright green eyes widened in excitement. "Yes! We haven't visited your new one yet, but heard about it just yesterday." She popped a bite of pastry in her mouth. "Will you be using the same bakery for that one? I love these cakes."

Wynona opened her mouth to respond, but wasn't quite sure what to say. She hadn't opened a second location and knew nothing about another tea house. Before she could press further, however, the front door slammed.

"NONA!"

Wynona jumped, along with several of her patrons, when Prim came racing through the entryway, causing a few to murmur and complain.

"Prim," Wynona said, putting out her hands to stop her friend.

"You have to see this," Prim said, still talking loudly. She was breathing heavily and her skin was flushed an unhealthy shade of red. She held up a tablet, but Wynona shook her head.

She turned to the room. "Excuse me," she said, grabbing Prim by the arm and hauling her toward the kitchen. When they were inside, she let go and Prim rubbed her limb with a scowl. Wynona immediately felt bad. "I'm sorry. Did I hurt you?"

"No." Prim pouted. "I just don't like being manhandled."

"Well, I'm a woman, so..." Wynona gave her friend a look. "What in the world has got you disrupting my dining room like this?"

Prim rolled her eyes and handed the tablet up to Wynona. She was still in her fairy form, which made her only waist-high. That in and of itself should have given Wynona worry. Without wings, Prim rarely spent time in fairy form. She preferred to feel like she was on even ground with the people around her and since she couldn't fly, being human-sized was the best she could do.

Wynona took the device and began to scan the screen. "What is this?" she asked. The headline was talking about a new tea house location. But the weird thing was, it looked an awful lot like Wynona's. The decoration on the outside of the building was almost an exact copy, right down to the yellow front door.

Prim poofed into her larger body and pointed to the screen. "Some idiot named Alavara Theramin opened a tea shop on the other side of town."

"Alavara..." Wynona thought hard. "I know her! She's an elf. She's been in here a few times."

A grunt interrupted the two women and they turned to see Lusgu, Wynona's brownie janitor, waiting behind them. Without speaking, he made a motion that the women were in his way and Wynona quickly scrambled to the side. She had learned not to get between Lusgu and whatever he was working on. His magic was strong and she knew she had only seen glimpses of it.

Once Prim had followed, Lusgu huffed and shuffled forward, his suspenders and bowtie at odds with the dirty feet he always wore. A broom swept diligently behind him, cleaning what appeared to be an already spotless floor.

Odd as he was, her shop was always spic and span, so Wynona didn't complain...too much.

Both women watched him go by before going back to their conversation. Prim's bright orange nail landed on the screen again. "Did you see the name of her shop?"

Wynona scanned the article, then stiffened. "Saffron's House of Tea? Are you kidding me?"

Prim snorted. "The stupid ghost reporters seem to think this is a second location for you. Nobody has put together that this is a completely different business. One that's horning in on your reputation and patrons."

Wynona frowned and began to read the article in earnest. It was a little strange. Alavara, an elf, opening a tea shop that was so similar to Wynona's. She even offered custom teas. But the couple of times Wynona had met the woman, she had never mentioned a talent for tea or even anything beyond a normal interest. "I don't understand,"

Wynona said, handing the tablet back. "Why would she try to recreate my shop?"

"Money," Prim said curtly. "Plain and simple. She's creating a knockoff of your shop, trying to swing your business her way."

"It's not like I'm some big, wealthy celebrity worth emulating."

Prim groaned and threw her head back. "You're the president's daughter," she said as if talking to a young child. "You're beautiful, you're a successful business woman and you have a talent with tea that makes everyone who comes in here walk out with a wide smile on their face. *Of course*, she would want in on that. It's a guaranteed hit."

"It's not if she can't actually magic the teas the same way I do," Wynona retorted. She shook her head, pushing back the unease trying to slither down her spine. "It'll be fine."

"Nona," Prim said sharply. "We've got to take this seriously." She put her hands on her hips. "This lady is trying to run you out of business."

"That's ridiculous," Wynona scoffed. "People will be able to tell the difference between us. She can copy all she wants, but none of my regulars will be deceived." She chose to ignore the fact that the fairy family had already said they planned to give it a try. Wynona just couldn't imagine that Miss Theramin could do exactly the same thing with teas that Wynona could.

She wasn't trying to be egotistical, but Wynona knew that she was good with her herbs. Granny Saffron had taught her well, and even with a curse that kept her from accessing her magic, Wynona had always been able to "feel" exactly what tea someone needed when they entered her shop.

In fact, she hadn't even realized it was magic at all until one of her friends, Officer Skymaw, who worked with Rascal, had pointed out what she was doing. As a black hole, he could see when magic was in use and he had detected it when Wynona brewed her tea, as well as residual magic in her teacups, which she collected from antique shops. Apparently, she not only had been using magic she shouldn't have been able to, but she also was drawn to magical objects.

It was just another mystery in Wynona's journey to discovering her abilities. She had been cursed as a baby and had grown up without any magic at all. The person who cursed her had never been caught and her family, the ruling presidential family of Hex Haven, had swept Wynona under the rug as an embarrassment. In a world where magical power led to political power, the Le Doux's were the top of the food chain.

Wynona, however, was not. Having nothing to add to the family coffers, she was considered useless. Which was exactly why Granny Saffron had taken such pains to help Wynona escape in order to live her own life.

The irony was that *after* leaving, Wynona had actually begun to discover her own magic, which she now was slowly learning to control. The task was made trickier, however, since she was doing her best to hide her newfound talents from the public in general. If her family ever caught wind of the fact that Wynona's curse had broken, she was afraid they would come for her, and she had no intention of leaving the wonderful life she had built. Copycat tea house, or no.

"Even the ghost reporters didn't know it wasn't your business," Prim tried to argue. "It doesn't look like that elf lady is doing anything to clear up the assumption." Prim growled. "I'll bet she's counting on people coming simply because they think it's yours."

The back door opened and a floating line of trays began to filter into the kitchen. "Thorns and thistles," Prim grumbled under her breath.

Wynona bit her lips between her teeth. Gnuq and Kyoz, her baking imps, normally delivered their goods early in the morning, but today they had been running behind and were just now bringing the fresh pastries for the day. Gnuq, much to Wynona's amusement, had a crush on Prim, who had no interest in the tiny imp.

A squeak announced the twins' entrance into the kitchen, and Kyoz eyed Prim warily. At one point in time, Prim had threatened the imps with bodily harm when they wouldn't stop playing tricks on her. Kyoz stayed back, but Gnuq had evidently thought the threats were attractive.

Gnuq's brown eyes widened and his mouth pulled into a wide, wild grin. After catching himself, he put on a smirk and blew a kiss toward the human-sized fairy.

Prim glared at the tiny creature, then turned to Wynona. "We'll talk about this later." She put her chin in the air and started to walk out. "Oh!" Grabbing the back of her leg, she spun, growling. Her human form disappeared and Prim's fairy-sized body clenched tight. "Who touched me?" she said through gritted teeth.

Kyoz covered her mouth and giggled while Gnuq looked a little too proud of himself.

"Okay," Wynona said, stepping into the middle of the fray. Unfortunately, she knew all too well that if she didn't intervene, this could turn into a full blown fight. "Prim, we'll meet for dinner tonight." Pointing a finger at the imps, she said, "Your contract says you won't bother any of my patrons. Behave or we're done."

It was a mostly empty threat and the imps knew it, but they had also signed the contract, and most paranormal creatures didn't go against their word. Those who did were blackballed from the paranormal community at large. Like most cities, Hex Haven definitely had a dark underbelly, but heaven forbid anyone break a written contract.

Sniffing, Gnuq whirled his finger through the air and the trays of dessert settled themselves onto the counters.

"Thank you," Wynona said firmly. She kept her eyes on the imps, hearing the kitchen door close behind her as Prim left. "I'll mark the delivery. You may go."

With Prim gone, Kyoz was feeling a little more brave and the two imps sauntered slowly to the back door. Wynona folded her arms over her chest, watching them carefully. But when they paused in the doorway, she knew they were planning something.

Looking at each other with a smile, they both clapped their hands and all of Wynona's pots fell from their hooks, clattering onto the floor.

"Kyoz! Gnuq!" Wynona shouted, covering her ears from the noise. She couldn't hear it, but she knew the two of them were giggling as they darted out into the back alley.

Sighing, Wynona shook her head and walked over to start picking them up. Before she could bend over, however, all the pots began to float. Wynona turned, giving Lusgu a grateful smile. "You're a miracle worker," she said, knowing he would hate the compliment, but feeling the necessity to give it anyway.

Lusgu's constant scowl deepened. "Trouble makers," he grumbled.

"Very true," Wynona agreed. "But they are also wonderful bakers and our customers enjoy the treats."

He huffed, but didn't reply again. With a few more sweeps of his fingers, he had the kitchen back in order.

Wynona headed to the door, still working to shove down her concern about Ms. Theramin's unethical business practices. "Thank you, Lusgu. I appreciate you."

Just before she pulled open the door, a small purple body squeezed underneath. Violet stood up in front of the door and yawned widely.

"Have a good nap?" Wynona asked teasingly. Violet had been in her office sleeping off a night out, much to Wynona's amusement.

Violet didn't answer right away, but took the time to fluff and smooth her fur. *Did I miss anything?* she finally asked.

Wynona opened her mouth, then paused. "Nope. We just need to get back to our patrons."

Violet nodded regally and turned to go back out to the dining room. *We'll talk about it later.*

Wynona sighed. There was no getting anything over someone who was already in her head. "But first...work."

CHAPTER 3

"It's fine. This is all fine," Wynona mumbled to herself as she filled another teapot for her latest customers. It had been a week since Prim had come in to inform Wynona about Miss Theramin opening a copycat tea shop.

At first, Wynona had only heard a few rumors from her patrons, but as time went on, things were starting to get more bold. Some of her customers were openingly talking about the shop, though Wynona had yet to find one who had actually been yet.

She spent her time correcting the assumption that the shop was hers. Most of her guests were shocked to hear that it was owned by a completely different person.

Today, however, Wynona had run into a particularly obnoxious patron who refused to believe that Wynona didn't own Saffron's House of Tea. No matter how much Wynona tried to dispel the inaccurate information, the woman, an older geni, claimed she knew best.

Wynona put the pot on the stove and turned up the flame to heat the water. Stepping to the side, she leaned her hip against the counter and forced herself to take deep breaths. Waiting for the water to heat was the perfect time to take a break and try to calm herself.

A slight tugging at her pants had Wynona aware that her familiar was working her way up to Wynona's shoulder, a favorite place for the mouse to reside.

You're upset.

Wynona sighed. "I'm tired," she replied. "Sorry. I've probably been a little grumpy lately."

Well, it's no wonder with that nasty elf stealing your business.

"She hasn't stolen my business," Wynona corrected.

She's certainly trying. Violet huffed and began to clean her face, her tiny paws rubbing and grooming her purple fur.

"I know," Wynona said. She wasn't kidding when she said she was tired. Between practicing her magic and stressing over the new shop, Wynona felt as if she hadn't had a decent night's sleep in a while. "But what am I supposed to do about it?"

Maybe you need to go talk to her. Anyone can see that she's trying to copy you. Take her to court.

"I don't want to sue her," Wynona stated. "I just want to go about my business."

Sometimes the status quo changes, Violet said wisely.

Wynona gave her mouse a look. "I feel like things change too fast for me to even have a status quo."

Violet snorted her agreement. *Why aren't you using your magic to heat that water?*

Wynona bit her lips. She didn't want to admit that she was still a little scared of using her powers. They were so strong and it took a lot of concentration and energy to control it. She had been terrified of bringing her newfound skills into the workplace. What if she hurt someone? Or blew something up? Or simply made a big mess?

Lusgu would never forgive her.

Violet grumbled under her breath. *You'll never get the hang of it if you don't give it a try. Stop being such a sprite and do it.*

Wynona closed her eyes for a moment, then nodded. "Okay. But if I make a mess, you're helping clean it up."

Violet ignored her and curled up to take a nap.

Pointing her finger at the stove, Wynona pulled on the pulsing powers that were a constant part of her now. She had gone so long without her magic that trying to find ways to integrate it into her life was proving to be harder than she would have suspected. But this was one way she could easily use it on a daily basis. Provided she could accomplish the task safely.

Closing her eyes, Wynona imagined a wall holding back her magic, then poked the slightest of holes in the wall. A tiny stream of magic began to trickle through and Wynona began to direct it toward the pot.

As the magic warmed the bottom of the pot, she felt herself smile. It was working! But her break in concentration cost her and Wynona gasped as she realized her wall was starting to form cracks.

"No, no, no," she whispered, frantically trying to reinforce her control, but no matter what she did, she could feel the cracks spreading and it would only be a matter of time before she lost control and had a dangerous burst. "Violet," she said through gritted teeth, but the mouse didn't stir. "VIOLET!"

The cracks shifted and Wynona knew there was nothing more she could do. She sent out a quick hope into the universe that nobody would be hurt as she felt her magic begin to explode.

"PROHIBERE!"

Wynona gasped, her eyes shooting open as she fell to her knees, her body feeling weak. "Lusgu," she breathed. That was the second time the small brownie had stopped her magic from becoming dangerous, though the first time, Wynona hadn't known it was her magic at all. She had still believed it was her grandmother's. "How do you do that?" she asked, climbing back to her feet. She pushed her black hair out of her face, sucking in deep breaths in order to try and calm her racing heart.

Violet was clinging to Wynona's hair, chattering so fast Wynona couldn't keep up with her, instead choosing to tune her angry ranting out.

Lusgu shook his head. "Should have left you instructions," he grumbled. With a flick of his fingers, the teapot whistled and he disappeared into his corner.

Wynona watched him go, a sinking feeling in her stomach. She knew so little about her brownie employee, but she found herself wanting to know more. Recently, she had discovered he had known her grandmother, but trying to get any answers out of him was like trying to clip the toenails on a kraken.

Pulling in another deep breath, Wynona walked over and grabbed the pot, putting it on the tray to take out to her customer.

Well, that was fun.

Violet had finally calmed down enough to be coherent, though Wynona wasn't sure she needed the snarky voice in her head at the moment. "I'm trying," she said under her breath. "I'm sorry that it's taking me longer than you'd like, but I'm doing my best."

Violet sighed, but didn't speak again, for which Wynona was grateful. She had enough pressure on her shoulders at the moment. Why did it always seem like life went in waves? Just a few days ago, everything seemed wonderful. Now Wynona felt like she was spiraling out of control. She had no idea what she was going to do about the other tea house, she couldn't seem to get a good hold on her magic and she felt as if she was failing everyone around her by struggling so much.

"Nettles with lemon," Wynona said with a forced smile, setting the tray in front of the genie. "Be sure to let it steep for at least seven minutes in order to rid it of the toxins."

The woman nodded and waved Wynona away. "I've been drinking this since before you were born," she said imperiously. "Even if you do own two tea houses."

Wynona opened her mouth to argue, yet again, but snapped it shut. At this point it just wasn't worth it. "Enjoy," she said tightly, then walked away to check on her other customers.

As she wandered, her cell phone rang and Wynona walked to the hall to answer the call. "Saffron's Tea House," she said, her voice less angry than before. "How may I help you?"

"Yes, I'd like to cancel my reservation," a soft voice said on the other end of the line.

Wynona frowned. The voice was familiar, but Wynona wasn't sure. "I'm sorry to hear that. May I ask who's calling?"

"Suaren Melez," the voice replied.

"Mrs. Melez," Wynona said, shock coloring her tone. "I'm sorry to hear you're canceling. This is for your appointment next week?"

'No, no, the one today," the elf replied.

Wynona frowned. She headed to her office. "Hold on just one moment, please." Arriving at her desk, she pulled open her appointment book. Usually, Wynona had all the reservations for the day memorized and she didn't remember Mrs. Melez being part of that. "I don't have you down for today, Mrs. Melez. Are you sure you're thinking of the right date?"

"I called just yesterday," Mrs. Melez snapped. "I spoke to someone named Alavara."

Wynona threw her head back, but held in her groan. "I'm sorry, Mrs. Melez, but that's not my tea shop. You must have a reservation at Saffron's House of Tea, which is a separate business from mine."

"How is that possible?" the elf argued. "The names are the same."

Wynona slumped into her desk chair and pinched the bridge of her nose. Even Violet was grumbling under her breath. "I understand that they're very close and I'm sorry for the confusion. But Mrs. Alavara Theramin opened a tea shop called Saffron's House of Tea. My shop is Saffron's Tea House."

"And you're telling me that they aren't the same company?"

"Yes, Mrs. Melez. Two separate companies." Wynona held the phone away from her ear and cringed as the normally sweet elf shouted about how they shouldn't confuse customers that way and how unfair it was that they didn't work together. "Again, I'm sorry for the confusion," Wynona said when she could get a word in edgewise.

CHAPTER 4

Wynona's jaw nearly came unhinged. She had ridden her scooter out to Ms. Theramin's tea shop and now Wynona couldn't believe her eyes. She'd seen the pictures. She should have been prepared. She wasn't.

The picture on Prim's tablet had shown her a place that looked very similar to Wynona's shop. The building standing in front of her wasn't just similar. It was an exact replica.

A car behind her had Wynona spinning and she was grateful to see Prim arriving. The fairy's electric car pulled into a parking spot and Prim hopped out. She whistled low. "Geez. Stalker much?"

Wynona shook her head and reached up to rub Violet's fur. "It's exact. I can't find a single thing that's different."

"She had to have used magic," Prim mused, putting her hands on her hips. "There's no other way she could have gotten it this perfect."

Wynona sighed. "Well, let's get this over with. Rascal is coming over tonight and I don't want to be here very long."

"You do realize that talking probably won't do any good?"

Wynona shrugged. "I have to try," she replied. "I really don't want to go to court about this, but it's affecting my business. If she won't listen to reason, then we'll move to the next step."

Prim nodded. "Right. Here we go." She reached out and knocked on the door.

It only took a few seconds for the door to open. "Hello, ladies. We're closed for the night," Ms. Theramin said with a soft smile.

Wynona's jaw was once again on the ground. She barely recognized the elf. Alavara had obviously done magic on more than just her building. Her hair was longer and was black with curls, just like

Wynona's. Her skin was pale and her lips red. The only real difference was their body types. Where Wynona was curvy like her mother and sister, Alavara was taller and willowy, a testament to her elf heritage.

Wynona snapped her jaw shut when Prim elbowed her in the ribs. "Ms. Theramin...Alavara, we need to talk."

Alavara's eyebrows pulled down. "Why?"

"Really?" Prim snapped. "There's no way you don't recognize Wynona. Stop pretending you don't. No one's that stupid."

Alavara rolled her eyes and huffed. "Fine. Come in." She stopped before moving very far. "But this better be short. I'm tired." One side of her mouth pulled up. "Work was busy today."

Wynona grit her teeth, but she didn't speak. Best to get inside and take it from there. The inside of the shop was just as meticulous as the outside. The tables, the chairs, even the cabinet of antique teacups looked like exact replicas of Wynona's. The more she looked, the angrier she grew.

Where's her purple mouse? Violet quipped.

Wynona bit back a smile. They had been working to keep Wynona's magic a secret, including Violet being her familiar. Apparently, they'd done a good job since Alavara hadn't copied that detail.

Alavara stopped in the dining room and rested her hands on the back of a chair. "Now. What can I do for you?" She pursed her bright red lips.

Wynona ignored the sprites in her stomach. She hated confrontation, but this needed to be done. Time to be brave. "I'm here to ask you to stop copying me."

Alavara's eyes grew wide. "Copying you? Whatever are you talking about?"

Prim growled and Violet huffed. "Seriously? That's the best response you could come up with?" Prim said tightly.

Alavara shrugged. "There's nothing illegal about seeing a good business model and capitalizing on it."

"You didn't just capitalize on it," Wynona argued. "You stole my look." She waved at the elf. "Both me and my building. You claim to do custom teas, but I've had a call that you gave someone something they were allergic to."

Alavara tsked her tongue and shook her head. "Pity. I thought you knew tea better than that, Wynona."

"I do," Wynona said through clenched teeth. "They got the tea here."

"And yet they spoke to you?" Alavara smiled. "That doesn't sound right."

"Because your copy job has everyone thinking these shops are owned by the same person," Prim shouted.

Alavara smirked. "I've never told anyone that you own this shop."

"Maybe not," Wynona retorted. "But I'm guessing you haven't done anything to dispel it either."

Alavara shrugged, but didn't respond.

"I came to give you a warning," Wynona said. "I'm asking you as a friend. Please stop, or I'll be forced to take more drastic measures."

Alavara's darkened eyebrows rose high. "Drastic? Such as?"

"Such as suing the pants off you," Prim said, sticking her nose in the air. "This is your cease and desist notice. Otherwise, we'll take you to court."

Alavara pulled out the chair and sat down elegantly. "Your threats are useless," she said breezily. "The law has no hold on what I'm doing. I haven't taken your name. I haven't told people we are working with each other. I haven't even mentioned you to my customers." She smiled and tilted her head. "So you have no grounds for a jury."

"*Your* customers are showing up at *my* tea shop, complaining about the service," Wynona said, her anger starting to get the better of her. "Not one of them has been under the impression that we are two separate businesses." She waved her hand around. "It's clear that you're trying to capitalize on my hard work. I believe the correct term is my intellectual property."

Alavara's face hardened at those words.

Wynona felt a small victory. Apparently, the elf hadn't expected Wynona to understand where the law had been infringed. "Look, Alavara, I don't want to fight. But what you're doing is wrong. Not just unethical, but illegal. I'm asking you to stop, but again, if you refuse. I will take legal action."

Prim put her hands on her hips. "We won't warn you again. Come on, Nona."

Wynona gave Alavara one last look, but the elf appeared angry, rather than defeated. It made that small victory inside of Wynona die. She had a feeling this wasn't over. She hated to put Alavara out of business, but something had to give. If Alavara continued, neither of them would have a business.

"Just because you have a boyfriend who works for the police doesn't mean you'll win this," Alavara shot out before they could leave. She grinned when Wynona turned back around to face her. "I believe that's called a conflict of interest."

Wynona sighed, then gasped when saw a small man in a suit shuffle into the room. He was swinging a broom and grunting as he moved around the room.

"Are you serious?" Prim cried. "You tried to copy Lusgu?"

Wynona felt an even deeper disappointment swirl in her belly. She had been upset about her business, but now it had reached a new level of low. The janitor was a dwarf, not a brownie like Lusgu, but still...this was too much. "Alavara..." Wynona shook her head. She didn't even have the words.

Alvara snorted. "Get out," she said cattily. "You're no longer welcome here."

Wynona turned. She didn't bother trying to say anything more. This needed to end.

Well, now I'm starting to feel offended that she doesn't have a copycat of me. Violet paused. *And what about Primrose? Where's her doppleganger?*

Wynona tsked her tongue. "Violet," she scolded.

Prim bounced at her side. "What's she saying?"

Wynona debated, but finally spilled the mouse's words.

Laughter bubbled out of Prim so hard that she had to stop walking. "She's right," Prim said. "We got left out."

Exactly!

"Ladies, what she's doing is illegal. We don't want her to do more illegal things."

Prim nodded and took a calming breath. "True. True." She paused next to her car. "So what are you going to do?"

"I'm going to go home and make dinner, spend the evening with Rascal, and then see if she's still running things in the morning," Wynona said. She played with the keys to her scooter, her mind whirling. "Do you think she'll stop?"

Prim shook her head, looking sympathetic. "No. She didn't look like she had any intention of stepping down."

Wynona nodded. "Yeah. I got the same feeling." She glanced back at the shop. A shadow behind the window stood watching their every move. "She's going to fight us."

Prim stepped up to Wynona's side. "Yep. But we'll win. And it won't be because Rascal is falling in love with you."

Wynona glanced down. "You think he's falling in love with me?"

Prim rolled her eyes. "Are you blind? That wolf would do anything for you. If that's not love, I don't know what is."

Wynona considered her friend's words. The idea of Rascal loving her was exciting and terrifying. There were still so many unknowns in her life and Wynona was worried about taking on something that deep until she knew more about herself.

Questions such as, who cursed her? Why was the curse breaking? How did she learn to control her magic? How did Lusgu know her grandmother? What exactly were all of her magical abilities? What would her family do when they eventually found out about her new magic?

Wynona shook her head. She liked Rascal...a lot. In fact, if she really thought about it, she knew Prim was on the money. Wynona was falling in love with the wolf shifter, but she couldn't let herself be distracted by it. Once she knew who she truly was, then Wynona could pursue that road. But until then, she would just have to be patient. And so would Rascal.

"Come on," Wynona said to Prim and Violet. "Let's go. There's nothing else for us to do here."

Prim grumbled, but opened her car door. "I'll bring by the new flowers tomorrow," she said as she got inside. "The orchids will be ready by then."

Wynona smiled. "I'll look forward to it. Thanks for coming, Prim. It was nice having back up."

Prim flexed her thin arm. "Someone has to be the muscle."

Wynona laughed and shook her head. "Have a good night."

"You too! Don't let the werewolf bite." Prim snickered as she closed her door and pulled away.

Violet huffed. *As if Rascal would bite,* she grumbled. *He's far too tame for that.*

"Tame?" Wynona mused as she started her scooter. "Have you seen him in a fight?" She had seen Rascal when he was protecting someone and there was nothing tame about it. It was no wonder he was the Deputy Chief at the Hex Haven precinct.

Violet clambered into her basket on the front of the scooter. *He's a puppy,* she teased. *For once, Prim was right. Whipped, whipped, whipped.* Violet's grin made Wynona laugh.

"You two are too much. I shouldn't let you spend so much time together."

Violet shrugged and went about grooming herself.

Wynona knew she didn't mean anything by the teasing. Violet adored Rascal and despite her snarkiness, she also loved Wynona. It was clearly seen every time Wynona's life had been threatened.

With one last look at the business, Wynona sighed and pulled out. She didn't want to do this, but unless Alavara stopped, Wynona would have no choice. "Please stop," Wynona whispered to the wind as she drove. For once, she wanted life to just be normal for more than a few days before another tragedy hit. If only she could be that lucky.

CHAPTER 5

"**A**m I missing anything?" Wynona asked Violet. She looked around the kitchen to double check that she hadn't forgotten any supplies. She'd spent a good portion of the night creating new tinctures for her tea shop after Rascal went home, and now Wynona was eager to take them to work and test them out on her customers.

Violet stood on her hind legs, her nose twitching as she looked around. *Nope*, she finally responded.

Wynona nodded. "Great. Let's go." She picked up the heavy bag, careful not to shake the jars, and headed to the door to the garage. Just as she opened it, there was a knock on her front door.

Wynona paused and looked at Violet with a frown. "Who could that be?"

Violet grinned and scurried across the floor.

Wynona sighed and closed the garage door, setting the bag on the ground. "Coming!" she called, hurrying to see who would be coming to her house. Other than Rascal and Prim, Wynona didn't have a lot of friends, especially ones that would be coming to her house. She pulled the door open. "Oh! Hi, Daemon."

Officer Daemon Skymaw nodded his greeting. "Hey, Wynona." He shifted his weight from side to side, looking a little uncomfortable.

Wynona raised her eyebrows. "Did you want to come in? I was just leaving for work, but I can—"

Daemon shook his head. "No. Thanks. I, uh, I need you to come with me."

Wynona frowned. "Okay. Is this police business? Where's Rascal?"

Daemon pushed a hand through his dark hair. As a black hole, his looks lived up to his name. His eyes were blacker than Wynona's and his hair like pitch. Only his olive-toned skin broke up the dark coloring. "Rascal is waiting for us," Daemon explained. His eyes darted inside. "Primrose isn't here, is she?"

Wynona paused, the question catching her off guard. "No. She's supposed to meet me at the shop. She's bringing new flowers today."

He made a face and moved back. "You might need to call and cancel. I have orders to take you to the scene."

"The scene?" Wynona's heart fell. "There's been another murder?" she whispered. Wynona rubbed her forehead. Through no fault of her own, Wynona had been involved in helping solve several murders for the Hex Haven police station. It wasn't something she wanted to repeat, but somehow, she kept finding herself pulled back in.

The last murder was how she'd become friends with Daemon. Prim had been framed for the crime and Wynona had been the only one to refuse to believe the evidence. It had taken a lot of work and a close call with her own life before Wynona had proved Prim's innocence.

When it rains, it pours, Violet said sagely from her place on the floor. She eyed Daemon. *He's nervous. If I yell BOO, do you think he'll jump?*

Wynona snorted. "I doubt it."

"Huh?" Daemon asked, looking confused.

Wynona shook her head. "Sorry. Violet was talking."

His eyes dropped down, then back up. "She speaks to you?"

"Of course...oh." Wynona sighed. "Sorry. I guess we haven't kept you as up to date as I thought." She waved her hand toward the mouse. "Violet is my familiar."

"Ah." Daemon nodded slowly. "That makes sense." He grinned. "I suppose I should have seen that coming, with your magic coming out and all."

Daemon's ability to sense and see magic meant there was no hiding her burgeoning abilities from him. It was a good thing Wynona trusted the officer and he was a good friend to Rascal.

"Yeah, well...I need to take some stuff to the shop. Can we stop there first?"

Daemon shook his head regretfully. "I'm sorry. But I'm supposed to bring you right over."

Wynona groaned. "This is ridiculous." She bent down and held out her hand. "Come on, Violet. Let's see why they need us." She tucked the mouse in her pocket, walked over to get her bag and came back to where Daemon waited.

After locking her door, Wynona climbed into Daemon's SUV, buckling up. "Who was killed?" She had a momentary panic. "Was it anyone I know?"

Daemon glanced sideways at her. "I don't think I should say any more."

Wynona was confused and her eyebrows pulled together. "I don't understand."

"I know, but I..." He shook his head. "No. I really need to wait until we get there."

Wynona felt a sharp pang in her chest. Daemon wasn't just acting nervous, he was acting suspicious. Why had he been sent to get her? Why wouldn't he tell her what was going on? Why would the police want her to come to a crime scene anyway? Chief Ligurio always hated when Wynona stuck her nose in his business. He didn't like listening to her and definitely didn't like that she had some success under her belt. There was no way he would want her around. At least not for her help.

Wynona gasped. "Daemon," she said, her voice shaky. "Who died?"

He pinched his lips together, making a thin, white line.
"They think I did it, don't they?" she pressed.
His face paled, but he didn't speak.

Wynona didn't ask any more questions. She didn't have to. It was clear what was happening. Rascal liked to get her opinion sometimes, but he wouldn't have sent Daemon to come retrieve her like this. But Chief Lirugio would if he thought Wynona had something to do with the crime.

She glanced down at the pocket on her shirt, making a face at Violet.

We both know you're innocent, Violet assured her. *Let's see what's going on and why you're a suspect.*

Wynona nodded. There was nothing else to do, but wait it out. Grabbing her phone, she sent a text to Prim, explaining that she wouldn't be in early.

I have a vendor appointment later. I'll drop them off with Lusgu.

Wynona sent an affirmative reply, grateful that she didn't have to explain any more to Prim. Wynona knew she would have to share eventually, but she needed to understand what was going on herself before she could spill it all to her best friend.

Daemon took a turn that caught Wynona by surprise. "Alavara," she said softly.

Daemon jerked his head toward her. "You do know her," he mused.

Wynona slumped back in her seat. "Barely. But yes." It only took another two minutes for them to arrive at Saffron's House of Tea. It was no wonder the police wanted to speak to her. Sighing heavily,

Wynona climbed down carefully in her pencil skirt and headed inside.

The front door was marked with caution tape, but with Daemon at her side, the on duty officer moved it out of the way to let them in.

Violet chittered angrily and Wynona reached in her pocket to pet the creature.

"Wy!"

Wynona let out a breath of relief and hurried over to take Rascal's hand. "What's going on?" she asked. "Daemon wouldn't tell me anything, but I'm guessing I'm somehow a suspect in this scene."

Rascal scratched behind his ear, looking tired. "Come on," he replied, pulling her toward a back room. It was a replica of Wynona's office and obviously where Alavara did her business.

The scene was buzzing with officers, including the vampire Chief of Police, Chief Ligurio. It seemed like chaos, though Wynona was sure that every police officer in the room had a purpose they were fulfilling.

It wasn't the moving bodies, however, that had caught her attention. It was the still one on the floor.

Wearing the same shirt and skirt that she'd had on yesterday, Alavara's body lay on the ground face down. A bloody butcher knife was sticking up out of her back and the wound had allowed blood to soak not only her clothes, but the ground around her as well.

Wynona gasped and put a hand over her mouth. "Why would someone do this?" she whispered, allowing Rascal to pull her into his chest. His thick, warm arms were comforting, but even closing her eyes couldn't rid Wynona of the grisly scene.

"We were hoping you could tell us that," Chief Ligurio said, walking in their direction. He paused next to Wynona and Rascal, glancing back at the body. "Why would someone kill a woman who was infringing on another woman's business?"

Wynona scowled. "Do you really think me capable of this, Chief Ligurio?" She turned away from Rascal's hold, determined to stand on her own two feet despite the nausea running through her stomach. "I know we haven't always seen eye to eye, but we've spent enough time together that I would hope you'd have a little more faith in the fact that I'm not the type of person to murder."

Chief Ligurio sighed, looking tired, which was unusual for the vampire. "I know," he admitted, which shocked Wynona. He also wasn't the type to admit when he was wrong. His dark eyebrows rose high on his pale forehead. "But you understand how this looks?"

Wynona nodded, also feeling weary. "Yes. And I'll be the first to admit that I visited her yesterday afternoon, after closing."

His eyes widened. "And?"

"And I gave her a warning."

Rascal groaned. "Wy..."

She shook her head. "It wasn't like that. When she first opened her doors, I ignored the fact that she was copying me. I didn't figure she would last very long, because as far as I knew, she didn't have the same gift I have for being able to give people the exact teas that they need."

Chief Liguri nodded. "Understandable. From what I understand, her elfin magic was more suited to fashion anyway."

"Which makes sense for someone trying to copy another's style," Rascal grumbled.

Wynona nodded. "True. But when her shop started to affect my business, I knew I had to take a stand." She made a face. "I took Prim with me."

Rascal threw his head back. "Why didn't you ask me to go along?"

"Because Prim isn't afraid to stand her ground," Wynona explained, hoping her eyes conveyed what she couldn't say right now. "She's a little..."

"Rash?" he supplied, giving her a significant look.

Wynona shrugged. "I suppose that's one way to put it."

"So what did you do when you spoke to her?" Chief Ligurio pressed.

"I simply told her that she had gone too far and that the shop, my look and even the set up of the business were protected under creative copyright and that she needed to cease and desist or I would bring charges against her." Wynona rubbed her throbbing forehead. "I told her she had until today to make up her mind how she wanted to proceed."

"And how did she respond?" Chief Ligurio asked.

"She was angry." Wynona spread her hands. "I didn't expect her to be any less, but she was completely belligerent. I had no doubt that today I'd be at the station, filing a suit against her."

Rascal pushed a hand through his thick, brunette hair. "No need for that now, I suppose."

Wynona shot him a look and he shrugged. She turned back to the chief. "I spent the rest of the evening with Rascal. He was at my house until close to midnight."

Chief Ligurio nodded. "He told me that." The chief tapped his long fingers against his lips. "But this crime scene doesn't make any sense. Why stab her? She was an elf. She had some magic, even if it wasn't strong." His red eyes glanced her way. "Magic beings fight with magic."

The underlying meaning was clear to Wynona. Chief Ligurio didn't know that Wynona had magic. A non-magical being was more than likely the one who had killed this way.

She and her friends had worked hard to keep her magic a secret, but right now she had the urge to spill it all, if it would get rid of the suspicious gleam in Chief Ligurio's eyes.

No...

She forced herself to take a calming breath, which wasn't easy with a dead body only a few feet away. They were keeping her skills a secret for a reason. She had an alibi. Rascal was a trusted man on the force. They would believe his word, even if they didn't believe hers.

"Do we have a time of death?" Wynona asked, hoping she came across as nonchalant. Chief Ligurio had accused her of murder before and Wynona knew showing fear wouldn't help her in this case. She had to be confident in her innocence or he would keep pressing.

"Around eleven last night," Chief said. His shoulders dropped ever so slightly before his eyes met hers. "So it would seem you're off the suspect list, Ms. Le Doux."

Wynona held eye contact. "So it would seem." She wanted to shake her head and growl at how stubborn the vampire was. Her brows furrowed. "Are you sure there was no magic used? The knife was truly the cause of death?"

"Skymaw!" Chief Ligurio barked.

Wynona jumped at the shout. She had brought up the question because in the last murder she had helped with, the harpy had been stabbed, but the cause of death was actually poisoning. Perhaps the perpetrator just wanted to make it *look* like the knife was the weapon.

"Yeah, Chief?" Daemon asked from the doorway. His eyes met Wynona's and he gave her an apologetic look.

She shook her head. She wasn't upset with him picking her up this morning. He was just doing his job. Besides, he was one of the few helping keep her secret. There was no hiding magic from a black hole.

"Did you scan the body for magical residue?" Chief Ligurio asked.

"Uh...no?" Skymaw made a face. "Sorry, Chief. We've only done it the one time and I wasn't asked to."

Chief Ligurio grumbled under his breath. "From now on that is your top priority at every crime scene, is that understood?"

Skymaw nodded. "Absolutely, Chief."

Chief Ligurio waved an arm toward the body. "Get on with it then."

Wynona held her breath as she waited for the results. Rascal was also uncharacteristically still. They had learned during their last investigation together that Daemon's ability to see magic extended to the leftover residue in objects cast from spells or potions.

Daemon walked all around the body, carefully avoiding the puddle on the hardwood. Slowly, he shook his head until he finally looked up. "There's no magic, Chief. None. At all."

Wynona frowned. It seemed so unlikely, but in a paranormal world, weirder things had certainly happened.

Chief Ligurio nodded curtly. "Let's get this body bagged and to the coroner." He walked away and began barking orders.

"You gonna be okay here?" Rascal whispered.

Wynona nodded. "I'll just stay out of the way."

He kissed her temple. "I'll give you a ride to work when we're done." He paused before moving. "Where's Vi?"

Wynona huffed. "Asleep in my pocket." She opened it up for the shifter to see. "This girl takes more naps than a cat in the sunshine."

Rascal chuckled. "It was a good day to do it, I guess." With one last glance, he disappeared into the crowd.

Wynona stepped away, her back against the wall. She might not have had anything to do with the murder, but she couldn't help having a healthy dose of curiosity. Since getting involved in helping solve several murders in the last few months, Wynona found an odd sense of accomplishment in helping put bad guys in jail. It was probably the same feeling that drove men like Rascal to become police officers. That sense of justice was addicting and heady.

But this time...no matter how curious, Wynona knew she wouldn't be helping solve this case. She'd done enough and was burdened with her own worries at the moment. Trying to figure out who cursed her and how to handle her magic were enough to keep any witch busy.

CHAPTER 6

Wynona watched as the officers came in and lifted Alavara's stiff body into the bag. She winced at the sounds. Police work wasn't always fun and this was an instance when she was glad she had a different profession.

"Van's here," an officer said, poking their head inside the office. "Bring her out."

Several officers, including Daemon, held onto various parts of the body as they worked their way into the hallway. Squeaking wheels let Wynona know they'd loaded Alavara onto a stretcher and after a few moments, the sounds all died down.

Surprisingly, she was left alone in the room, which was more uncomfortable than she cared to admit. Why would someone want to kill the elf? Yes, it was a crime and annoying that she had been trying to steal Wynona's business, but that wasn't a good reason to kill her. The courts would have taken care of the situation and Wynona definitely wasn't angry enough to hurt Alavara.

But would someone else have been?

Maybe this wasn't the first time Alavara had tried to rip someone off. Maybe someone from her past had caught up to her?

Wynona shook her head. She really shouldn't get caught up in all this. It wasn't her case. She had a solid alibi and even Chief Ligurio admitted he didn't really think she was involved, despite the circumstances.

But she couldn't seem to help her eyes wandering around, trying to take in the scene. Without her permission, Wynona found her feet moving forward. Slowly, she walked around the outline on the floor. The blood puddle was dark and made Wynona slightly queasy. Daemon had to be right. If someone had used magic to kill Alavara before stabbing her, there wouldn't have been so much blood.

A lump in the blood caught Wynona's eye and she squatted down in her skirt, careful not to let anything touch the ground. Bending her head around, she struggled to tell what the object was. It could have simply been a clot, but Wynona wasn't sure.

Straightening, she grabbed a pencil from the desk, then came back and got down again, using the tip to poke at the blob. Wynona's black eyebrows shot up when she realized it was hard. There went the clot theory. Carefully, she pushed it over and gasped. It was a button! The threads were dangling as if it had been snapped from the tiny latch on the back.

Wynona flipped it back to the front and tried to use the pencil to clean off the front, but it was too saturated. It looked like there was some kind of design... Maybe the button was gold?

She shook her head and blew out a long breath. The police would have to clean it up to see what it was exactly.

Hearing a noise in the front room, Wynona jumped up. She needed to tell someone about this and have them bag it up. She hurried to the hall and paused, debating who to call.

Just as she opened her mouth, a breeze blew her hair into her face and she stopped to fix it. Looking around, Wynona waited, then shrugged. It had to have come from the open front door. "Rascal! Chief Ligurio!" She rushed into the main room, spotting several officers, none of which were the ones she wanted. "Umm...has anyone seen the chief? Or Deputy Chief Strongclaw?"

"Wynona?" Daemon's head came in the front door. "Did you need something?"

Wynona nodded. "Yes. I found something I think the chief and Rascal should look at."

Daemon frowned. "Really? We already went through the room."

"I know, but it was covered in blood under the body," Wynona explained.

Daemon nodded. "'Kay. Give me a sec."

Wynona tapped her foot as she waited impatiently. She couldn't seem to help herself. Sometimes she was too curious for her own good. No matter how much she didn't really want to get involved, Wynona's mind just never stopped trying to figure it out.

"Wy?" Rascal asked as he stepped through the door. Chief Ligurio was right behind him. "Officer Skymaw said you found something?"

Wynona nodded. "In the office." She led the way and stopped at the side of the door. "There. In the blood."

Rascal went in and squatted down, looking around. "I don't see anything," he said.

Chief Ligurio frowned.

"What?" Wynona came inside the office and looked over Rascal's shoulder. "It...it was right here."

"What was right here?" Chief Ligurio snapped.

"It was a button," Wynona said, her eyes darting back and forth. Rascal was right. The button was gone. "It was under the body and when everyone cleared out of the room, I spotted it." She rubbed her forehead. "At first I just thought it was a clot or something, but when I poked at it with a pencil, I realized it was something more."

"A pencil?"

Wynona held up the tool. The tip was still covered in blood.

Chief Ligurio frowned, then leaned down toward the blood and sniffed. "Strongclaw?"

Rascal did the same, paused, then shook his head. "I can smell nearly every person on the force," he said. "There's no way to tell who might have been in here."

Chief Ligurio nodded and huffed. "How long were you out of the room?" he asked Wynona.

"Only a minute, maybe slightly more," she said. "As soon as I figured out what it was, I came out to get someone to come bag it." Her shoulders fell. "I didn't want to pick it up because it was covered in blood and I was worried about fingerprints."

Rascal stood and came over, wrapping her in his arms. "Don't worry about it," he whispered. "You did just fine."

Wynona let herself relax against him. Rascal's hold was always so warm and inviting. It didn't matter that they'd been dating for several months now. Each time he touched her, she felt as if she could never get enough. She was falling hard and fast for this wolf shifter, but he seemed content to keep their relationship where it was.

Probably better this way...

Just like helping with the investigation, Wynona's life was a little too unsettled for her relationship with Rascal to change. She needed to learn to be patient and content with things how they were. After she better understood herself, she'd be able to look at things becoming more serious between her and the wolf shifter, but not until then.

"Tell me about this button," Chief Ligurio asked. "Did you see any defining features?"

Wynona made a face. "Not really. Like I said, it was covered. I rolled it over and that's now I knew it was a button. The hook was on the back along with a few pieces of broken thread."

"Color?" the vampire pressed.

Wynona shook her head. "The thread was saturated. But when I flipped it back to the front, there was some kind of design." She shrugged. "And it might have been gold. It was really hard to tell."

Chief Ligurio growled low and Rascal's hold tightened. "Not very helpful, Ms. Le Doux."

Wynona pinched her lips together before she could say something rude back. She knew Chief Ligurio was often grumpy and he'd never spared her that. But couldn't he just once treat her like she did something good? It wasn't like his team had found the button.

"What do you want to do, Chief?" Rascal asked.

"There's nothing we can do," the chief said sourly. "No one else saw it, and since Ms. Le Doux has a motive, there's no way I can use what she's saying as anything useful."

"You really think I did this?" Wynona blurted out before she could stop herself. She had thought they were past this. She stepped away from Rascal and put her hands on her hips. "How many times do I have to prove to you that I'm not your enemy, Chief Ligurio?"

He gave her a wry look. "I'm not accusing you of anything," he offered. "But that doesn't mean I don't take note of the fact that you seem to have a knack for being involved in a lot of investigations."

She couldn't argue with that. For someone who had only been in the real world for close to a year, she had certainly found herself surrounded by dead bodies. It would be easy to assume it wasn't a coincidence.

"However, I also believe that if you were truly associating with those in the underbelly of Hex Haven, your family would do something about it before the law could take hold of you."

Wynona scowled, but quickly schooled her features. Again...he had a point. Just as Wynona was afraid her magic would have her parents whisking her back to the castle, any hint of scandal, anything that might suggest she was sullying the Le Doux name, and Wynona would find herself being stolen in the middle of the night, the public none the wiser as to her whereabouts.

"Thanks," she said grudgingly. "But I promise, there was a button."

"I believe you," Rascal said, his eyes searching the room. "If it's not here, then the only solution is that someone took it."

Chief Ligurio sighed. "Go check and see if someone else bagged it," he said, then his eyebrows furrowed. "If no one did, shut down the scene. It could be that the culprit is still here and is trying to cover their tracks."

Rascal nodded and ushered Wynona out of the room. "Why don't you sit in the dining room while I take care of this."

"So I'll be out of the way?" she grumbled.

"I'm sorry," Rascal said. "But you know how Chief gets."

Wynona blew out a long breath. "Yeah. I know." She glanced at her watch. "Any chance I'll be out of here soon? My shop opens in an hour."

"I'll get it taken care of as soon as I can," Rascal assured her. He settled her on a couch, then leaned down to kiss her forehead. "Relax for a few. I'll be done soon."

Wynona grabbed his hand before he could leave. "Who else is here?" she whispered. "Chief Ligurio said the murderer might still be around."

Rascal's gold eyes flashed. "The janitor and the baker are here. I have officers taking their statements."

"Please tell me the baker isn't a set of twin imps."

Rascal chuckled. "Nope. She's a witch."

"Ah." Wynona nodded and leaned back. "Glad to hear it."

"I'm not sure anyone can copy Gnuz and Kyoz."

"Too true," Wynona agreed. "Okay. Go do what you need to do. I'll wait."

"Thanks." Without another word, Rascal was gone.

Wynona watched him for a moment as he worked the room, asking about the evidence that was missing. She shook her head and pulled out her phone to read a book. She wasn't going to get involved. She'd already done more than she should have.

Let it go, she scolded herself.

She'd proven her innocence, she'd offered a slight clue that the police had missed...that was all she could do this time. Chief Ligurio's crew would just have to make due without her. This time she was putting down her foot... She absolutely would not get involved. Nope. Not even a little bit.

CHAPTER 7

"Sorry I'm late!" Wynona hollered as she hurried into the kitchen of the shop. They were set to open in ten minutes and she hadn't done any of her normal preparations for the day. While some patrons walked in, others had appointments, and Wynona always worked hard to have everything set up on time for those time slots.

Lusgu grumbled under his breath as he fired up the stove with a wave of his fingers.

Wynona paused when she realized he had all the tea pots loaded and now heating. "Lusgu," she said breathlessly, tucking a loose chunk of hair out of her face. "Thank you." She could have sworn that the tips of his long, pointed ears grew slightly red, but by the sounds coming from his mouth, no one would think he was anything but annoyed.

"Can't see what's right in front of their noses," Lusgu complained before pointing to the broom. It followed him into the dining room, sweeping behind him and gathering invisible dust that only Lusgu seemed to be able to see.

"I'll bet Alavara's dwarf wasn't half so good," Wynona said with a smile, then paused. She pushed out a harsh breath and hung her head. That unkind thought wasn't normal for her and she mentally apologized to Alavara, praying the woman's ghost wasn't around to haunt her.

Her family were the ones to speak rudely of others, including Wynona herself whenever it pleased them. Their power and authority made it difficult for there to be any consequences. When she escaped, Wynona promised herself she would be different.

She would help when her family would have refused. She would work for herself, where her family reveled in wealth. And she would be kind when her family would be rude.

The clock struck the hour and Wynona gasped. Hurrying out to the dining room, she unlocked the front door, then ran back to start putting out teacups, arranging the flowers and generally trying to look like she actually knew what she was doing. Maybe she would get lucky enough—

The bell above the door chimed and Wynona forced herself to slow down. Closing her eyes, she took a deep breath. She could do this. She had had hectic mornings before, including one where she found a dead body in her own office.

Putting a placid smile on her face, she headed to the front entry. "Hello," she said calmly. "Welcome to Saffron's Tea House." Wynona paused when she realized no one was there.

"Ms. Le Doux," came a disembodied voice before flashes of light that could only be from a camera began to wreak havoc with her eyes. "How do you feel about your partner being murdered?"

"What?" Wynona put a hand over her eyes. She grit her teeth. Ghost reporters. They were the bane of every paranormal's existence. With their ability to become invisible, they could sneak up on practically anyone. "I don't have a partner," Wynona managed to get out as more questions were tossed at her.

"When did you last visit her?" another voice asked.

"How long have the two of you been working together?"

Wynona closed her eyes once more and tried to find inner peace. This was ridiculous. How did the media get it all so wrong? Clamping her hands at her sides, she tilted up her chin. "Miss Theramin and I were not partners," Wynona said carefully, but boldly. "Her tea shop was her own, just as mine is my own. We were not connected in any way, shape or form."

"Do you have any idea who would have wanted to hurt your partner?"

"When did you come up with the idea to open a second shop?"

"What will happen to the tea shop now that Miss Theramin is dead?"

A purple haze began to work its way over Wynona's eyes. She knew her frustration was growing and her emotions often led her magic since she was still learning to control it. She tried taking some deep breaths, but the haze wouldn't go away.

A scampering on the floor barely caught her attention, and then there was a tug on her leg that worked its way up her body. *Breathe, Wynona,* Violet ordered. *We don't need to hurt anyone today or announce to all of Hex Haven that you're out of control.*

Wynona forced a shuddering breath into her lungs, but her vision stayed purple. "How do I get them to leave?" she whispered.

Have you tried asking?

The joke did exactly as intended and even more of the tension inside Wynona released. Her vision, however, remained stubborn. "I don't think—" She gasped. Through the purple overlay, Wynona could make out shapes. Well, blobs really. "It's them," she said quietly. "The reporters."

Violet chittered in delight. *Show these bozos the door.*

Doing her best to hold onto the magic vision, Wynona walked through them and opened the front door. "Please leave," she stated in a firm voice. "You're trespassing on private property and I don't wish to answer any more questions."

Loud shouting broke out as they all tried to deny her rights.

Wynona kept her eye on the floating bodies, making sure none tried to venture further into the building as she pulled out her phone. "Hello? Deputy Chief Strongclaw?"

"Wy? What's going on?" There was panic in Rascal's voice, more than likely because she had used his formal name. "I can't feel you. Where are you?"

Wynona blinked a few times, caught off guard with his words, before forcing herself to concentrate. "I have a situation at the tea shop where the ghost reporters are refusing to—"

The shouts dimmed to grumblings and the flashes and voices began to work their way through the door. Wynona stayed strong as she watched them leave, but paused when she realized there was one more blob in the corner. "I'd like to press charges," Wynona said into the phone, her eyes directly on the reporter still lurking.

With a loud huff, the reporter became visible and glared at Wynona while they made their way to the door. He was a small, slim man, his hair mostly gone. He looked human, making it impossible to know what kind of paranormal he had been before he died. The reporter paused in the threshold and cocked his head. "How did you know I was there?"

Wynona did her best not to react. "Which station do you work for?" she asked in return. Maybe if she could keep him on the defensive, he would forget the strange situation.

"I'm going, I'm going," the creature said, giving her one last glare.

The sound of screeching traffic caught Wynona's attention and she looked at the street just in time to see a massive brown wolf leap through the cars, nearly causing an accident. As he came to her stoop, his body shifted, changing back into Rascal, who stomped up the steps.

We're in for it now...

"Hush," Wynona scolded her familiar.

"What is going on?" he demanded, his glowing eyes going back and forth between Violet and Wynona.

Wynona glanced around to make sure her reporters were gone, then backed up. "Please come in, Deputy Chief." She didn't want anyone watching to understand that this was anything other than a business call. The reporters needed to understand she'd been serious in her order to be left alone.

When the door closed behind Rascal, however, Wynona allowed herself to collapse into his chest.

A rumbling growl was vibrating deep inside of him, the sound comforting in how it filled her to the tips of her toes. Large arms wrapped around her and pulled her in close. "What in the paranormal world was that about?" he asked, his face buried in her hair. Abruptly, he pulled back, cradling her face between his hands. "And why are your eyes purple?"

"Shoot." Wynona blinked rapidly. "Violet? A little help?" She hadn't even realized her vision was still purple. It had been very handy a few minutes ago, but especially if others could see it, Wynona needed it gone.

Violet sighed. *Hunky dude is here. Do I really have to?*

"Violet," Wynona said more firmly. Sometimes her magic was too stubborn to be pulled back and she needed Violet's extra help in controlling it.

Violet huffed. *Fine.* She jumped from Rascal's pocket, where she'd gone as soon as he'd been close enough, and landed on Wynona's shoulder. Putting her paws on Wynona's neck, Violet began to vibrate.

Wynona closed her eyes and concentrated, allowing the extra strain of magic she now felt to help guide her to her own. Together, they wrangled the power into submission and when Wynona opened her eyes again, her vision was back to normal.

"Thank you," she breathed, reaching up to pet the mouse.

Violet chittered, then leapt back to Rascal. He grinned and helped her get situated in his pocket.

Wynona couldn't exactly blame her familiar. Being against Rascal's broad chest was one of her favorite places as well.

"Wy," Rascal said again. "What happened?"

Wynona took his hand and led him farther inside. "Two words. Ghost reporters."

The growl started up again, just as the door chimed. Rascal stiffened and Wynona held up a hand. She wasn't eager for the media to be back either, but it could just as easily be a customer.

"Sorry I'm late, dear," Mrs. Winrok, an older sprite, said as she fluttered inside. She paused and squeaked when she spotted Rascal. "I didn't know you had company."

The tiny woman cowered a little at the sight of the angry wolf shifter and Wynona shifted more surely between the two. "Good morning, Mrs. Winrok. Your usual table?"

The creature nodded, keeping a wary eye on Rascal even as she followed Wynona to a seat next to the front window.

After she was seated, Wynona hurried back to Rascal. "If you have the time, wait in my office. Once I'm done here, I'll be in to tell you what happened."

His nostrils were still flaring, but Rascal nodded and spun to do as she'd asked. Putting a hand on her heart, Wynona took a couple of deep breaths. Normally she loved the independence and freedom that running her own business gave her, but right now she wished she had a couple more employees.

Her heart was still pounding from the horrible encounter with the ghost reporters and then seeing Rascal in wolf form coming to her rescue. Plus, she was fatigued from using her magic and could desperately use a cup of matcha as a pick me up.

Wynona waved to her current patron and hurried to the kitchen to build a tray. Lusgu had kept the pot hot, much to Wynona's delight, and it took her no time at all to have everything ready.

But by the time Wynona got Mrs. Winrok set up, three more people had arrived and it took her nearly an hour to get back to Rascal.

"I'm so sorry," she panted, coming into her office. "There was a string of patrons and I needed to get them taken care of."

Rascal sat at her desk, leaning over a book he'd been reading. Now that she was inside the office, he leaned back, folding his impressive arms over his chest. "Let's get down to business then, shall we?"

Wynona held back a wince. She didn't like working with official Deputy Chief Strongclaw. She knew, technically speaking, that her magic outranked him, but she didn't feel like a powerful person and when Rascal got upset, he became much more like the predator he was.

She wasn't worried about him hurting her. Rascal in wolf form or human form would never do such a thing. But when he was on the hunt, sometimes he lost his soft side and it scared Wynona slightly.

Rascal groaned and scrubbed his hands over his face. "Sorry. I wasn't trying to frighten you." He stood and offered her the chair. "Sit down," he said in a softer tone.

Wynona gave him a small, awkward smile and obeyed. When his hands landed on her neck and shoulders, massaging slightly, she let out her own groan and dropped her chin down to her chest to give him better access.

"What did the ghost reporters want?" Rascal asked, his voice much more pleasant than before.

Wynona deflated a little more. "They wanted to know about my *partner*," she said, using quotation marks with her fingers. "Somehow, no one seems to believe me when I say I'm not connected with that tea house."

A low rumble came out of his throat. "And? I know you wouldn't call the station just for that."

"And when they kept overriding me and refusing to leave, I thought maybe frightening them with the law was the best way to go."

"Is that all?"

Wynona stiffened and she knew Rascal felt it because he stopped massaging.

"Wy?" he pressed.

Just tell him already, Violet whined from her cozy spot in his pocket.

"And I almost lost it with my magic," Wynona said in a small voice. She looked up and over her shoulder. "Plus, I discovered a new ability."

He dropped to his knees beside her. "I'm guessing that's why your eyes were purple?"

Wynona nodded and rubbed her forehead. This headache was going to knock her out if she wasn't careful. How much stress could one person handle in a day before they simply broke? "Apparently, I can see ghosts when they're invisible."

His eyebrows shot up. "What?"

Wynona made a face. "It's kind of hard to explain. But my vision went purple, and then I could see the outlines or the blobs, is maybe a better word, of the ghost reporters, even when they were in their invisible form."

"Huh." Rascal studied her. "Daemon said you were stronger than anyone he'd ever met. I'm thinking he might be right."

Wynona flushed and dropped his intense gaze. She drew a random pattern on the desktop. "I didn't ask for all this power," she said softly. "I just want to go about my life."

"I know," Rascal said in a soothing tone. He rubbed her back. "But maybe this is a good thing," he pressed. "Think of all the cases you can help me solve."

She glared sideways at him and he grinned.

"Between my sense of smell and hearing and your powers, we'd make the perfect power couple."

Wynona rolled her eyes. "I'm not getting involved in this one, Rascal," she said, though her tone was flirtier than it should have been. She couldn't seem to help it. Being around Rascal was like getting a jolt of caffeine and a warm soothing blanket all at the same time.

He chuckled, the sound reverberating through her chest. "Alright. I won't press." He leaned in and kissed her cheek. "For now." After standing, Rascal put his hands on his hips. "Sounds like you might need a watchguard for the next few days."

Wynona's eyes widened. "What?"

He scratched his chin. "They were bending the law this morning and every reporter knew it. If they think they can get away with it again, they'll keep hounding you until they get what they want."

"I don't have what they want," Wynona said, jumping to her feet. "I had nothing to do with the murder, and I had nothing to do with Alavara. I'd only met her a couple of times."

"I know," he assured her. "But others don't." His jaw ticked. "I'll send over an officer to make sure things stay quiet the next couple of days. If everyone leaves you alone, then we'll stop rotations."

Wynona plopped back down. "Is that really necessary?"

Rascal nodded. "Yes. Besides just the reporters, there's another reason it's a good idea."

She looked up. "Why's that?"

Rascal's eyes fell to the floor. "Have you considered that the murder might have been directed at you?"

All the blood drained from Wynona's head. "What?" she asked, swaying.

"The elf who was killed was dressed as you, Wy," Rascal said carefully. He knelt down again. "They were in a tea shop named and built to be just like yours." His eyes flashed a brilliant gold. "We have no idea if the murderer meant to kill the copycat..." He swallowed hard. "Or the original."

CHAPTER 8

Wynona had to sit down. Why in the world would someone want to kill her? Her mind spun. Could someone be coming after her? But...why? That was the question.

Rascal knelt and put his hands on her knees. "Just breathe, Wy. Just breathe."

"I don't understand," she whispered, unable to make her voice any louder. "Do you really think someone was after me and just mixed us up?"

Rascal scratched behind his ear. "I'm not sure," he admitted. "You've been running your shop for over half a year at this point, so I don't know if it's possible to get you mixed up." He shrugged. "On the other hand, stranger things have happened. We live in a paranormal world, after all. Strange is our middle name."

"I suppose they're not strange if you've never known any different," Wynona mused.

Rascal laughed and tucked a piece of hair behind her ear. "Don't get all philosophical on me, Le Doux."

A small smile tugged at her lips. "Sorry. It just came out."

"I think that's Lu's job," Rascal joked.

This time, the smile made it all the way onto her face. "You're right." She sighed and rubbed her forehead. "It's just all so fantastical, I suppose. One minute I was frustrated she was ruining my business, the next I'm concerned someone killed her thinking she was me."

"Remember," Rascal climbed to his feet, "we don't actually know that. It's just one line of thinking at this point." He frowned. "If she made a habit out of stealing clients, Miss Theramin could have had any number of enemies."

"True." Wynona blew out a long breath. "I like that idea much better. Plus, I believe it has more merit."

"While I'm inclined to agree," Rascal stated, "I'm not taking any chances. You're going to have an officer at your door until this is over. Between the reporters and the possible threat to you personally, I want you taken care of."

Violet poked her head out of his pocket and chattered wildly.

Wynona felt her face go up in flames as Rascal chuckled.

"I don't think I'd mind sticking that close to two such lovely ladies," he cooed at the mouse. "But duty doesn't always give me the choice."

Sniffing in disdain, Violet climbed out of his pocket and down his side until she strutted across the floor, refusing to look back at Rascal.

He was still smiling when Wynona shook her head. "She's touchy."

Rascal rubbed his jaw. "Yep. But that's what makes her so fun."

Wynona blocked the angry rant echoing through her head from Violet's response to their conversation. The mouse seriously had an attitude problem on occasion, though she was always there when Wynona really needed her.

"So now what?"

"Now I make a call, get your protection set up, and try to get back to finding a murderer." He took his cell out of his pocket and walked over to plop down on the couch.

The front bell chimed and Wynona stood, forcing her shaky knees to be strong. "I'll be out with my patrons," she whispered to Rascal. He nodded his understanding while he continued his conversation on the phone.

Stepping outside her office, Wynona took a deep breath, threw back her shoulders and marched out to the dining room, ready to take care of her customer. She spent the next hour settling and resettling customers, making teas and helping those who wanted her attention.

This was where Wynona was at her best. She loved the interaction with her patrons, she loved creating teas and she loved seeing people's faces when they tried her brews for the first time. Truly, she simply loved her job. It was everything she had ever hoped for.

Her work was simple, but enjoyable, and didn't affect those outside of her shop. So the question sitting heavily on her shoulders was, why would someone wish to stop her from doing her work? What could they possibly find so offensive about her tea-making that they would feel the need to kill her?

An intense shiver went down her spine and Wynona shifted her shoulders to get rid of the feeling. There wasn't anything she could do about the situation right now. Rascal and the department would take care of her. Wynona knew her time would be best spent focused on her work and her friends.

"Wy?"

Her head jerked to the front entry, where Rascal was waiting for her. "Excuse me," Wynona said to the woman she'd been brewing a cup for. "I'll be right back." She raised her eyebrows as she weaved through the tables until reaching Rascal's side. "Yes?"

"I need to head out, but I've got Officer Oozog out front. He's going to wait on the step until being relieved. Okay?"

Wynona nodded. She leaned her shoulder onto the opening threshold. "How fast do you think this case will take?"

Rascal scrunched his nose and pushed a hand through his hair. "I have no idea," he responded. "We don't have much to go on, but as soon as I have news I can share, I'll let you know."

"Thanks." Wynona gave him a soft smile. It grew bigger when he ducked down to kiss her cheek.

"Be safe," he commanded, giving her the same look he used on his officers. "No going around without other people, okay?'

Wynona rolled her eyes good naturedly. "Yes, sir."

He relaxed slightly, but the intense look in his eyes didn't change. "We're going to do our best to take care of you," he said in a low tone. "But you can make it a lot easier if you'll follow the rules."

"I know that," she said, just as softly. "And I promise not to do anything stupid, but I know what it's like to be a prisoner." She tilted her head. "I don't want to go through that again."

"And I don't want to risk losing you." There was a slight growl under his words. "Please, Wy. For me. Just take the officer along."

Wynona studied her fierce wolf. He was so intimidating with his broad build and commanding stature, yet she knew without a shadow of a doubt that he would never do anything to hurt her. "Okay," she agreed, still keeping her voice low. She didn't need her entire dining room knowing there was something nefarious going on.

"Thank you." One more quick peck on the cheek and his authoritative presence slipped out the front door.

Wynona watched the door for a few seconds, feeling the loss of him by her side. She shook her head. It was ridiculous to sit around moping. She needed to get back to work.

Just as she headed back to the dining room, noise started to build outside the front door. Frowning, Wynona went to see what was going on. Carefully, she pulled open the door and peered out.

"Back inside, Ms. Le Doux," a voice growled.

Wynona jerked, unsure who was speaking to her. It wasn't a voice she recognized.

"Ms. Le Doux! What happened with your other shop? Do you have any idea how your partner died?" A scuffling sound followed the shouts.

"You've got to be kidding me," Wynona whispered to herself. She poked her head out a little farther. A beefy looking ogre in a police uniform was guiding a large group of people with microphones away from the front door of the shop.

Now that her head was out the door, the shouting picked up and Wynona couldn't follow all the calls.

"Ms. Le Doux," the officer shouted over his shoulder. "Inside, please!"

Wynona deflated. This was a mess. How was she going to be able to live like this? It seemed the ghost reporters had gotten the message, as this was a different group. Many of the women were dressed in tiny skirts and tight dress jackets. The men had gelled hair and some even appeared to have make-up on. These weren't the reporters. They were social media influencers. "Crap," Wynona grumbled. This group was almost as persistent as the ghost reporters. They ran blogs and social media accounts and many of them loved the shock factor. As a part of the presidential family, Wynona knew about this group all too well. Her sister, Celia, adored being interviewed and welcomed being treated like a celebrity every time she granted someone a bit of her time.

"Ms. Le Doux!"

Wynona shook her head and backed up to close the door.

"Ms. Le Doux!"

She paused. That voice. She knew that one. Stepping out carefully, Wynona's eyes nearly jerked out of their sockets when she spotted Mrs. Humryn stuck in the crowd. Without thinking, Wynona rushed down the steps and hurried to the crowd.

"Ms. Le Doux. What do you think you're doing?" the ogre growled.

"I'm so sorry," Wynona said breathlessly. "But that's one of my customers. She's not part of the paparazzi."

The officer looked to where Wynona was pointing. He groaned. "Go inside. I'll bring her in."

Wynona hesitated.

You promised.

Violet's voice snuck in and Wynona turned back to the door. The purple mouse was sitting on the threshold, her hands on her hips. Nodding, Wynona turned and went back inside. Camera flashes followed her and she couldn't help but take a relieved breath as she escaped their lenses.

Keeping the door slightly ajar, Wynona waited in the entryway until Officer Oozog dropped off Mrs. Humryn.

"The air is filled with devils," Mrs. Humryn said breathlessly, trying to fix her hair. "What a kerfuffle."

Wynona held back a laugh. She loved the pixie's use of older words. In a world where some creatures lived hundreds of years, there was always a mixture of languages from different eras.

"Thank you, Officer Oozog," Wynona said to the troll still standing at the door. "Can I get you something?" she asked.

He shook his head. "No, thank you. I'll get back to the wolves." He jabbed a thumb over his shoulder, then paused. "Don't tell Deputy Chief I said that."

Wynona couldn't help but snort a laugh. "Your secret is safe with me," she assured him. "Again, thank you."

He nodded, then stepped outside and pulled the door closed firmly behind him.

Wynona let out a breath. "Alright, Mrs. Humryn. Let's get you settled."

"I think maybe I'd like a different tea," the pixie said in her high pitched voice. "Something to settle my nerves."

Wynona gave herself just a second to let the magic flow through her. "I think I have just the thing," she assured her customer.

Fifteen minutes later, Mrs. Humryn was set up with her cup of chamomile and passionflower and a tray of tiny pastries.

Her duty done, Wynona went back to her office to take a breath. Violet was already sitting on the desk.

Well...it appears we have a situation.

Wynona plopped on the couch and sighed. "This is ridiculous."

It is. But it doesn't seem like we can do anything to stop them.

"I still don't get why no one will believe Alavara's tea house wasn't part of mine. I'm not a franchise." Wynona pulled a hair tie out of her pocket and pulled her hair up into a high bun. Today was proving to be more difficult than she would have expected. What was it going to take to make this all go away?

What are we going to do?

Violet lifted her head off the back of the sofa. "What?"

What are we going to do to get rid of this situation? Violet huffed. *We can't keep letting customers get caught in the hubbub. You were lucky Mrs. Humryn was the one trapped in the middle. Some of your other customers wouldn't be so kind about it.*

Wynona groaned. "You're right. But what *can* I do? We're just going to have to wait until the police solve the case."

You could solve it.

Wynona quickly shook her head. "Not a chance. I've done that several times now. I don't want to get involved."

You might not have a choice, Violet sniffed. *At the rate things are going, the tea shop is going to end up shut down because all your customers are too scared of Rock Guy.*

Wynona frowned. "Rock Guy?" Her eyebrows shot up. "You mean, Officer Oozog. He's an ogre."

He's a walking, talking rock, Violet argued.

Wynona rolled her eyes. "Be nice," she scolded. "It's not like a purple mouse is common either."

Violet grumbled but didn't say anything more. There really wasn't anything else to say. Unless Wynona wanted to get involved, there was nothing she could do but wait it out.

Violet was right, though. If the police didn't get moving soon, Wynona's business was going to suffer. Unless someone managed to corral the news media and kept them completely away from the shop, things were going to get difficult.

Wynona closed her eyes. They could do this. She just needed a few minutes to get her mind calmed, to come to grips with the situation and possible danger, and then she'd be ready to get started again.

Violet stood up, her ears twitching. *Lusgu is talking to someone.*

Wynona jumped to her feet. "Good heavens. What now?" The grumpy janitor was not a good man to have around the customers. He had a tendency to drive them away and the paparazzi was doing that well enough on their own. "Back to work," she grumbled under her breath. She paused at the door. "Coming?"

Violet waved her on. *Go ahead. I'm going to close my eyes for a few minutes.*

Wynona glared, but ultimately moved on. It wasn't worth getting angry over. Not everyone could live the life of a mouse.

CHAPTER 9

Wynona pressed the button to open her little garage. It was time to head into the shop, though it wouldn't open for a few more hours. Last night, after all the excitement of the day, she'd come home and crashed.

Rascal had checked in on her, but left without staying very long. She had barely been able to keep her eyes open and only wanted a cup of chamomile and a thick blanket.

This morning, however, she was feeling much better. She'd never put the theory to the test, but Wynona had a sneaking suspicion that the magic that leaked from the Grove of Secrets at the end of her property had more than a little to do with her swift recovery.

Her magic was strong, her body well rested and her hope restored. She was sure that everything about today was going to go better than yesterday.

Grabbing her bag, she walked to the Vespa she kept in the garage. It took up very little space and allowed her to store her things along the walls, which had been a bonus when she'd bought the house from a druid last year.

Being out near the forest kept away unforeseen visitors and it had a built-in greenhouse, which worked perfectly for Wynona's little tea business. Wynona was sure that the druid had done her own plant work and pulled on the powers from the forest to help, but she had never done any investigating into the matter.

The Grove of Secrets was a place where people disappeared. It was dark and foreboding, yet held an eerie beauty all its own. The fact that no one who went in ever came back out, only added to its mystique.

Its borders were beyond the jurisdiction of Hex Haven, meaning criminals always seemed to want to test their ability to survive by escaping through the trees, but none had ever been heard of again.

Wynona didn't know exactly what the magic of the forest did, but as long as she felt good and her plants got a little extra boost...she was fine right where she was.

Just as she moved to straddle the scooter, flashes began to blind her. "What in the world?" She put her hand up, but couldn't see anyone. "Ghost reporters," she grumbled, turning her head away just as the voices began to shout.

"Is it true you had a quarrel with Ms. Theramin?"

"Will you be attending the funeral?"

"Can you tell us more about how she died?"

"Violet," Wynona whispered.

On it. Violet jumped from her small basket at the front of the scooter and raced to Wynona's hand, then onto her shoulder.

With her familiar in place, Wynona channeled the magic she worked so hard to contain and let out the slightest trickle, aiming for her eyes. She wanted to shout with pride when her vision began to shift and the world went purple. Four blobs appeared and she pursed her lips, continuing to ignore their questions.

How did they know where she lived? The only reason there wasn't a guard at the house was because her address was unlisted. The only people who knew Wynona's residential address were Rascal and Prim and probably Chief Ligurio. None of them would have given her away.

The title company.

Wynona cursed under her breath at Violet's suggestion. These reporters had been working overtime. She stepped forward and the shouting calmed down as they waited for her to respond. "I will only ask once," Wynona said, doing her best to imitate her mother.

Marcella Le Doux could command a room better than anyone Wynona knew and she desperately needed a little of that charisma right now, even if she hated the thought of being compared to her estranged parent.

"Leave my property or I'll call the authorities."

"You have to give us something!" one of the blobs shouted.

"I have already told you all I know." Wynona squeezed her fists, her nails pinching her palm as she held back the onslaught of magic that wanted to break free. Violet helped, but right now Wynona was starting to get upset and that was a key trigger to her getting out of control. "I wasn't involved with Ms. Theramin in any way, shape or form."

Refusing to give them any more time, Wynona walked back to the house and pressed the button to close the garage. Once inside, she whipped out her cell phone. "Rascal?"

"Hey, Wy. What has you calling so early? Did you sleep well last night?"

His low, rumbling tone immediately began to help calm her ire and Wynona sat down in a chair, feeling slightly better. It would all be okay. It just might take a little time. "Someone leaked my address and I've got several ghost reporters at the front of the house. I can't leave."

His growl was dark and angry.

Wynona pulled the phone away from her ear and realized with a start that she was still seeing the world in purple. Blinking rapidly, she tugged on the strand of magic she had aimed at her vision and slowly, it went back to normal. "Thanks," she murmured to Violet.

Violet scrambled down and headed to the kitchen. *Might as well grab a snack. We're going to be here a while.*

Wynona couldn't blame her. She had no idea how long the reporters would hang around before giving up.

"I'm coming," Rascal said tightly from the other side of the line. "Meanwhile, make sure all the curtains are pulled and your doors and windows locked. They've gone too far this time."

"Thank you," Wynona responded. She hung up, grateful Rascal was on her side. He could be scary when he wanted to be and she almost felt bad for the reporters outside.

She walked to the window and peeked through. Nothing. Shaking her head, she worked her magic again. This time her sight snapped into place, bringing a fierce headache with it. "Ow," Wynona whimpered, rubbing her forehead.

That's what you get for doing it without me acting as buffer.

"I know," Wynona responded, keeping her eyes on the outside. There. Standing at the side of the house were all four blobs. Apparently, they'd hoped if they left the front of the garage, she'd assume they had gone away.

Sighing, Wynona pulled away from the window and blinked her eyes back into submission. "One of these days I have to learn to control it, though."

True. But taking on a tsunami by yourself isn't the smartest thing you've ever done.

"Thanks for the reminder." Wynona plopped onto her couch and laid her head back, closing her eyes. "They're a persistent bunch, aren't they?" she asked, referring to the media.

No more so than anyone else. They just get in your face about it. What happened to the cookies?

"Uh...you finished those last night," Wynona reminded the mouse.

Violet grumbled under her breath, but didn't speak again.

Wynona kept her eyes closed and tried to practice her meditative breathing while she waited for her rescue. She had a sneaking suspicion that those reporters weren't going to leave until someone with actual authority got to them.

The sounds of crunching gravel caught her attention fifteen minutes later and Wynona smiled. Her wolf in shining armor had arrived. She peered through the window to see his huge, black truck settle in her driveway.

Rascal's hair was standing on end, his eyes glowed bright enough to be seen from a distance and there was the beginning of fur on the back of his hands as he stormed toward the house. Before coming inside, he let out a loud growl that should have had any trespasser quaking in their boots.

Wynona unlocked the door and ushered him inside.

"Are you alright?" he asked. The words were slightly garbled as his teeth had begun to elongate.

"I'm fine," Wynona assured him. "Thank you for coming."

"How the he—" Rascal snapped his mouth shut and cleared his throat. His wolfy features slowly disappeared. "How the...crap did anyone know where you live? I thought it was unlisted."

Wynona sighed. "It is," she said, throwing her arms to the side. "You, Prim and Chief Ligurio are the only ones who know where I'm at." She scrunched her nose. "And the title company."

Rascal put his hands on his hips. "So someone called in a favor." His eyes darted to the door. "And called in friends. How many did you say there were?"

"Four," Wynona responded. She held up a finger and went to the window. This time she brought her purple vision up a little slower and the pain was much improved. "It looks like your appearance scared off most of them." She let the curtain fall back into place and blinked her vision back to normal. "Only one is still here." She frowned. "I'll bet it's the same one who didn't leave the shop when I asked the other day as well."

"Where are they?" Rascal asked.

Wynona pointed. "Just at the corner of the house."

His eyes flashed, but a smile tugged on his lips. "Watch this." Puffing up his chest, Rascal headed outside. He paused on the doorstep and sniffed the air. A deep growl permeated the fresh morning air and he continued to make a point out of smelling the breeze. Slowly, he turned toward the corner that Wynona had said the reporter was hiding.

Wynona held back a laugh and rushed to the window, pulling her purple vision back on. The sharp pain in her head was ignored as she watched the blob slowly back away. It trembled when Rascal let out a howl and began to stalk toward the side of the house.

The creature was frightened enough that it lost its control on being invisible and simply began a blur as it raced off her property and down the long driveway it had arrived on.

Wynona jumped at Rascal when he came back inside, wrapping her arms around his chest. "Thanks," she said through a laugh. "That was awesome."

His thick arms held her close and he kissed the top of her head. "No one messes with what's mine," he said in a severe tone.

Wynona paused only slightly. Was she his? They were dating and she felt certain she was beginning to fall in love with him, despite the fact that she didn't feel like she had time for that yet. But it still seemed so...permanent.

Then what would you call it?

Violet's question was a good one. Did it really matter if he referred to her as his? They were exclusively dating and wolves tended to be possessive. Really, it all made sense, she just hadn't put it in those exact words.

"Sorry," Rascal said gruffly, pulling back and looking embarrassed.

The last of Wynona's worries melted away. This was Rascal. Yes, she was his. Just as he was hers. Just because the words hadn't been said out loud before now didn't make them any less true.

She smiled to ease his worries and grabbed his hand. "Do you think I can get a police escort to the shop? Is someone meeting us there?"

"Actually, I'm waiting..." He trailed off when his phone buzzed and he held up a finger to Wynona before pulling away from her touch. "Strongclaw." His eyes were on the floor. "Uh-huh. How many?" He pressed his fingers into his eyes. "Yeah. Got it. Thanks." He ended the call and blew out a breath. "Where can you go instead of work today?"

"What?" Wynona screeched.

Rascal winced.

"Sorry." She'd forgotten about his sensitive hearing. "But what do you mean other than the shop? If I'm not there, it won't open."

Violet chittered so quickly that Wynona couldn't keep up with her, but it was clear how she felt about the situation.

"The murder broke the news this morning," Rascal said, holding his hands up to hold off arguments. "It was announced last night, but appeared on every available piece of media this morning." He gave her a look. "There are nearly twenty reporters and influencers outside your shop from everywhere around the region, wanting to interview you. Since you shut them out, they're all getting more desperate."

"What?" Wynona's head spun. This was much worse than a few persistent ghost reporters. They were at her shop, now they'd found her home. What next?

"Wy?" Rascal ducked his head so he could look into her eyes. "Where do you want to go? You could always hang out at the station, but I'll probably be in and out all day."

Wynona shook her head. "No. I don't want to be there."

"I'll try not to take that personally," he grumbled good naturedly.

Wynona looked up, feeling helpless. "I don't want to be a distraction and I...I wasn't going to get involved in the case, but..."

"But?" Rascal pressed.

"But it now looks like I'm going to have to close my shop until this goes away." She set her hands to the side. "How can I sit back and do nothing?"

Rascal shrugged. "I don't know, but don't get involved in something you're going to regret either."

Violet grumbled and curled up in a ball on Wynona's shoulder.

"Can I go to Prim's? Do you think anyone's there?"

Rascal's lips pursed as he considered. "I haven't heard that they're bothering her. That's probably as good a place as any." He jutted his chin out. "Grab your stuff and I'll drop you off. My windows are tinted enough we should be able to get you where you want to go."

Feeling ridiculous and frustrated, Wynona did as she was told. She didn't want to be at Prim's. She wanted to be at her shop. She *needed* to be at her shop. But if they took too long to solve the case, she would continue to be displaced from her work and her home.

Wynona didn't like it, but maybe...it was time to take matters into her own hands.

CHAPTER 10

"So..." Prim drawled as she wiggled her fingers at a fern. The delicate branches grew at a visible rate, reaching for the magic the fairy offered. "Who do you think cursed you?"

Wynona had to give her friend credit. She was definitely doing everything she could to keep Wynona from going stir crazy or from thinking about the mess that was her current life.

Because it's better to think of the mess that was your past life?

Wynona shot Violet a look, who wasn't the least bit repentant about her sassy behavior. She looked back at Prim, who was waiting expectantly. "I have no idea," Wynona said with a sigh. She plopped herself onto a stool. "Anyone who hated my parents could have done it, though how anyone got close enough is a mystery."

Prim pursed her pink lips and focused on spritzing a hollyhock. "How close would someone have to have been in order to curse you?"

Wynona paused. She hadn't really thought about it. "You know, I'm not quite sure." She put her clasped hands on the work table. "They couldn't have been across town. That's too far for even my mother." Her red nails tapped the dirty surface. "But with the protection wards in place, I would think the creature had to be in the castle."

"So...someone snuck in?"

Wynona shook her head. "That or..." She trailed off as another thought occurred to her. She felt the blood drain from her head and swayed slightly before catching herself on the edge of the table.

"Nona!" Prim shouted, rushing over. "What in the world happened? You're as white as a moonflower."

Wynona sputtered and came out of her shock when Prim began to spray the water in her face. "Holy hexes, enough!" Wynona put her hands up to stop any more moisture from hitting her.

"Sorry," Prim said, real concern in her tone. "I was trying to pull you out of your trance."

Wynona raised her eyebrows and wiped at her face. "Thanks, I think." She gave a wry grin. "It worked, after all."

Prim's smile was anything but easy. "But what caused it in the first place? Were you having another vision?" She looked around. "I don't see a teacup."

Wynona wiped her now wet hands on her skirt. "No, no vision. Just a realization." She hadn't realized just how frightening her tea reading must have been if this is how Prim reacted. Yes, Wynona knew she blocked out the outside world when the magic took over, but dousing someone in plant water seemed a bit extreme.

"And?" Prim pressed, leaning in.

"I think it must have been someone who was already there." Wynona's voice was low and hoarse. If her thoughts were correct, that brought them down to two types of suspects.

"So a servant...or..." Prim said carefully, also having caught wind of the idea.

"Or a family member." Wynona swallowed hard. Betrayal cut through her chest like a knife. Her family members were supposed to be the ones who loved her and took care of her. Why in the world would one of them curse her?

"But that doesn't make any sense," Prim said, shaking her head hard. "Your parents were furious that you didn't have powers. They might not be a loving couple, but I can't see them doing anything to hinder your possibilities."

The pain eased a little as Wynona realized her friend was right. It didn't make sense for her parents to bind her powers. And since she was the oldest of the Le Doux children, none of her siblings could have done it either. "So that leaves us with a servant," she mused.

"Or an employee," Prim pointed out. "Your family employs all sorts of people who wouldn't be considered servants. Cooks, bakers, accountants...the list is endless."

Another long breath eased the tightness in her chest even more and Wynona began to relax. "You're right. The only problem is, that leaves the list endless as well."

"True." Prim began to walk again, spraying water as she went. "And why would they risk hurting the presidential child?" She spun on her dainty toes. "What was in it for them?"

"The chance to take down the Le Douxs?" Wynona offered.

"No...because they didn't curse Celia. And with their magic, Mama Le Doux and dear old Daddy will live for hundreds of years." She bounced on her toes, a position that would have led to taking flight if she had wings. "If someone wanted to stage a coup, they would have gone for the parents, not the useless baby."

Wynona groaned and threw back her head. "This is why I try not to think on it. It's just a big mess and nothing makes sense."

"I sure wish your grandma was alive," Prim said. "She'd probably have some insight for us."

"True." Wynona felt the usual depression coming on as she thought about her grandmother. The woman was the only maternal influence she'd had. Without powers, Wynona had been nothing but dead weight to her parents. Since she couldn't help them gain or retain their power, they basically threw her away, letting her know in no uncertain terms how useless she was.

Ha! If only they could see you now, Violet said smugly.

"We don't want them to see me now," Wynona reminded her familiar. "If they catch wind of my powers, they'll drag me home in the middle of the night."

"Not if you get strong enough before they know what's going on," Prim pointed out. "But you won't be able to keep something like this a secret forever, you know."

"I know, but right now things are too out of control," Wynona argued. "I need them to stay ignorant just a bit longer. When I have a better handle on things, then I think I can give them a run for their money if they try anything."

"Fine, fine," Prim whined. "Let's talk about something else."

You do realize that Grandma might have shared things with Lusgu or Mrs. Reyna?

Wynona stiffened and slowly turned to Violet, her mind spinning. She barely remembered that Mrs. Reyna, Rascal's wolf shifter neighbor, had made comments about Granny Saffron. The two had obviously known each other, but Wynona had been too busy with a case at the time of their last visit to press the issue. "Lusgu won't tell me anything," Wynona whispered.

Violet shrugged. *True. But it's worth a shot.*

"Hello? Earth to Nona?"

Wynona jerked her head to look at the impatient fairy. "Right. Sorry. New topic."

"Tell me about this murder."

Violet snickered.

Prim spread her hands to the side. "What? I'm curious."

Wynona nodded. She couldn't blame Prim for wanting to know more. Everyone did. It was why Wynona couldn't go to work...or home. "I don't know much," she admitted. "Alavara was killed. As far as I know, it was a knife through her back." A shudder ran up her spine. Despite helping out the police several times, Wynona never enjoyed seeing a crime scene.

"What kind of knife was it?"

Wynona frowned and shook her head. "I have no idea. A big one."

Prim smirked. "Good observation."

Wynona rolled her eyes. "I wasn't there to study the crime scene."

Prim bounced over to the table and jumped onto a stool, setting the spray bottle aside. "Are you really telling me that the great Wynona Le Doux, murderer catcher extraordinare, didn't see *anything* suspicious when presented with a murder the police thought she might have committed?"

Wyanona made a face at her friend, who only laughed. "Yeah, okay. I noticed something, but..."

"But?"

"But it disappeared."

Prim frowned. "How could it disappear?"

Wynona leaned her elbows onto the table. "When they removed her body, I was looking around—"

"I knew it!" Prim cried triumphantly. She pointed one tiny, manicured finger across the table. "You're curious."

"Of course, I'm curious," Wynona said with a laugh. "Who wouldn't be?"

Prim shrugged. "Lots of creatures, I'm sure."

Wynona waved the idea off. "Do you want to hear what I saw, or not?"

Prim made the motion of zipping her lips, then sat very still.

"When the body was gone, I noticed there was a lump in the blood."

"Ewww..."

Wynona gave Prim another look and the fairy quieted down again. "Once I realized it wasn't just a clot or something, I grabbed a pencil from the desk and poked at it."

Prim snickered. "You sound like a boy in the woods, poking at dead animals."

"Oh, for heaven's sake." Wynona threw up her arms. "Seriously?"

"Okay, okay, I'm sorry." Prim was laughing too hard for her apology to be taken seriously. "The way you said it was kind of funny."

Wynona couldn't help but smile. Prim was right, it was a little humorous. "*Anyway*, I turned over the blob and discovered it was a button."

Prim's eyes widened. "The killer's?"

Wynona lifted her shoulders. "I don't know. I tried to move the blood with the eraser of the pencil, but it was too saturated to tell for sure what it even looked like in order to know who it belonged to. I think it was gold, but I can't be sure."

"And you said it disappeared?" Prim cocked her head. "How did that happen?"

Wynona told the story of leaving the room and coming back to nothing. "So you see, there's really nothing to go on. Other than the button, the murder scene was clean, according to Rascal. They're interviewing people, but no one is standing out as having any reason to hurt her."

"She obviously had no trouble breaking the law," Prim said with a sniff. "I'll bet one of the people she conned before came back and settled the score."

"I've thought of that," Wynona murmured. "And I know the police have as well. If there's a possible connection that way, I'm sure they'll find it, though I find death a little strong for a copycat."

"Sure..." Prim said slowly. "They'll find the connection, but in the meantime, you're out of house and business." Her sarcastic look fell into one of concern. "What're you going to do?"

Wynona slumped. "I'm not sure. My patrons can't even get into the shop with the crowds that were there yesterday, and Rascal said it was worse this morning. Plus, you know they found my house." She blew a piece of hair out of her face. "I'm not sure how to get them to leave me alone. Stating that our shops had nothing to do with each other has made no difference. Everyone just overrides me."

"Idiots," Prim muttered, grabbing her bottle again. She thrust it toward Wynona. "Well, might as well make yourself useful. I have to make some arrangements for the Weeping Widow."

"Since when did the pizza parlor need flowers?"

"Since Widow Wraithsong is trying to redecorate." Prim pointed to a corner of the greenhouse. It was filled with plants that looked like they'd rather eat a body than sit beautifully in a vase. "She's definitely going for a darker vibe than you are."

"Huh." Wynona shook her head. "Good for her, I guess." Shifting off her stool, she walked around and sprayed the flowers that looked like they hadn't been watered yet. The motion was monotonous, but calming. What was it about plants that had the ability to make a person feel better?

At the thought, Wynona's eyes darted to the plants Prim was currently working with. A shiver ran up her spine. "Most plants anyway," she whispered to herself.

Ten minutes of peace passed and Wynona was just getting ready to refill her bottle when Prim spoke up.

"Have you made up your mind yet?"

"Made up my mind? About what?" Wynona asked.

"About helping the police," Prim said as if the answer was obvious.

Wynona unscrewed the top and placed the empty bottle under the faucet flow. "I have to admit I considered it, but I'm not a detective. I really should just stay out of it."

"You're better than any detective I know," Prim offered.

"Oh? And how many are you acquainted with?" Wynona asked with a smile.

Prim put her nose in the air. "More than you know."

"I'll believe that when I see it," Wynona retorted, then laughed. "But thanks. I appreciate the vote of confidence."

"But I'm serious. You can't just not work and not go home. The only way the media are ever going to leave you alone is if you get this thing solved." Prim paused in her work and turned to face Wynona. "You said yourself the police don't have a lot to go on. You could help."

"I'm sure the police are plenty capable," Wynona said with a raised eyebrow. "Rascal knows what he's doing."

"He does, but somehow it's been you who's figured out the last several murderers," Prim sang.

Before Wynona could retort, her phone buzzed and she pulled it out of her pocket, hoping it was an update from Rascal. The number was unknown. Frowning, she answered the call. "Hello?"

"Ms. Le Doux? We'd like to schedule an interview with you about the recent killing of your partner, Ms. Alavara Theramin."

Wynona jerked away from the device, then immediately put it back to her ear. "How did you get this number?"

"Are you available in the next thirty minutes?" the woman asked, completely ignoring Wynona's question.

"No." Wynona pressed the end button and then turned off the sound when it buzzed at her again.

Prim tsked her tongue. "They're not going to give up."

"Why? Why won't they give up? I didn't have anything to do with this!" Wynona felt her eyes begin to sting and purple sparkles dripped from her fingertips. She was becoming overwrought and if she didn't get back under control quickly, she might damage Prim's greenhouse.

She pressed her fists into her eyes. "Violet," she whispered.

The scuffling of feet hurried across the floor and Wynona felt the mouse climb her leg, until she settled on her shoulder and nuzzled her neck. It still took a few moments, but slowly, Wynona felt her magic begin to calm. "Thank you," she said softly, petting the creature behind the ears.

Prim's right. We need this case done and gone.

Wynona sighed and nodded, looking over to Prim, who was frowning in concern. "You're right," she said. "I need to get this over with. I can't concentrate, I can't practice my magic, I can't even work until it's all out of my hair." A weak smile pulled at her lips. "One more set of eyes on the case can't be a bad thing, right?"

Prim nodded, though she looked reluctant, as if she understood what this was costing Wynona. "You're amazing," Prim said. "You'll have it figured out in no time."

"Let's hope so," Wynona muttered. "Or my magic just might kill me before I ever get around to mastering it."

CHAPTER 11

"I understand budget constraints," Wynona argued over the phone. "But I'm not looking to be paid." She sighed and pinched the bridge of her nose. "I just want my life back."

"It doesn't work that way," Chief Ligurio snapped. "I can't just have volunteer consultants hanging around doing whatever they want. The station would be filled with wanna-be detectives who have watched one too many episodes of 'Condemned Creatures.'"

Wynona sent Prim a pleading look, but the fairy waved her off. So much for being best friends.

"The vamp hates me," Prim said. "Don't turn to me for help."

"He doesn't..." Wynona cut off her response. In the end it didn't really matter whether the grumpy vampire chief hated anyone or not. "Chief," she said as calmly as she could. "Can you bring me on with a ridiculously low amount of money? Like five dollars? That way there's the official paperwork, I'm free to move about the crime scenes, and I can do my best to offer any insight I discover."

A long, beleaguered sigh came through the line.

When he didn't object immediately, Wynona held her breath. She had a chance. She really wasn't in this for a second paycheck. Her business and life were in jeopardy and that was the only reason she wanted in on the case. She'd spent most of the last year under the radar, but now the media outlets were hounding her like she was the last witch on earth.

It was time to take a stand and the only way to do that was to put to rest the murder that everyone was upset about. Things would be so much easier, however, if she could do her investigating with police permission. Trying to sneak around on her own was possible, but Wynona knew from experience that having the chief's blessing opened far more doors than that of a tea shop owner.

"Fine," Chief Ligurio growled. "But I'm putting Strongclaw on your tail, Ms. Le Doux. With the reporters trying to pin you down, I don't think it's a good idea for you to wander around as an open target. If I recall correctly, we're already wasting resources to keep you safe." He grunted. "Are you sure you want to risk being found?"

Wynona hesitated only slightly before answering in the affirmative. "I can't keep living my life like this," she explained. "My business is suffering and I want it fixed. One more set of eyes on the clues should only help matters."

She didn't want to explain to him how the whole purpose of her escaping her family was to gain freedom and the current situation was taking that back away. The deep, visceral need in her belly was gnawing at her. She couldn't keep hiding. She couldn't keep sitting back and let someone else handle it.

Wynona had proven her worth several times before, which Chief Ligurio knew. If he didn't trust her, he wouldn't be willing to take a risk on her. The fact that he did so grudgingly was only because his grumpy personality demanded it. Well...that and the fact that he hated her family with a passion, but who was worried about past grudges?

"Fine." There was a shuffling of papers on the other side of the line. "Nightshade will take care of the paperwork. Make yourself useful, Ms. Le Doux," Chief Ligurio warned. "Or we won't be doing this again."

Wynona rolled her eyes at the warning, then stuck her phone in her pocket.

"Melodramatic, much?" Prim asked, voicing the sarcastic comment sitting on Wynona's tongue.

"You heard that, huh?" Wynona began to gather her things.

"Couldn't help but hear it. Anyone with any form of supernatural hearing did. He wasn't trying to keep his voice down at all."

Wynona nodded. "Yeah, well...at least he said yes. Dancing around behind his back is much harder." She found her keys and jangled them. "And on that note, I'm going to get to work."

Prim pursed her lips in a pout. "How come you get to have all the fun?"

Wynona laughed. "You really want to go around looking at dead bodies and trying to figure out if someone is lying to you?"

Prim shrugged. "No, but you make it look good...so..."

Wynona walked around and grabbed the fairy in a tight hug. "And this is why I love you so much." One last squeeze and then she pulled back. "Be safe. I'll check in soon."

"Be careful. Chief said he was sending Rascal, but he's not here yet."

Wynona nodded. "I'll shoot him a text."

"Where are you going first?"

Wynona paused at the doorway, waiting for Violet to scramble up her leg and settle on her shoulder. "Where else?" She gave Prim a wry smile. "The scene of the crime."

The tea house was still roped off to the general public and two guards were posted at the door. "Good morning, gentlemen," Wynona said with a cheer she didn't feel.

The officers glanced at each other. "This place is off limits to civilians," a man with bright green eyes said.

Wynona assumed he was a shifter, since the color was brighter than it should have been on a normal person. "I'm aware of that, thank you," she said politely. "I'm Wynona Le Doux. I've been hired by—"

"Le Doux? As in President Le Doux?" the other officer chimed in. His eyes were wide and slightly frightened.

Wynona held back a wince. Her family's reputation always seemed to precede her. And not in a good way. "Yes," she said carefully. "But I'm here on behalf of—"

"Not even the presidential family has jurisdiction at a crime scene," the shifter interrupted again. He straightened his shoulders as if to show that he wasn't worried about any potential backlash. "Please leave."

Wynona put her hands in the air. "Officer…" She paused, waiting for him to fill in the blank.

The shifter narrowed his eyes, refusing to answer.

"Officer," she said a little more softly. "I'm not here on behalf of my family. Chief Ligurio has hired me as a consultant and I need to look at the crime scene." Sheesh. Working with the chief was supposed to help make this easier, but right now Wynona kind of wished she had just snuck through the back.

The shifter snorted and exchanged amused glances with his not-as-brave companion. "Chief Ligurio hired you? Really?"

Before Wynona could take offense or respond to the disbelief, tires squealed to a stop. All three heads turned toward the sound and Wynona blew out a breath of relief. The cavalry had arrived.

Rascal was looking every inch the deputy chief in charge when he stormed up to the front of the building. "You couldn't have waited for me?" he asked, raising a single eyebrow.

Wynona knew it was meant to sound tough and in charge, but the slight twinkle in his golden eyes, which were almost always filled with laughter, gave him away. She shrugged nonchalantly, giving him a coy smile. "But don't worry, these two were adamant that I wait for you before entering."

She heard the choking sound of disbelief behind her and Rascal's eyebrows shot up. There was no fooling him. "Glad to know Officer Melion and Aldor have such good heads on their shoulders." Rascal sent them a toothy smile.

The quiet one seemed to shrink a little while the other shifter held himself stiff as a board.

Rascal waved an arm toward the door. "Should we go inside before the ghost reporters find you?"

The shifter must have had a death wish because he opened his mouth one more time, before Rascal's glare made him snap it shut again.

"Thank you," Wynona said softly as she and Rascal walked by. She knew they were just doing their duty, though they could have been a little more pleasant about it. Many of the officers at the precinct knew her, or at least knew of her reputation, but these two were young and Wynona had never met them before.

I'd say you've left an indelible impression this time, Violet said wryly.

Wynona laughed softly. "I'd say so." She paused in the dining room of the shop. "Such a waste."

Rascal growled lightly. "Such a rip off. She was breaking all sorts of laws."

Wynona nodded sadly. "I know, but still...it's horrible that she was killed."

He wrapped an arm around her shoulders and kissed her forehead. "Thanks for deciding to come help."

Wynona glanced up. "No qualms about me putting myself in danger?"

Rascal made a face. "I can't say I love that, but we were running ourselves in circles. I'm hoping your out-of-the-box way of looking at things will give us a lead." He grinned. "Plus, it means I get to stay closer to you."

Wynona smiled back. "I don't mind that either." Rascal was becoming a permanent fixture in her life and she loved it. He was right. This would be a great way for them to spend time together. Sitting in front of a fire, sipping tea and exchanging kisses would be preferable, but...she'd take what she could get.

"Where to first?" he asked.

"Let's go back to the office," Wynona suggested. "I looked before, but this time I'll be more focused."

"Right."

They went down the hallway and Wynona pushed the door open. "Oh!" She gasped. The dwarf janitor, who had been playing Lusgu's role, was curled into the corner of the office, stuffing his face with what appeared to be cake. "Hello," Wynona said carefully. She glanced at Rascal over her shoulder, but held up her hand when he tried to walk in front of her.

Rascal huffed, but his hands were shifted into paws with very large claws as if ready for an attack.

The dwarf ignored Wynona and continued to eat. Wynona stepped forward, being sure to skirt the blood stain on the floor. "Sir? Sir?"

Black, beady eyes jumped up to hers before going back to his meal.

With Rascal's heat at her back, Wynona stopped a few feet from the creature. "Sir, this is a crime scene. Would you mind telling us why you're here?"

The dwarf's eyes narrowed and he swallowed. "Home," he grunted, stuffing another bite in his mouth.

"You live here?" Wynona asked. If Alavara had been trying to find a copycat for Lusgu, she'd done a good job. Lusgu rarely spoke and when he did, it wasn't always helpful. Short, terse answers that were vague seemed to be his specialty. Mr. Hungry seemed to be cut from the same cloth, which was unusual for a dwarf. They tended to be loud and overly aggressive, like the baker Chef Droxon that Wynona had worked with before he'd been killed.

The dwarf grunted.

"Okay, enough." Rascal stepped forward and grabbed the dwarf by his collar, dragging him screaming and hollering down the hall.

"Stupid dog!" the small man shouted, swinging his arms in the air.

Rascal held the creature out in front of him and the punches held little effect. Being so tall and strong, it probably felt like being hit by a child.

Wynona bit back an inappropriate laugh. The situation was serious, but the scene was kind of funny to watch.

Scratching and spitting, Rascal dumped the dwarf on a couch out in the dining room. "Now." Rascal bent over and got right in the creature's face, his sharp teeth on full display. "Tell us why you're here and I might stop them from tossing your butt in jail."

Wynona stayed back. She wasn't going to get between the two men right now. Not until some things had been figured out. The dwarf really shouldn't have been here. And why was he eating as if his last meal had been three weeks ago?

The janitor glared at Rascal and adjusted his clothes until he was satisfied. Apparently, even an angry wolf shifter wasn't enough to make the man worry about his life. "I live here," he ground out, his black eyes glittering with anger. "You, none of you, have the right to keep me from my home."

"It's a crime scene," Rascal argued, folding his arms over his chest. "We have every right. You being here violates the law, not to mention you could be contaminating evidence."

"Are you saying you didn't get all the evidence during your first sweep of the place?" the small man said with a not so pleasant grin.

Rascal's growl was deep.

Wynona finally felt like it was time to break up the male bonding. "Excuse me." She stepped up close to Rascal and put a hand on his arm, but kept her focus on the dwarf. "Hello, I'm Wynona Le

Doux." She smiled, but the janitor kept his glare. "I'm helping the police work on solving Alavara's murder."

At the words, the creature shifted uneasily.

Wynona squatted down to be more at his level. "You worked for her, correct? Were you part of the clean up crew?"

He huffed. "I was *the* clean up crew. Not sure how a body was supposed to do it all by themselves, but I managed."

Wynona kept her smile in place. "That must have been a lot of work." She looked around. "And you did an admirable job. Not a speck of dust anywhere." She let out a small breath when she saw some of his anger dissipate. "Would you mind telling me your name?" She knew Rascal had the information, but right now she was trying to break down the dwarf's defenses. His cooperation would be much better than anything forced.

He eyed her before answering. "Masterick. Leadtank."

"Nice to meet you."

"Are you really a Le Doux?"

Wynona nodded. Maybe she should have changed her name when she escaped. The name held too many connotations for the public at large.

"And yet you're out here? Helping the police?"

Wynona nodded again. She pointed to the other side of the couch. "May I?"

Masterick hesitated, but ultimately nodded. His demeanor said he was wary, but intrigued. Okay, so maybe having a famous last name wasn't such a bad thing.

"I'm sure the police have already interviewed you," Wynona stated, ignoring the dwarf's grunt. "But can you tell me your story again? Maybe there's something they missed."

"Likely," Masterick said, glaring with hatred up at Rascal, who bared his teeth in return.

Wynona gave her boyfriend a look and he raised his eyebrows in an innocent gesture. Men. Shaking her head, she turned back to the janitor. "The night Ms. Theramin died, where were you?"

"Here," Masterick grunted. "As always."

"Did you hear anything? A disturbance of some kind?"

Masterick poked his pinky in his ear and shook it rigorously. "Nope. Not a thing." He grinned. "Deep sleeper."

"Well, after all the hard work you do, it's no wonder," Wynona praised. When Masterick preened, she knew that flattery was going to be the best way to get any information. "What did you do when you woke up to go to work?"

He shrugged. "I saw the body." His eyes went up again. "And had to call it in. Unfortunately."

"That's it?" Wynona was disappointed. Surely he had more to offer than that.

"What do you want? I went to bed as usual, slept as usual and woke up to a dead body. That wasn't usual." Masterick snorted and folded his arms over his chest.

"What about finding you eating cake in your boss's office?" Rascal demanded. "Is that usual too?"

Masterick rolled his eyes. "No one has brought food in since yesterday," he snapped. "What do you expect me to live on? Air?"

"So the cake was left over from yesterday?" Wynona pressed. "Did Alavara do her own baking?"

Another snort. "She couldn't cook to feed herself, let alone anyone else."

"Who did she have a contract with?" Wynona asked.

The dwarf grumbled, but didn't respond.

"A Ms. Mardella Soulton," Rascal offered, smirking when Masterick ground his teeth. "We already cleared her, but I can take you to talk to her if you'd like."

"I would." Wynona stood and offered her hand to Masterick. "Thank you for your time, but I think maybe you need to find somewhere else to stay for the foreseeable future."

When Masterick didn't budge, Rascal grabbed him again and hauled him outside. "Take him to the station," Rascal said, handing off the shouting dwarf. "If he can find somewhere else to stay, he can go there instead."

"Yes, sir," Officer Melion said quickly, working to subdue the squirming man. "I'm on it."

"Come on," Rascal said, taking Wynona's elbow. "I'll drive."

CHAPTER 12

"Have you heard of her?" Rascal asked as they got onto the road.

Wynona's lips pinched into a thin line. "No...she's not a name I'm familiar with." She shrugged. "There have to be dozens of bakers in Hex Haven."

"True." Rascal's ears twitched. "But there had to be a reason Alavara used her. Why not Kyoz and Gnuq? It's not like she couldn't have hired them. Business would have been business."

Wynona tapped her silver nail on her knee. "That's an excellent question. She seemed to be copying me, but this wasn't as close of a match as the other parts." She scrunched up her nose. "Maybe that was her defense in court? It wasn't exact, so there was no copying?"

"Maybe," Rascal murmured. He made a right turn, taking them out of the main parts of the city, and parked along the street.

Wynona climbed out, Violet hanging onto her hair as they stared at the bakery. It was everything a person would expect. Pink striped awning, cakes and other goods displayed in the window with a visible bell above the door. "Alavara might have been copying me, but Ms. Soulton is definitely not copying Kyoz and Gnuq. Their place is barely recognizable as a bakery."

Rascal waited by the door for her. "How did you discover them, then?"

Wynona laughed softly. "They'd catered one of my parents' parties when Chef Droxon wasn't available." She shrugged. "I figured if my parents would use them, they had to be worth hiring."

"Good call," he murmured, "if they weren't such pains in the backside."

"Oh, I know," Wynona said over her shoulder. "Prim never lets me forget it." She faced forward, needing to get her head in the game for the interview ahead. The poor janitor sounded as if he was a victim of circumstance, but Wynona wasn't ready to let him off her list just yet. Not until she had someone more clearly in mind.

Someone had killed Alavara and the most likely was someone who was close to the victim, and that likely meant someone from the shop. Though that left their list devastatingly small.

"Hello!" a lovely woman said from behind the counter. She had glasses on the tip of her nose and chunks of hair falling out of the bun on her head. Her apron was covered in flour and some of that flour had made its way onto her cheek. "What can I get for you today?" She pushed the glasses up, leaving a trail of flour along the tip of her nose.

Wynona couldn't help but smile at the sight. There was no question that this woman was a baker. Which also meant she was the person they were looking for. "Ms. Soulton? Ms. Mardella Soulton?" Wynona clarified.

The woman frowned. "Yes, that's me." She looked between the two of them. "Is there a problem?"

"My name is Deputy Chief Strongclaw," Rascal said, giving her an odd look. "Do you remember speaking to me yesterday?"

Ms. Soulton pursed her lips and studied him for a moment before her eyes widened. "Oh! Yes. The werewolf." Her shoulders fell. "Alavara's death."

"Wolf shifter," Rascal corrected.

Wynona smiled at his defensiveness. "Yes," Wynona said, inserting herself in the conversation. "My name is Wynona Le Doux. I'm a consultant with the precinct and I'd like to ask you a few questions."

"Consultant?" Ms. Soulton's frown deepened. "I didn't know they used consultants. And a Le Doux? You're related to the president?"

Wynona held back her sigh. Maybe she needed to just say her first name. Anyone who thought about it would recognize her, especially since she was the spitting image of her mother, but it didn't mean Wynona had to advertise the connection. "Yes, I'm their daughter."

The baker's eyes widened and she stepped back a little. "And what did you need exactly?"

Wynona put on her most pleasant smile. "I know you already spoke to the police, but I'd like to ask you a few questions myself." She looked around, noting the empty bakery. "Is now a good time?"

Ms. Soulton sighed and took off her glasses, cleaning them against her apron. The baking accessory was cute, with cats and bows all over it. She set the glasses back on her nose. "I suppose. It's not like I've got other customers to take care of at the moment."

Wynona made sure to keep her smile in place. She could understand someone not enjoying being invaded by the police. "Can you tell me where you were the night of the murder?"

Ms. Soulton shrugged. "I was at home."

"And do you live alone?"

Ms. Soulton nodded. "Well, unless you count my cats."

"Cats? You have more than one?" Wynona clarified. Violet huffed in her ear.

"Seventeen," Ms. Soulton said, a smile bursting onto her face. "I am a witch, after all."

"Ah." Wynona had wondered, but wasn't sure how to ask. The more human looking paras were sometimes hard to figure out. "Any specialties?"

Ms. Soulton spread her hands to the side, showcasing her display cases. "Hearth Witch. That's why I bake."

"And is there magic in your goods?" Putting magic in food was fine, as long as it was advertised that way. Wynona had noticed no such notice when they'd walked in.

"Not usually," Ms. Soulton replied easily. "Only when I get a custom order and they ask for something specific."

Wynona nodded and looked at Rascal. He smiled, but didn't speak. This was her show. He'd had his chance.

She worked to make her brain come up with more questions, but Wynona was coming up blank. "How long have you worked with Alavara?"

"Since she opened. So, just a few weeks."

"And how did you get the job?"

"Pardon?" Ms. Soulton looked offended. "Why wouldn't I get the job?"

"I'm sorry," Wynona said quickly. "I just wondered if you had a connection before the contract or if you applied for the job?" Considering how calm Ms. Soulton seemed, Wynona was sure the two women hadn't been friends. A friend would still be mourning at this point.

Ms. Soulton shrugged. "I sent in a resume and a sample. She called and said I got the job."

"Okay...well...thank you." Wynona's smile was tight. She didn't know anything more than she had when they'd come inside. Ms. Soulton seemed sweet, if not a little scatterbrained. Without any kind of connection, there seemed little reason why she would kill her employer. A few weeks wasn't quite enough time for someone to go from hello to murder. "Do you know of any other people we should speak to?" Wynona ventured. "Anyone that Ms. Theramin had a relationship with?"

Ms. Soulton began fussing with some bagged candies on the front desk. "She was dating someone at the police station." The witch scrunched up her nose. "He might have more information for you. I'm sorry I'm not much help."

"It's alright," Wynona assured her. "Thank you for your time." She followed Rascal back out to the truck and climbed inside before speaking. "She had a police boyfriend?" she screeched. "What was wrong with this woman?"

Rascal chuckled. "You ignored her for a long time and now that you know she was dating an officer, you freak out?" He winked. "I think I'm flattered."

Wynona huffed and folded her arms over her chest. "It's one thing to copy my business. It's another to copy my life."

Maybe she was mentally insane.

Wynona shook her head. "She didn't seem that way at all when we spoke to her."

Violet grumbled, but ultimately agreed.

"Do you know who she was dating?" Wynona asked Rascal.

Rascal nodded. "Yep. Give me five minutes. Officer Montego hasn't been on duty since the incident. He'll be at his house." He glanced over his shoulder and merged into traffic before turning them south.

Wynona mused while they were driving, stuck in her thoughts until Violet interrupted.

Who has seventeen cats? Talk about a crazy cat lady.

"Technically, she's a witchy cat lady," Wynona offered.

Violet scoffed. *Still. Ridiculous. No one sane surrounds themselves with predators.*

Rascal chuckled and Wynona looked over. Sometimes he could catch glimpses of Violet's chatter and apparently he'd caught that last sentence. "Careful, little purple," he teased. "You're surrounded your-self."

Violet sniffed and began to groom herself. Apparently, she didn't find Rascal all that intimidating.

Wynona shook her head and reached over to rest her hand on Rascal's thigh. He quickly entwined their fingers and kept hold while he maneuvered the vehicle to a small cottage style home.

"Here we are." He put the truck in park and they let go of each other long enough to get out of the vehicle.

Wynona straightened her shirt as they waited at the door. Before it could open, she quickly leaned toward her companion. "What is he?" she whispered.

"Vampire," Rascal offered back, just as quickly.

Violet snorted. *Of course.*

Wynona nodded her understanding just as the door opened.

"D-deputy Chief," the man standing in the doorway said. His eyes were red rimmed and his face more ashen than was normal for his kind. He wasn't nearly as large as Rascal was, which was a testament to his strength, or lack thereof. The man's slight stature was defeated as his shoulders rounded and his head looked too heavy to hold up. Officer Montego slumped against the side of the doorframe. "What are you doing here?"

Wynona frowned. The glazed look in his eyes made her think he was drunk, but vampires had to drink *a lot* of alcohol to reach that state. Had he been that in love with Alavara? Men didn't usually respond quite this way...at least not in her experience.

"Montego," Rascal said, his voice much softer than with the other two suspects. "Ms. Le Doux has been hired as a consultant on Ms. Theramin's case. She'd like to ask you some questions."

The officer eyed Wynona, then deflated even further. He sniffed, wiping his nose on the back of his hand. "Might as well come in," he said hoarsely, waving a wild arm. "Nothing better to do anyway." He shuffled across the floor, his socks slipping on the hardwood floors.

Wynona glanced at Rascal, who nodded her to go ahead. She stepped inside, feeling like an invader, but knowing she needed to speak to the man. He probably knew Alavara better than anyone. Wynona trod carefully, but her eyes moved around. The place was definitely a bachelor pad.

Clothes were thrown on the dining chairs, bags of blood were strewn across the coffee table along with dozens of soda cans, while dishes filled the sink. The pervasive scent of stale copper clung to everything and Wynona did her best not to shudder.

"Have a seat," he said, waving toward the couch.

Wynona sat gingerly on the edge. He hadn't offered to clean off the surface and she didn't want to do something that would upset him. It was clear the man was taking the death hard. "I'm sorry to bother you, Mr. Montego, but I'm hoping you can answer a few questions."

He slumped in a seat across from her and grabbed the half empty beer bottle on a side table. He took a swig. "Ask away." Normally other liquids went right through a vampire, but he must have been pumping his system full if his behavior was anything to go by.

Wynona cleared her throat and tried to ignore Violet's running diatribe of disgust in her head along with the six pack of beer next to Officer Montego's seat. "Where were you when Ms. Theramin was killed?"

The vampire jerked upright, his face forming into something slightly nonhuman. "Are you suggesting I had something to do with my girlfriend's death?" His face screwed up. "I *loved* her! Why would I kill her?" His anger broke and he slumped back in the seat, great red crocodile tears pouring down his face. His hand went back to the bottle. "I loved her," he whimpered.

Forget the elf. This one's a certified nutcase.

Wynona felt like she had whiplash. Fear, revulsion and sympathy had poured through her so quickly, she could hardly catch her breath. Rascal had stayed standing behind the couch and she had felt his wolf rush to the surface. The tingling on the back of her neck let him know he was still close, but a glance over her shoulder said Rascal hadn't shifted...yet. "I understand," Wynona said warily. "But it's still important for me to know. I'm trying to piece together that situation and knowing where all the players were is helpful."

He nodded, still whimpering. "I was home. Alavara was working late and had planned to come join me for a late dinner." He began to sob. "She never showed up."

"Okay." Wynona stood up and took the beer bottle from his hands. "That's enough of that," she said primly.

"Hey!"

"Watch it," Rascal growled.

Officer Montego cringed, sinking back into his seat.

"Alcohol won't make it better, Officer Montego," Wynona said, settling back on the couch. "It causes depression and I don't think you need that right now."

"It keeps me from feeling," he snorted, looking away from her.

Wynona felt another rush of sympathy. "I'm sorry," she said again. "Did Ms. Theramin call at all that night? Did she say anything out of the ordinary?"

"No, no." He shook his head and closed his eyes. "Nothing. There was nothing."

"Did she have any enemies?"

The officer only continued to shake his head. "Everyone loved her. Who would want to do this?"

Wynona swallowed hard. This was going to be a hard question, but it needed to be done. "Did you know that I had threatened to sue her for copyright infringement?"

Officer Montego scowled. "What?"

"She was copying my business, Officer Montego." Wynona raised her eyebrows. "It was affecting my clientele and when I spoke to her, I gave her a warning." She narrowed her eyes. "Had she ever done anything like this before? Maybe there was another business owner who wasn't happy with her copying them?"

His hands gripped the side of the chair and Wynona grew worried at the wild look in his red eyes. "What it sounds like, Ms. Le Doux," he spat her name as if it were poisonous, "is that you were the only one who possibly had a motive." He leaned forward, his lip beginning to curl.

Rascal started to growl, the sound growing louder until the smaller man edged away, obviously recognizing the superiority of the wolf to his weaker powers. "Just leave," Officer Montego said hoarsely. "Please."

Wynona felt drained. This had been terrible and not the least bit helpful. The man was drunk and crazy with grief. There was no way he'd be able to help her now. "Thank you for your time," she said, standing up and quickly walking to Rascal's side.

Together, they hurried to the truck and climbed inside.

"That was..."

"A waste of time," Wynona finished for him.

"Not necessarily," he said, tilting his head to the side. "I think we can safely cross him off our list."

"Yeah...probably." Wynona reached up absentmindedly to pet Violet, who had been very quiet while they were inside the house. "Thoughts, Violet?"

Violet scrubbed her face. *I think he wanted to drain me.*

Wynona laughed softly. "I didn't get that vibe at all."

Either me or you, Violet huffed. *I've never seen a vampire so strung out.*

"I thought the same thing," Wynona said, her eyes out the window. Shaking her head, she turned back to Rascal. "What now?"

He shrugged, one hand hanging on the steering wheel. "Back to the precinct, I guess. I'm not sure where else to go at this point."

Wynona nodded, her mind going over the interview. The man was clearly distraught, but it would have been nice if he'd been able to offer at least a little insight into what was going on. She straightened. "Can we visit Alavara's home?"

Rascal nodded. "We'll need a warrant. Good idea." A loud grumbling sound followed his response and Wynona watched the tips of his ears turn red. "Uh...maybe we could hit my apartment first and grab some lunch?"

She laughed softly, trying to shush Violet's snickers. "Good plan. I'm starving."

He gave her a sideways glare, but it only made her laugh harder. "Can I help it if shifters have a crazy metabolism?"

"Sorry." Wynona waved a hand in the air. "I'm not laughing at you, I promise."

"Oh? Then what would you call it?"

Wynona tried to think of something else, but there was nothing for it. "Okay, maybe I was." She put two fingers close together. "Just a little bit."

Rascal sighed dramatically. "My own girlfriend. Turned against me." He shook his head and tsked his tongue. "What's the world coming to?"

Wynona unbuckled, scooted over and leaned into his shoulder after buckling herself in the middle seat. "We're investigating a murder," she said softly. "Better not answer that question."

The humor was gone, but Rascal's strong hand landed on her knee and Wynona closed her eyes to enjoy the sensation. Sometimes the world was a scary place, but other times, the moments of sweetness made up for it.

CHAPTER 13

Rascal slammed the cupboard closed, his ears red as he turned to Wynona. "So...it appears I don't have anything for lunch."

Wynona tried to hold back her grin, but it was hard.

Violet huffed and stalked out of the room. It was quite a feat, since her legs were so small, but her indignation was clear with every strut.

Rascal rubbed the back of his neck and chuckled. "I don't think I'm her favorite animal right now."

Wynona slipped off her barstool and walked over to wrap her arms around his waist. "Maybe not, but that's okay. You're my favorite animal."

Violet's indignant screech made Wynona wince.

Rascal laughed and kissed the tip of her nose. "Come on." He took her hand and walked her toward the door.

"Where are we going?" Wynona asked as she happily tripped along behind him. Instead of heading toward the elevators, he took a turn to the left.

"Mrs. Reyna's."

Wynona's eyes widened and she stopped walking, keeping Rascal from moving either. "Why are we going there?"

Rascal's eyebrows went up. "For lunch, of course." He grinned. "I fix everything in that apartment. I have a free-standing invitation to come eat whenever I want."

Wynona nodded, but it didn't ease her concern. She had mixed feelings about Mrs. Reyna. The elderly wolf shifter had known Wynona's grandmother. Really, she would be a great person to have a conversation with, except that Mrs. Reyna seemed to take great delight in supplying Wynona with vague pieces of advice or memories and refusing to tell her anything else. It was maddening and painful, bringing up memories that Wynona wasn't sure she wanted to examine all too closely, yet not being able to forget them all together.

"She always has a full pantry," Rascal said easily, not realizing why Wynona was reticent. He knocked on the door and waited, his other hand still holding hers.

There was some shuffling on the other side before the door moved. "Rascal," Mrs. Reyna scolded. "You could have warned me." Her dark eyes darted to Wynona and she raised a single eyebrow. "So that's how it is, huh?" Making a disappointed sound, Mrs. Reyna turned, leaving the door open, and walked inside.

Rascal followed, bringing Wynona with him.

Mrs. Reyna walked toward the couch. "You know where the food is," she said, waving a hand over her head and completely ignoring the grinning shifter.

Rascal leaned over the back of the couch and gave her wrinkled cheek a kiss. "Thanks, Mama Reyna. I owe you one."

"You owe me a working compactor!" she hollered after him.

Wynona stood awkwardly in the family room. Rascal had left her behind while he went to gather lunch and she wasn't sure what to do. Did she assume it was okay to sit? Did she help Rascal in order to avoid conversation with a woman she wasn't sure liked her? Should she—?

Wynona shook her head. All this conjecture was dumb and unhelpful. "How are you, Mrs. Reyna?" Wynona asked, trying to break the silence.

"Sit down," Mrs. Reyna snapped. "Hurting my neck, standing up like that."

Wynona sighed and sat down in a chair across from the couch. "Is your arthritis bothering you? Would you like me to make a tincture?" When they had first met, Wynona had unknowingly passed

Mrs. Reyna's test. Granny Saffron used to make Mrs. Reyna a tea in order to help with her aches and pains, which had been a complete mystery to Wynona.

However, as someone who liked to help those around her feel better, Wynona had offered to make her a tea, since that was her chosen medium. Mrs. Reyna had followed the process closely, finally giving her approval when the tea had been exactly the same as the one Granny Saffron used to make.

Mrs. Reyna's usually confident look fell and she massaged her hands. "That would be nice," she said softly.

Wynona blinked. Mrs. Reyna was never soft. She was a fiery older shifter who didn't take guff from anyone and would as soon smack a person over the head with a cane than sit and speak kindly. Rascal was her one exception to her rule as he did so much to help her around the apartment.

Mrs. Reyna gave Wynona a sharp look. "Well?"

Wynona jumped to her feet. "I'll get right on that." She escaped to the kitchen, then instantly scolded herself. Mrs. Reyna might be a bit rough around the edges, but she had a good heart. She didn't show it very often, but Wynona knew it was there. Otherwise, Granny Saffron wouldn't have been friends with her.

It was the same with Lusgu. He wasn't much of a conversationalist, but he had been in Wynona's corner more times than she could count, even if he grumbled the whole time.

Wynona laughed softly as she filled the teapot. It seemed her grandmother had a fondness for befriending diamonds in the rough.

"What's so funny?" Rascal asked from his place at the counter. He glanced over his shoulder and Wynona shook her head.

"Sorry. Just had a thought." She put the kettle on and then began to shuffle through the cupboards, collecting the herbs she needed.

A warm presence pressed against her back. "Oh?" he asked in a low voice.

Wynona glanced over her shoulder with a smile. "I was just thinking how Granny Saffron had a thing for cranky friends."

Rascal snorted. "I never met your grandma, but that does seem to be what we're discovering." He paused. "Was she like that?"

Wynona shook her head, crushing some leaves in a pestle and mortar. "No. She was as warm as a cookie straight from the oven." She stopped her work. "Unless you approached her as the powerful witch she was. Granny didn't suffer fools and her powers were stronger than anyone else's."

Rascal's hands rested on her shoulders and he tapped a finger in thought. "Your mom isn't as strong as Saffron was?"

Wynona shook her head. "No. Why?"

"Does witch magic usually diminish like that?" He frowned. "I thought the witch community married wizards in order to increase their magic. And your grandfather definitely wasn't weak."

Wynona tilted her head to the side. "I hadn't really thought about it. Granddad was powerful. It's why he held the presidency so long before passing it to my dad. And my mom's family is the strongest line of witches in history." Her brows furrowed. "It does seem kind of odd that Mom ended up less than either of them. She should have been immensely powerful." She shrugged. "Genetics are a funny thing, huh?"

But Rascal wasn't ready to let it go quite so quickly. "And your dad's line? I mean, he's held the presidency since Grandpa died, so he can't be weak either."

"No, Dad's line is just under Mom's. It was a combination of the two most powerful families." Wynona dropped her work and turned around. "What are you thinking?"

His warm hands rested on her hips. "I'm just thinking about your powers," he mused. "I know we're still trying to explore and understand them, but remember when Daemon asked about you?"

Wynona nodded, recalling when the black hole had figured out that her curse was breaking.

"He said you were the most powerful witch he had ever felt." Rascal's brow was wrinkled. "Do powers skip a generation?"

She shrugged. "I'm not sure. Other genetic traits do, so it's possible, I suppose."

The whistle of the teakettle made both of them jump and Wynona spun to take care of it. "I'm gonna run this in to Mrs. Reyna."

Rascal walked back to the counter and grabbed two plates. "Sandwiches are ready, so I'm coming."

Together they joined Mrs. Reyna. Wynona set the tea tray on the coffee table and poured the hot water into a cup, adding an infuser she had prepared. "There you go," she said, handing the cup and saucer to the wolf shifter.

"Thank you," Mrs. Reyna said politely.

Wynona nodded, trying not to react to the kindness. They must have really arrived on a good day. She smiled when Rascal handed her a plate with a sandwich and a handful of chips and apple slices. It made her feel like a five year old again, except that the sandwich had enough meat for ten people. She wasn't quite sure how she was going to get it in her mouth.

Shifters, Violet grumbled.

Wynona turned, smiling as the purple mouse wiggled under the front door. "Are you hungry?" she asked.

Violet scampered over and came up the side of the chair and stopped on the arm, nodding eagerly.

Wynona handed over an apple slice, then settled into her own meal.

The group was quiet for a few moments while they all dealt with their food and drinks, but soon it was broken.

"When did the disposal break?" Rascal asked.

Mrs. Reyna sighed and leaned back into the couch. "A couple days ago."

"I have some time off tomorrow," he said quickly. "I can get the parts then."

The elderly woman nodded and rubbed her forehead, the saucer and cup shaking slightly.

Rascal frowned and set his plate down before taking her cup. "What's going on, Mama Reyna?" He leaned his elbows onto his knees. "Something's bothering you."

Mrs. Reyna didn't answer him. She was studying Wynona.

Wynona slowly brought her sandwich back to the plate. "Is something wrong with the tea?" she asked, though she knew it wasn't that. The tea was perfect. She was sure of it.

"It's gone," Mrs. Reyna said, shaking her head. "It's gone."

Wynona tilted her head. "What's gone? Did someone take something from you?"

Rascal growled softly. "Tell me what happened. Did you report the theft?"

Mrs. Reyna shook her head and held up a hand to stop further questions. She closed her eyes and took in a long sniff, obviously testing the air. Her eyes were glowing when she opened them, her wolf close to the surface. "I can smell it," she said in a low, hoarse tone.

Wynona was frozen. What was going on? What was missing? What could Mrs. Reyna smell?

Appearing much younger suddenly, Mrs. Reyna sat straight up and pinned her gaze on Wynona. "Your magic smells...of Earth. Or wildflowers and wilderness."

Wynona blinked. "Um...thank you?" She glanced at Rascal, who shrugged and shook his head. His sense of smell was incredible, one of his greatest gifts in fact, but he'd never mentioned what her magic smelled like.

"I always wondered..." Mrs Reyna's eyes were still glowing as she tilted her head. She was examining Wynona like a bug under a microscope. "It was hidden before."

Wynona's eyebrows shot up and Violet stopped eating, finally tuning into the conversation. "The curse," Wynona said bluntly.

Mrs. Reyna nodded.

"What did it...smell like?" Wynona couldn't help but ask. It did nothing to help her, but she found she was curious.

Mrs. Reyna shook her head hard, her eyes closing just long enough for the glow to dissipate. "It doesn't matter," she said quickly.

"Please," Wynona pressed. She had a sudden thought that maybe if she knew what it smelled like, she would have a greater chance of finding the witch or wizard.

Or servant, Violet offered, reminding Wynona of her conversation with Rascal.

Wynona acknowledged the suggestion with a quick glance, then went back to Mrs. Reyna.

"Crackling fires," Mrs Reyna whispered, her eyes downcast. "Fir trees...damp earth."

Wynona frowned. Why did that sound familiar? There was something just on the edge of her consciousness that kept slipping through her fingers. Could she be remembering someone from her growing up? A servant? A nanny? A cook?

Mrs. Reyna shook her head again. "I need to rest," she snapped, sounding much more like her normal self. "You need to leave."

"Wait!" Wynona shouted, then cringed. "Sorry." She hadn't meant to shout, but there was something there... She was sure of it. "Can you tell me any more? Is the curse truly all the way gone? Do you know where those first smells came from?"

Mrs. Reyna climbed to her feet, refusing to answer. She opened the door and held it open, her mouth in a thin white line.

Rascal was scowling, but he held out his hand to Wynona and guided her to the door.

Wynona slowed as they walked through, trying to catch Mrs. Reyna's eye. "Please," she whispered one more time.

"It's not time," Mrs. Reyna said curtly. Without another word, she began closing the door, causing Wynona to hurry out or get hit.

She'd left a full plate of food inside, but Wynona's appetite was gone. She felt slightly faint. Mrs. Reyna knew something. She *knew* something. Her family had looked for information about the curse for years and even their resources hadn't been able to figure out that a cranky old wolf living in a run down apartment knew what was going on.

Rascal stormed toward the elevator. His movements spoke of power and anger. His alpha side was choking the hallway with its essence. He punched the button to take them downstairs before speaking. "We'll try again," he said, his voice low and guttural. "I won't let her keep whatever she knows to herself."

"She said it wasn't time yet," Wynona said softly. Her mind was spinning and she barely noticed Violet catching up with them and climbing up her leg. When soft fur brushed against the side of her neck, it didn't soothe her like it normally did. "She's been holding it back all this time." Her haunted eyes went to Rascal's. "How could she claim to be friends with Granny, yet keep something like this a secret?"

Rascal stiffened, but didn't respond. There wasn't anything to say. Granny was the paranormal world's most powerful witch. Which meant there was no way Mrs. Reyna could have kept something like this from her.

Granny had known.

She'd known and she'd let Wynona continue to suffer.

She'd known and had never told Wynona.

And now Granny was dead, her friend wouldn't talk and Wynona was still struggling.

She thought she'd known what pain felt like, but the sense of betrayal that cut through Wynona's chest was enough to take her breath away. And she couldn't help but wonder, what else in her life had been a lie?

CHAPTER 14

They sat in silence in the truck until Rascal broke the silence by clearing his throat. "Do you want to keep investigating? Or would you rather I take you back to the greenhouse?"

Wynona took in a deep breath, pushing away the pain from her visit with Mrs. Reyna. There would be a time to sit and sift through what she'd learned and mourn the fact that she still lacked answers, but right now wasn't that time. They had a murder to solve and a reputation to save. She could fall apart later.

Where did she want to go? They'd spoken to all three of the people in Alavara's life and gotten nowhere. "I'm not sure," Wynona mused. "Is there anyone else that the police were considering as a suspect?"

Rascal shook his head. "No. We're at a standstill at the moment."

"It's too bad that button disappeared," Wynona murmured. She reached up and rubbed Violet's head. "It might have given us a direction."

Rascal glanced her way.

She caught the look and had an immediate defensive reaction. "You don't believe me, do you?"

Rascal jerked back as if he'd been slapped. "Where did that come from?"

Wynona slumped. "Sorry. I didn't mean to snap." She rubbed her forehead. "I guess I'm still on edge from Mrs. Reyna's."

He reached over and patted her thigh. "Yeah…I'm not really happy with how that turned out either. When you're ready, we can go back and confront her again."

Wynona grabbed his hand and held it tight. "Thank you. But right now I just want my business back. Which means we need to solve this murder."

He nodded and took a turn. "How about we go talk to Chief? We can ask about a warrant and maybe he's got some news for us."

"Good plan."

The ten minute drive was quiet, but not as uncomfortable as when they'd first left the apartment. Wynona was grateful that the emotions had begun to calm by the time they got to the station and headed inside.

"Wynona!" Officer Nightshade smiled wide, her sharpened fangs glinting in the yellow lighting. "Haven't seen you in a while."

Wynona waved. "I know! It's been nice, huh?"

The vampire laughed softly. "I don't know. I've missed hearing you argue with the chief."

Wynona rolled her eyes. "That's not arguing. Just a difference of opinion."

"When you're the only one who is brave enough to offer a different opinion, it's as close to an argument as we get," the secretary said.

Wynona laughed. "I suppose so." She pointed down the hall. "We're headed to see him now. Keep your ears open."

Officer Nightshade gave Wynona a salute and a grin. "Will do." She nodded at Rascal. "Deputy Chief."

Rascal nodded back. His normally humorous expression was gone, replaced with the serious demeanor he wore at work. His hand landed on Wynona's low back and he guided her down the hall to Chief Ligurio's door.

Rascal knocked, then pushed it open. "Chief? You got a minute?"

Wynona waited, but Rascal wasn't moving. She frowned and glanced up.

He winked at her and held up a finger in the universal sign of *wait a minute.*

Wynona relaxed.

"Then get me answers!"

She grinned. Chief must be on the phone.

"I don't care. The judge can take ten seconds of his dinner to sign a warrant. Just get it and get it now." There was a slamming sound before, "What is it, Strongclaw?"

Rascal pushed the door the rest of the way open and led Wynona inside. "Hey, Chief."

Chief Ligurio snarled, twisting a pencil between his fingers. "What now? Wasn't giving you permission enough? Come to ask for more pay, Ms. Le Doux?"

Wynona paused. Even for the chief, that was harsh. She put her hands up. "I come in peace, Chief Ligurio. We only had a few questions for you."

The vampire tilted his pale face down and pinched the bridge of his nose. "It's been a long day," he explained.

As far as apologies, it was pretty terrible, but Wynona let it go. The man held an eternal grudge against her family and she knew it was as good as she was going to get. Instead of snipping back, she studied him. Her tea senses were twitching. "You have another migraine." It was a statement, not a question. Wynona could practically feel the pulse herself now that she was allowing herself to tune into the vampire.

Chief Ligurio raised his head and glared. "Every time you do that, I have a harder time believing that you're magicless, Ms. Le Doux. Are you sure your curse is still in effect?"

Wynona barely caught herself from reacting. "When was the last time you had a drink?" She made a face so he knew she wasn't talking about tea this time.

Chief Ligurio scrubbed at his face. "I don't know."

"Rascal, please call for a cup. I'll grab some additives." Wynona bustled to the side cabinets and counter where the chief had a hot plate and a small refrigerator. She'd made him a tincture before and knew exactly what she was looking for.

"Do you mother all your employers?" Chief Ligurio grumbled, laying his head back against his seat.

Rascal met Officer Nightshade at the door and took a steaming mug from her. "Thanks," he said softly before bringing it to Wynona.

She smiled and dropped a small bag of herbs inside. "Okay, Chief. Let this sit for a few minutes, and then you'll feel better." She set it down on the desk and walked away. "But to answer your question, no. I don't mother my employers." She settled herself in a chair across from the desk. "But I do try to give them my best." She raised an eyebrow. "Even when they're grumpy."

"Should dock your pay," he grumbled, drumming his fingers on the desk.

Wynona smiled. "Considering it's far less than minimum wage, I don't see how that's possible."

Those red eyes glared, but the chief said nothing more.

Rascal stood beside Wynona. "We came to ask if there have been any other developments. This afternoon we spoke to the three suspects and nothing new came up." Rascal made a face. "Though Montego was so deep in his cups he won't be back to work for a few days."

Chief Ligurio nodded. "I gave him a week off. He couldn't seem to concentrate at work."

Wynona folded her hands primly in her lap. "So?"

One black eyebrow rose high. "So?"

"You didn't answer Rascal's question," Wynona pointed out.

"As astute as always," Chief Ligurio grumbled. He took a deep breath. "But, it just so happens that we do have a lead." His red eyes went up to his second in command. "I was on the phone before you arrived trying to get a warrant. Judge Tolarus says he's in the middle of a meal, but I'm hoping my contact at the DA's office will come through. The warrant is to search her house." The vampire chief cocked his head. "We discovered there were very few records at the office, leading us to believe she might have stashed them elsewhere." He shrugged. "The most logical place is her house."

Wynona pointed at the mug, indicating it was time for him to take a drink. He gave her a look, but complied, causing Wynona to smile, though she tried to keep it from being too smug. "Funny. We were coming to ask about her house. And you know, I didn't look through her filing cabinet." She looked up at Rascal.

He nodded. "We went through those the first time through the office. The records were all brought in, but Chief is correct. There were very few for someone who was running a business."

"Can you tell me what was there?" Wynona asked. "Or can I see them for myself?"

Chief Ligurio leaned forward, his elbows on his desk. "You're welcome to look through them, but I suggest heading to the house first." He took another long draw of the mug.

"Oh? And why's that?" Wynona asked.

"We also have reason to believe she didn't get along with her neighbor."

Wynona blinked. "You think her neighbor killed her?"

The chief shrugged. "Don't know." He gave her a sarcastic grin. "That's why I have people investigating."

Wynona pursed her lips. "Well, I suppose it's a direction at least. When will that warrant come through?"

The vampire waved them off. "Go ahead and drive over. You can talk to the neighbor without a warrant. Hopefully it'll come through in time for you to search the house."

Wynona nodded and stood. "Thanks, Chief. We appreciate it."

He huffed. "The faster this is solved, the faster you're off my payroll, Ms. Le Doux. Don't consider it anything more than that."

Wynona knew better than to take the words at face value. Chief Ligurio might be testy, but the fact that he'd hired her at all said a lot. Her family didn't have a kind reputation and Chief Ligurio had an even worse experience when he dated Wynona's sister, Celia. The fact that Wynona could be in his presence without him threatening bodily harm was a miracle in and of itself.

"Do we have her address?" Wynona asked as they walked down the hallway. She stopped and reached for her shoulder. "Violet!"

A sleepy hum answered Wynona's frantic cry.

Wynona had been so caught up in helping the chief and getting answers, she'd completely forgotten about her familiar.

Rascal chuckled and pointed to the pocket on the shirt of his uniform. "She scrambled in to take a nap when we first entered the office."

Wynona closed her eyes and took a deep breath. "No wonder I didn't get a headful of snarky comebacks during our little chat with Chief Ligurio."

Rascal's chuckle grew and he took her hand. "The tiny thing does have a bit of an attitude."

I heard that.

"And apparently she's awake," Wynona warned, but from the grin on Rascal's face, he'd caught her response.

A purple nose poked out of his pocket. *Are we done with the insults and boring conversations? Or should I go back to sleep?*

"We're heading to Alavara's house," Wynona explained softly as they stepped through the front door of the station, heading to the parking lot. "We're waiting for a warrant to come through, but apparently, there's a neighbor who didn't get along with her very well."

Violet snorted, cleaned her face and ducked back down. *Let me know when something interesting happens.*

Rascal was still smiling as he shook his head. He opened the passenger door of the truck and helped Wynona inside. "Up you go." After making sure she was settled, he closed the door and went around to the driver's seat. "And yes, we have her address," he responded as he started the truck. "It's in her file and I can access it on my phone."

The truck roared awake and they pulled out.

"I wonder why she didn't keep her records at the shop," Wynona mused. "She had the office space."

"That's the question, isn't it?" Rascal said, his eyes on the road. "Why keep them out of range of others unless she was hiding something."

"My thoughts exactly," Wynona said. Her stomach took that moment to grumble at the fact that she had left most of her lunch at Mrs. Reyna's "Sorry," she said sheepishly, putting a hand on it.

Rascal pointed just in front of her knees. "I have a couple of power bars in the glove compartment." He scrunched his nose. "They're not awesome, but they'll do in a pinch."

Wynona opened it and fished around, pulling out one that was supposed to taste like cookie dough. "Yep," she said around a dry bite. "Not quite awesome, but thank you for sharing."

Rascal smiled. "We'll grab something to eat when we're done here."

"Lunch wasn't that long ago," Wynona pointed out.

Rascal pointed to his chest. "Shifter. I can eat anytime."

"True." She sometimes envied his metabolism. Her hips were a testament to the fact that she didn't run on the same frequency as him, yet couldn't quite keep herself away from Gnoz and Kyux's delicious baked goods.

"You're beautiful," he said fiercely, bringing her out of her wandering thoughts.

"What?" Wynona blinked herself back to the present.

"You were headed down that road that all women go when people talk about body image." His eyes flashed gold. "You're beautiful. Don't ever forget it."

Wynona smiled and relaxed in her seat. "Thank you," she said softly. Her hand met his as he stretched across the truck seat. "But one of these days, you're still going to have to tell me how you always know what I'm thinking."

Rascal swallowed hard, then nodded. "Okay. Soon."

Wynona nodded in return. "I'll hold you to that. But for right now, let's go interview a potential murderer."

CHAPTER 15

"This is the potential murderer?" Wynona asked. She and Rascal were still inside the truck, but parked in the driveway of the house that belonged to Alavara. Next door, a goblin was cutting his hedges. His craggy face was slightly shorter than the bushes themselves, but every once in a while, he rose on tiptoe, his large feet stretching to let him see the top.

Wynona couldn't see anything wrong with his cutting, but the scowl on his face and the way he kept thrusting his sheers out in front of him would suggest that his cutting left much to be desired.

"He does look a little..."

"Grumpy?" Wynona offered.

Shifty, Violet pressed.

Wynona sent her familiar a sharp look. "Shifty would suggest he breaks the law."

Violet shrugged while Rascal chuckled.

Wynona reached over and socked his arm. "Be nice," she scolded. "And he definitely doesn't look like he killed someone."

"He does look like the type of guy who will report you to the HOA if you put a foot out of line, though," Rascal said.

Wynona wanted to argue, but it was true. The goblin's home was pristine. In fact, it looked like he even kept his garbage can scrubbed and buffed. There was nothing wrong with that, but usually creatures like that had a problem with others who didn't. "Let's just give him the benefit of the doubt," she said, grabbing the door handle. She jumped to the ground and smoothed out her skirt and shirt. "Hello!" she called, waving to the neighbor.

Black eyes narrowed even further at her before ducking down behind the hedge.

Rascal hid his laugh behind a cough while Violet grumbled.

"You two are no help," Wynona murmured, knowing Rascal's wolf hearing picked it up. Sticking her chin in the air, she walked over. "Hello, Mr...?" She waited for him to supply his name.

"Who wants to know?" the goblin demanded, putting his hands on his hips in a defiant fashion. His eyes darted to Rascal, widened and then came back to Wynona. "You two cops?" His eyes moved over her skirt and shirt.

"Let me introduce Deputy Chief Strongclaw," Wynona said, waving a hand at Rascal, who had finally composed himself and was standing tall and looking like the authority he was. "My name is Wynona Le Doux. I'm a consultant for the Hex Haven precinct, currently working on the case of Alavara Theramin."

The goblin snorted. "Le Doux. Right. Like the presidential family would be working for the police." He smirked at her, but when Wynona and Rascal's faces didn't change, the goblin's face slowly blanched. "You're really the president's daughter?"

Wynona nodded, trying to keep a pleasant look on her face. She hated that her family elicited such fear.

The goblin swallowed hard, then must have decided he wasn't going to give into his fear and straightened his thin shoulders. "Well, I'm glad you're here. It's about time someone took some interest in all the broken laws of this neighborhood."

Wynona glanced at Rascal. "Broken laws?" she asked. "What laws are you referring to?"

A skeletal finger pointed toward Alavara's house. "The garbage can for *that* house hasn't been cleaned in months."

Wynona frowned. "Ms. Theramin is gone," she said carefully. Did her neighbor not realize this? It was all over the news. Unless he spent his spare time with his head buried in the sand, there was no way for him to miss what had happened.

The goblin sniffed. "All the more reason to make sure the next occupant follows the rules."

"There's no city law stating anything about cleaning garbage cans," Rascal said in a gruff voice.

"Our HOA requires it," the goblin argued. "That woman knew that." Once again he jammed his finger toward the house. "She was forever breaking the rules."

"Rules and laws are two very different things," Rascal said bluntly. "The police don't get involved in HOA disputes."

The goblin grumbled.

"You still haven't told us your name," Wynona said gently. This neighbor seemed to be a ticking time bomb. And he didn't seem the least bit upset that his neighbor had recently been murdered. Was that because he'd been involved or because he was just that cold?

The goblin scowled, but glanced up when Rascal growled lightly. "Vrebs," the small creature finally spat.

"Thank you," Wynona said politely. This conversation reminded her of talking with her sister. Cecilia was difficult to get along with as well. "Mr. Vrebs, we heard that you and Ms. Theramin weren't on the best of terms. Could you please tell us what you fought about?"

He shrugged and folded his arms over his chest. "I told you, already. She broke the rules."

"Can you tell me exactly what ones she broke? Besides not cleaning her garbage can?" Wynona pressed. It was like pulling teeth with this one. And very sharp teeth at that. Ones that were currently being flashed in her direction.

"She didn't trim her hedges properly. She never swept her driveway." He sighed and threw his arms in the air. "Is any of this actually necessary? Alavara is gone. We'll do a better job interviewing the next occupant. End of story."

Rascal leaned over the hedge, getting in Vrebs' face. "Not if you had something to do with the reason the house needs a new occupant," he said in a low tone.

Vreb's swallowed audibly and backed up a couple of steps. "You think I killed her?" He shook his head adamantly. "Why would I do that?"

"Why would you leave notes all over her house?" Wynona asked. The flutters of paper attached to the front door hadn't escaped her notice, but she was banking on a guess that they were the work of Mr. Grumpy Pants.

Fear turned to anger. "Someone had to let her know," Vrebs growled. "The HOA was too lenient on her. I'm part of the board and took it upon myself to let her know what needed to be changed." He stuck his long nose in the air. "There's no law against that."

Wynona nodded and gently tapped Rascal's back, who was still glaring hard at the small creature. Violet, thankfully, had been rather quiet. Wynona could only handle so much antagonism at one time. "You're right," Wynona agreed. "There's no law against that, but your little feud could easily be seen as a reason for you to harm her."

The goblin snorted, but the quivering in his hands gave away his true feelings. "I didn't hurt her."

"Where were you the night she was killed?" Rascal asked.

"Here. At home." The goblin's scowl deepened. "And before you ask, yes, I was alone."

I wonder why, Violet drawled.

Aaaaand, there was the snarky comeback Wynona had been expecting during the conversation. *Be nice,* she sent back, making Violet huff in annoyance. "Did you hear or see anything unusual in the days leading up to her murder?" Wynona asked. In order for the neighbor to be so aware of Alavara's faults, he had to be watching her closely. She really didn't think the tiny goblin had hurt anyone, but he could possibly annoy a body to death.

The goblin shrugged. "There was always someone coming and going," he grumbled. "She was dating an officer." Black eyes darted up to Rascal's before coming back to Wynona. "And a woman, don't know her name. But she visited often."

"How often?" Wynona asked. She tilted her head. "And do you know the woman's name?"

The goblin shook his head. "No. No name, though I assume the women had business together. They didn't always seem to get along, so I'm assuming it wasn't a bosom buddy situation." He smiled, his sharp teeth making it menacing instead of reassuring.

"Would you recognize her if you saw her again?" Wynona asked. What woman would Alavara be associating with? It couldn't be a family member. Records showed the elf didn't have any. Not a business associate. The tea shop had been under her name only. And Alavara hadn't lived in Hex Haven long enough for there to be any kind of deep relationship, had she?

The goblin scratched his head, shifting the three hairs that lay across it. "Yes, but why bother? She didn't fix the hedges. All they did was talk or shout."

"Did you hear what they were shouting about?" Rascal hurried to ask.

Vrebs shook his head, his scowl firmly in place. "I'm not a busybody. I don't know everyone else's business." He backed up. "I've told you all I know." Turning, he muttered under his breath. "Treat me like a gossiping old hag. How would I have all their answers? Can I help it if creatures don't know how to polish garbage cans properly? Nooo...but suddenly that makes me the neighborhood tattletale."

Wynona stood stockstill, listening to the complaints with her eyebrows raised. Slowly, she turned to Rascal, who was turning pink in his attempt to hide his laughter.

His golden eyes turned her way, filled with mirth.

"I'm not quite sure what that was," Wynona said, wincing as the goblin slammed his door.

Rascal raised a single eyebrow. "He better be careful. I'll bet the sound was above the acceptable audible limit for this place." He waved his phone in the air. "Chief says we're good to go with the warrant."

Wynona frowned and punched his upper arm. *Ow...* Sometimes his shifter strength was not to her advantage. "Come on. Stop making fun of a lonely, old creature and go inside the house."

Stopping at the door, Wynona read over all the notes that had been left for Alavara, who would never read them. Her heart sank. No, she hadn't particularly liked the elf, but Wynona wouldn't wish this kind of end on anyone. Determination to find the killer and get back to her own life surged and Wynona straightened her shoulders. "Can we get inside?" she asked.

Rascal nodded. "Yeah. But I'll have to call for the key." He pulled his cell out of his back pocket, grinning as Violet nuzzled his jawline. Punching a few keys, he put the phone away. "Skymaw's on his way with the key. It's faster to have him bring it than go back and get it, then return."

Wynona nodded. "'Kay." She looked around and eventually walked to the porch steps. Apparently, Alavara hadn't had the time, or maybe the money, to put any furniture on the porch. The paint job was well taken care of, but the spot was simply...empty.

Rascal moved around behind her. "The inside is much the same," he murmured, peeking through the windows. After a minute he came and sat down.

"What do you mean?" Wynona let her shoulder lean into him. She loved how warm and strong the wolf shifter was, even if it did mean her knuckles were still sore from punching him.

"Very little furniture," Rascal said, scratching behind his ear. His arm then moved to wrap around Wynona, tugging her in under his arm. "A couple of chairs, a table...just the essentials. It almost looks as if she didn't plan to be here very long."

"Huh." Wynona pursed her lips as she lost herself in thought. It made no sense. Alavara had built a business. She was dating a police officer. Those weren't the actions of someone who planned to move on soon. A thick, warm finger gently tapped her forehead.

"What's going on in that brilliant brain of yours?" Rascal asked before kissing the top of her head.

Wynona wanted to sigh in contentment at the show of affection, but she held herself in check. Mr. Peeping Tom was more than likely watching them this very minute. She wasn't the type to put on a show for all and sundry. "Just trying to put the clues together," Wynona answered honestly. She looked around. "This isn't the cheapest of neighborhoods," she mused.

"Nope. Upper middle class," Rascal agreed.

"Right. So if she couldn't afford furniture, why would she buy such a nice house?"

Maybe the outside mattered more than the inside, Violet offered.

Wynona ticked her head back and forth. "Possible, but unlikely. Women tend to nurture their spaces. They want to feel good in them." She twisted to look over her shoulder. "If Alavara was planning on staying, she would have created a space conducive to that." Wynona turned back around to look at Rascal. "But if she wasn't planning to stay, why build a business from the ground up? Or start a relationship with Officer Montego?"

"All good questions," Rascal said with a slow nod. "And none of which I have the answer to."

"And you said there wasn't much in the way of paperwork at the office?" Wynona asked, already knowing the answer, but wishing it were different.

Rascal shook his head. "We didn't tear down the walls or anything, but nothing came up with a regular sweep through."

She sighed. "And then we have that knife."

And don't forget the missing button.

Wynona nodded to Violet. "Right. Plus the button." She scrunched her nose. "But what does it all mean? Officer Montego was brokenhearted and as a shifter, he definitely wouldn't need a knife, nor would he leave one lying around as evidence if he'd been involved."

"I would hope not." Rascal snorted. "No officer would be that stupid."

"Exactly," Wynona responded. She paused. "Unless we were *supposed* to find the knife?"

But why? Violet asked as she scrubbed her face. *What would be the purpose of providing us with the murder weapon?*

Wynona shook her head again. "I'm not sure. There were no prints, so it's not like they were trying to frame anyone and the coroner confirmed the knife was the actual weapon. No magic or spell. Just a good old fashioned stabbing."

"Something you rarely see unless you're dealing with non magical creatures," Rascal muttered.

Wynona stiffened. "You don't think..." She chewed her lip.

"What?"

"You don't think they were trying to frame me?" Wynona asked softly. "Do you?"

"What? Why?" Rascal demanded, a growly undercurrent coming through.

Wynona shrugged and held out her hands. "I'm not sure, but there are very few creatures that have absolutely no magic and none of them have any bearing on this case that we know of." She took a deep breath. "But as far as the world knows, I have no magic. Maybe I wasn't a possible victim, but a possible suspect."

Rascal pushed a hand through his hair. "Well, no matter the angle, we know you didn't do it."

"But Chief Ligurio had to ask, didn't he?" Wynona whispered.

Rascal sighed and tugged her into his chest. "Doesn't matter. The chief knows you're innocent. We all do. And now you're helping catch the real killer. If throwing suspicion to you was their intent, they'll end up regretting it."

CHAPTER 16

Rascal helped Wynona down from the truck. The day had been a long one and she was ready for sleep, but tonight it would have to happen in a bed other than her own.

Prim's large greenhouse loomed in front of her. On the far side was Prim's cottage. Dainty and quaint, full of flora and fauna, as any good plant fairy's would be. But she and Rascal had parked at the back in order to keep Wynona's presence a secret.

Wynona had eventually turned off her phone because the media calls had become relentless. They had figured out where she lived, they knew where she worked and now they knew her phone number. It would only be a matter of time before they began searching places other than her own residence to find her.

But for now...no one had bothered Prim and that would become Wynona's home away from home. It wasn't how she wanted to spend her evening, despite their wonderful friendship, but it was what it was.

"Prim?" Wynona poked her head inside the greenhouse. The dampness of the air hit her immediately and Wynona soaked in the heat. The air outside was only just beginning to get a bit of warmth to it as winter gave way to spring, but it wasn't enough in Wynona's opinion. She preferred the warm weather and in the greenhouse, it was always summer.

"Back here!" Prim's voice was muffled but clear enough and Wynona stepped inside with Rascal on her heels.

As soon as they were fully inside, Violet rushed down Wynona's shoulder and disappeared into the plant life. Somewhere inside the greenhouse were other mice and Violet always seemed to enjoy a visit.

Rascal chuckled. "Is this where her boyfriend lives?"

Wynona smiled and shrugged. "I'm not sure. She seems to give him the cold shoulder just as much as she pulls him in."

He rested one hand on her lower back, the connection warm and strong, just like him. "Women," he said in a teasing tone. "Always playing hard to get."

"Men," Wynona shot back. "Can't seem to make up their minds."

His grin grew, but Rascal didn't say anything more.

Wynona led the way through the greenhouse, following the sounds of grunts and moving pottery. Finally, she found Prim, up to her elbows in dirt as she worked to repot a plant that was larger than the fairy by at least two feet.

"Let me help you with that," Rascal hurried to say, rushing to Prim's side.

"NO!" Prim shouted, her pink eyes wide and her hair standing on end.

Rascal skidded to a stop, his hands in the air.

Prim blew out a breath, trying to get a chunk of her hair out of her face. "It's a Cobra Lily," she said with a grunt. With one last heave, Prim wrangled the roots into the newer, bigger pot. Sighing, she wiped the back of her hand on her forehead. "It's carnivorous," she continued in an aside.

Rascal backed up without saying a word, but kept a careful watch on Prim and the plant.

Wynona held onto Rascal, but mostly for his safety. She wasn't worried about Prim. No plant would dare take a bite out of her.

"They also like to bond," Prim continued, not understanding that her words were making Rascal extremely uncomfortable. "Every time it gets a new pot, it rebonds with the first thing it touches." She straightened and put muddy hands on her hips. "There." Reaching out, Prim rested her palm on the plant's curved tip.

"No wonder it's called a cobra," Rascal whispered.

Wynona nodded. The stalk of the flower rose high, curling over like a cobra when in strike formation.

The plant began to shiver under Prim's touch, eventually curling into her hand like a snake.

Wynona watched in fascination. Her own magic was stronger than Prim's, but so out of control that she struggled to see the beauty in it. Prim's power, with her affinity for living things, was amazing and always sent a small sliver of jealousy running through Wynona's stomach.

She shook it off. Prim was one of the best creatures Wynona knew and she refused to be jealous of something so wonderful. Someday, she'd have command of her own powers and then she'd share with her friends the same way Prim did with her.

"All done," Prim said, dropping a small bird carcass into the plant's open flower before caressing the plant for a moment more. She wiped her hands together, dropping dirt to the floor, and turned to face Rascal and Wynona. "Now...who's hungry?"

Rascal gulped and looked at Wynona, his eyebrows raised. "And I'm not even squeamish," he said in a low tone.

As a wolf shifter, he'd probably seen more than his fair share of carnage, but apparently the line between plants and animals was a sensitive one for him. Wynona held back a laugh, but her smirk couldn't be contained.

Rascal huffed, but only shook his head at her.

"I'm starving," Wynona finally said, answering her friend. "What can I do to help with dinner?"

"You can sit on a chair and tell me about the investigation," Prim said, walking toward the entrance to her cottage. "I'm dead on my feet and want a bit of fun news to perk me up."

Besides her gift with plants, Prim was also a prime gossip. She loved hearing all the news and knowing what was going on. Wynona's work with the murders during the last year had given her some juicy tidbits that no one else knew about. It was the fairy's favorite source of dessert.

"I don't mind helping and talking," Wynona said. Besides, she knew full well that dinner was going to be rough for Rascal. Prim ate like a fairy, from the earth. Plants, vegetables and fruits. Rascal needed meat and if Wynona didn't cook it, it likely wouldn't make it to the dinner table.

Prim sniffed and glanced at Rascal before rolling her eyes. "Fine, fine. Make your man his gross steak dinner, just as long as you tell me everything."

Wynona raised her eyebrows at Rascal, who grumbled, but didn't retaliate.

An hour later they were all seated at the table with Prim's eyes wider than tea saucers. "He was upset that Alavara didn't scrub her garbage cans?" she screeched.

Wynona winced, but nodded. "Yeah. I'm guessing he doesn't have a lot of friends in the neighborhood."

Prim puckered her lips and blew out a raspberry. "No kidding. Who would want to live next to a guy like that?" An evil grin crossed her face. "*However...* I might just have something to add to our little pow wow."

Rascal's ears perked up as his eyebrows shot down. "What do you mean?"

Prim's bright pink lips were in full on smirk mode. "There was talk down at the nursery today."

Wynona sighed. "Spit it out, Prim. What were the ladies talking about?"

Prim scowled. "You're no fun." She waved a hand at Rascal. "Don't you enjoy egging on his wolf...just a little?"

Wynona gave her friend a look and Prim's scowl deepened. "Fine, fine." She cleared her throat and straightened in her seat. She was still in her fairy form, making her half the size of the rest of the guests at the table, but her chair came up high enough to accommodate her height. "Word is that the helper? The dwarf?"

Wynona nodded.

"They're saying his record isn't exactly...clean," Prim said carefully. "If you know what I mean."

Wynona looked at Rascal, who was staring.

"Are you suggesting he has a record?" Rascal asked, his voice slightly lower than normal. "We checked into him. How would anyone at the nursery know something like that?"

Prim's pleased grin was all too perfect. She adored having a leg up on her competition. "Lula works with Triwyn, who bought a plant in Cauldron Cove. She said she saw him on the news once."

Rascal's face was unamused. "That's it?"

Prim shrugged. "How do you know he didn't change his name?" she pressured.

Wynona felt like she was going to get whiplash as her head jerked from one friend to another. Neither Rascal or Prim seemed to want to back down from their stance, though they usually got along quite well.

"And you think the police were too stupid to figure that out?" Rascal asked, biting off a hunk of steak from his fork. His eyes glowed dangerously as his wolf rose to the surface.

They were bright enough that even Prim noticed and suddenly she wasn't quite so confident. Leaning back, Prim gave Wynona an uncertain look. "Rascal..." she said warily. "I'm only telling you what the gossips are saying. If you're sure, then don't pay attention to it."

Wynona frowned. This wasn't like him. In fact, he'd been fairly moody for the last couple of weeks. Normally, Rascal was happy go lucky, got along with everyone and rarely gave in to his wolf unless he was protecting someone. But lately he'd been brooding and on edge. What in the world could have caused this change in him?

Slowly, Wynona reached out and put her fingers on his forearm. When his head snapped in her direction, a pinprick of fear hit her chest.

Rascal took in a deep breath, closing his eyes as if analyzing the very air around them, before his entire body slumped. When his eyes reopened, they were back to normal. "Wy..." he said hoarsely. "I'm so sorry. I wasn't trying to frighten you." He reached out one hand as if to touch her, but stopped himself at the last minute.

Forcing herself to relax, Wynona grasped his suspended palm and brought it to her cheek. "What's going on?" she asked softly. "Something is bothering you."

"Hey!" Prim cried. "How come you're not sorry for scaring me? I didn't do anything wrong." She folded her arms over her chest and huffed.

Rascal hung his head before turning to Prim. "No, you didn't. I'm sorry for scaring you too."

Prim sniffed. "It's fine." She studied her nails. "I wasn't really scared anyway. Wolves are just big puppy dogs, after all."

Rascal's lips twitched, but the smile didn't fully appear.

Wynona stood up, keeping his hand in hers. "Take a walk with me?" she asked.

Rascal sighed but nodded. Apparently, he didn't want to have this conversation, but Wynona wanted answers.

"Hang on!" Prim called, jumping from her seat. "Before you go, I got a new tea today." She was grinning proudly as she brought a tray to the table with a kettle and cups. "We should all have a calming cup before you two go have a heart to heart."

Wynona hesitated, but ultimately sat back down. Prim meant well, even if her timing wasn't the best. "What tea is it?" She reached for the prepackaged box.

Call her a tea snob, but Wynona preferred her own tinctures, though she would never hurt Prim's feelings by saying so.

"Sweet cinnamon," Prim said, plunking the tray down. "It's got hints of anise and black pepper in it. I had a cup yesterday and it was good." She leaned in. "Not as good as yours, but you know...sometimes a fairy has to make do with what's on the shelves."

Wynona gave her friend a smile. "I'm sorry. I'll refill all your shelves just as soon as I can get back into my workshop."

Prim waved her off. "It's fine. Like I said, this stuff is pretty good." She plunked the bags in each cup and handed them out. "It's not magic laced or anything, but it'll warm you right up."

Wynona brought the cup to her nose and took a long sniff. "Ooh...it does smell nice." She nodded in appreciation. Mass produced tea was fine, but it couldn't come close to her work in the shop.

Her heart ached. Her shop. When would she ever get back to it? They were still at ground zero with the murder and until it was solved, there would be no going home.

Rascal squeezed her knee. "Hang in there," he whispered. "It'll all work out."

Wynona nodded. Dunking her bag a few times, she let it steep, then set it aside and took a sip. "That is nice," she admitted. And it was. Slightly sweet, hints of spice...she would have to look into making something similar when she got back to work.

A few minutes later, Wynona had finished her tea and was ready for that walk when her cup began to shake in the saucer.

COMING! Violet screamed.

Wynona's eyes couldn't leave the cup, though she noted the tiny claws climbing her leg and arm until Violet was settled on her shoulder. Paws rested against her skin, helping Wynona keep herself in check as the magic began to take over.

This wasn't the first time the tea leaves had spoken to her, but it was the first time that Wynona had understood what was happening.

Each time before, she had still been under the impression that she had no magic, but now she knew better.

Her hand still shook as she reached for the cup, but with Violet helping keep the magic under control, Wynona felt a surge of confidence that wasn't normally there.

She brought the cup closer to her face, turning it just right to see the dregs in the bottom.

"Ants," Wynona murmured. "There are troubles ahead." She ignored Violet's snort. "A cat... Somewhere we are being deceived..." Wynona tilted her head to the side, trying to remember the last symbol in the corner of the cup. "An arrow," she finally decided. She looked up, feeling much more in control than she had the first few times she had read the leaves. "A downward arrow."

"And what does that mean?" Rascal asked, his voice soft and low.

Wynona blinked up at him. "It means we're headed in the wrong direction." She sighed, carefully placing the cup back on the saucer. "I hate to say it, but I think we need to check out Prim's bit of gossip."

Rascal scrubbed his face even while Prim snickered. "I know better than to argue with the leaves," he said with a smile, though it was tired. "I'll put in a call before bed."

Wynona nodded. She wasn't sure how she was going to solve this, but if the direction they were headed was wrong, then they needed to look elsewhere and the only lead they had was Prim's. Somewhere, someone was deceiving them and it was going to take some work to figure it out.

CHAPTER 17

W ynona wasn't feeling as refreshed as she hoped after sleeping at Prim's place last night. The only spare bed had been the couch and it was a bit on the lumpy side. Good thing Wynona wasn't particularly tall or she would have gotten even less sleep.

She rubbed her eyes and yawned, cracking her jaw in the process. "Sorry," she squeaked when Violet grumbled. "You can sleep anywhere, but I'm afraid us humans struggle a bit more."

Violet scrubbed her face. *My night wasn't all bon bons and cheese platters either.*

Wynona nodded and rolled her hair into a low bun. Her waves were unruly on the best of days, but without her normal hair products, it was just plain frightening. Hopefully the twist would hold it long enough to be useful. "I'm sorry," she said again. "As soon as I can safely get us back to the house and the shop, I promise I will."

Violet sniffed but nodded. Her smugness faded quickly and she scurried up Wynona's arm, nestling at her neck. *I know, I'm sorry I'm cranky.*

Wynona froze. That was very unlike her furry familiar. Violet liked to be the queen bee, but Wynona wasn't going to look a gift horse...uh...mouse...in the mouth. Wynona rubbed behind the tiny creature's ears. "We'll get through this together," she said softly.

Violet chittered, purring ever so slightly before yawning and closing her eyes.

Smiling at the contentment in her friend, Wynona stepped out of the bathroom and headed for the front room. "Thank you so much," she gushed to Prim, who was blending something eerily green for breakfast. The color was nearly neon and Wynona was a little afraid to ask what it was.

It hadn't escaped her notice, after befriending the fairy, that the creature ate the very things she grew. It seemed rather hypocritical, like an animal fairy eating meat, but Wynona had no idea at the inner workings of fairy biology, so she kept her mouth shut.

"It was so nice not to have to worry about the ghost reporters breaking into the house or accosting me when I leave this morning."

Prim smiled over her shoulder. "One of these days they're going to figure out we're friends, though, so..." She shrugged.

Wynona nodded. "Thank goodness that day is not today." She grabbed an apple from the table and headed to the greenhouse door. "Rascal is picking me up any minute, so I'm gonna get a whiff of sweet flowers before I go."

"Hey, Nona?"

Wynona paused, her hand on the doorknob.

Prim's normally bright pink lips were pinched into a line. "Be careful, huh? The grape vine says the dwarf was shady, and I didn't really worry about it." She swallowed hard. "But your tea reading makes me wonder."

Wynona tried to smile, but the truth was, she was a little worried too. "Don't worry," she reassured the fairy. "I've got a wolf protector. We'll be fine."

Prim's pink eyes filled with longing. "Someday I want one of those..." she said on a sigh.

Wynona's eyebrows shot high. "You want a wolf?"

"What?" Prim seemed to come out of her dreamy state. "No, no. Not the wolf, just...someone who actually cares enough to protect me." She spun, suddenly very interested in the blender again. "Are you sure you won't stay for some shake?"

"Nope! Thanks! Gotta run!" Wynona dashed through the door before Prim could tie her down. There was a line as to what Wynona was willing to eat and blended plants that glowed were definitely on the wrong side.

The rumbling of an overly loud engine let Wynona know Rascal had arrived and she picked up her pace as she crossed the greenhouse, careful to give the newly planted Cobra Lily a wide berth.

Once outside, Wynona immediately ducked. The air was chilly and the breeze even more so, but it only took a few seconds to climb into Rascal's truck. He had started to get out, but Wynona waved him away, opening her own door. His gentlemanly manners always made her feel cherished, but there was no reason for them both to freeze this morning.

"Hey," she said breathlessly, tugging the door closed behind her.

"Good morning." Rascal leaned over and took what little breath Wynona had left in her lungs.

Her body was far from cold by the time he pulled back and she fought the urge to fan herself. How could one simple touch affect her so strongly?

Because you're in love, Violet said wryly.

Wynona's eyes widened and they darted to Rascal. Sometimes he could hear what Violet was saying and she wasn't quite ready to admit something like that yet.

He didn't hear me, Violet sniffed. *I don't always have to broadcast my words.*

Wynona kept her sigh as soft as possible. *Let's chat about this later, okay?*

Humans...always make it all so complicated.

Wynona smiled when Rascal took her hand and she forced her muscles to relax.

"Ready to go track down a dwarf?" he asked, jerking the truck into reverse.

"Ready as I'll ever be," Wynona replied. She gripped his hand when he reached across the cab and rested their combined hands on her thigh. He was quickly becoming her rock. When she had first begun to help the police, Wynona had gone around by herself digging into clues and following leads in hopes of clearing her name. Now she was clearing her business, but she couldn't imagine doing it alone. Rascal, even with his recent moodiness, was the perfect partner.

They were quiet. Wynona enjoying his touch, but fearing what they were going to find when they arrived at the tea shop. Mr. Leadtank lived at the shop. But where? There hadn't been any bedrooms.

"I didn't think to ask where Mr. Leadtank had been sleeping," Wynona said as they pulled alongside the curb. "You know, after we removed him the other day."

"He had a cot in the back of the store room," Rascal explained. He made a turn toward the police station. "Right now they've got him staying in a spare cell, though he's allowed out, unlike the other prisoners." He cleared his throat. "Captain wasn't pleased last night with my request to dig deeper, but after coming up empty at Ms. Theramin's house, it was the best idea we had."

Wynona nodded. They pulled into the police parking lot and Rascal came around to help her down. Grasping her waist, he lifted her to the concrete, then tucked her under his arm. "Come on. It's freezing out here."

"I'm ready for summer," Wynona said through chattering teeth.

"Me too." Rascal pulled open the front door and ushered her inside. "I'll have to take you on some of my favorite trails this year."

She smiled widely at him. "I'd love that." Time alone with Rascal in nature? The very place his inner creature loved and knew well? Sounded perfect.

"Wynona!" Officer Nightshade smiled wide enough to see her sharp canines. "What brings you here this morning?"

"We're talking to one of your visitors," Wynona replied, careful not to say prisoner. As far as she knew, Mr. Leadtank wasn't here under duress.

"Chief in his office?" Rascal asked curtly.

Officer Nightshade nodded. "Yes. He said to send you in. Apparently, he had someone working late last night."

Rascal nodded and put his hand on Wynona's low back, his usual way of guiding her through traffic.

"Let's do lunch sometime!" Amaris called out as Wynona followed her wolf.

Wynona nodded eagerly. "Yes, please!" She faced front as they walked down the hall, stopping to knock on Chief Ligurio's door.

"Enter!"

Wynona made a face. "Has he had his blood this morning?" she whispered.

Rascal started to shrug, but a shout from inside interrupted.

"Open the door, Le Doux," Chief Ligurio snarled. "I know it's you."

Putting on a pleasant face, Wynona walked in. "Sorry, Chief Ligurio. I was just worried about you." One of these days, she would remember the fact that she was surrounded by supernatural hearing.

Chief Ligurio grunted and rubbed his temples. "Strongclaw."

Rascal nodded. "Chief."

The vampire held up a folder. "Better prepare yourself. They're bringing Leadtank here in two minutes."

Wynona rushed to Rascal's side in order to look at the folder. Her eyes widened and she gasped. "He changed his name?" she whispered.

"Looks like it," Rascal said. He whistled low under his breath. "No wonder. His rap sheet is nothing to sneeze at."

"Cake! I want the cake!"

All three heads jerked toward the door where Masterick Leadtank was being dragged inside. Despite the fact that he wasn't supposed to be a prisoner, his hands were cuffed and he was wearing a jumpsuit from the jail.

Wynona glanced at the chief, who sighed, still rubbing his head. "He had cake smeared across his clothes," the vampire explained in a low tone. "He refused to shower, so we at least made him change. And the cuffs are because he won't stop trying to get away. Every time he evades an officer he ends up back at the shop, scarfing every pastry he can find, then smearing the remains on the hardwood."

Wynona frowned and shook her head. "Something's wrong," she said in just as low a tone.

The chief nodded.

Rascal edged in front of Wynona, as if to protect her from the small man trying to break free.

"Let me out! It's mine!" the dwarf shouted, wrenching his arms against his captors.

"He's going to hurt himself," Wynona said, rushing around Rascal. She knelt in front of the small creature. "Mr. Leadtank," she tried. "Mr. Leadtank?"

The dwarf didn't seem to hear her, thrashing his head from side to side. His eyes were wild and there was no sanity left in them.

Wynona jumped back when his legs kicked out, and looked to Rascal. "Can we get Daemon in here?" Something was buzzing against her skin. She rubbed the sensation, but it didn't go away until she backed closer to the desk.

"What do you need him for?" Chief Ligurio snapped. "He's off duty today."

Wynona glanced over her shoulder at the chief. "I think there's a spell at work here," she said softly, keeping a tight rein on her emotions.

Grumbling, Chief Ligurio nodded and punched his phone. "Get me Skymaw," he barked.

Amaris's voice could barely be heard replying before the line cut off.

Testing a theory, Wynona stepped closer to the dwarf, only to have Rascal grab her arm.

She looked up and shook her head slightly.

Rascal's hand tightened ever so slightly before he nodded and let go.

Again, Wynona stepped forward. The itch on her skin picked up and became stronger the closer she got to the wild dwarf. *Violet?*

The mouse stood at attention on Wynona's shoulder. *I'm here.*

Can you feel that?

The mouse chittered her agreement.

Can we feel magic?

There was a pause before Violet answered. *I don't know...but it sure seems like it.*

Fingers shaking, Wynona reached out her hand. She had learned to feel her own magic, moving inside herself, but this was from the outside and definitely didn't feel the same. She aimed for the dwarf's arm, just to see what would happen. The buzzing grew until it was almost painful and just before Wynona touched his skin, her fingers brushed what felt like a live wire, sending a shock through her system and creating a spark that nearly blinded her. It reminded her of the time she touched the remnants from the blight spell in the meadow a few months back.

When she finally blinked enough to clear the stars from her vision, she was on the floor and the officers holding Mr. Leadtank were staring at her in shock.

"What the he—" Chief Ligurio growled and finished his cursing under his breath as Rascal dashed to Wynona's feet.

"Are you hurt?" Rascal asked, his eyes flashing and his teeth elongating. He was close to losing control.

Wynona shook her head, then stopped when the motion made her dizzy. "I'm fine," she said. "Just shaken up." It was a wonder her own magic hadn't reacted. She fisted her fingers, making sure she was completely under control.

Rascal growled and carefully brought her to her feet. He spun toward Mr. Leadtank, but Wynona held his arm.

"He doesn't know what he's doing," Wynona said. "Someone has left a spell on him and it's going haywire."

"But why?" Rascal asked, his tone still low and full of anger. "Why now? What's causing it to break? He was lucid just yesterday."

Chief Ligurio was barking instructions over their head, but Wynona paid no attention.

"I don't know," she responded, her head leaning against Rascal's shoulder. "Violet, you alright?"

Violet was cleaning herself in a frenzy, some of her fur still standing on end. *Warn me next time, huh?*

Wynona petted her friend. "Sorry. That wasn't exactly planned."

Violet huffed, but didn't say more.

"This isn't a good idea," Rascal said tightly. "I need to get you out of here."

Wynona shook her head. "No. We need to figure this out. We need to strip him of the spell and find out what he knows."

"He might very well be the murderer," Rascal said, his face fierce when he looked down at Wynona. "He changed his name and now he's gone feral. Even if he didn't mean to do it, he could have had an episode and killed his employer."

Wynona nodded. "That does sound plausible, but we don't know for sure. We need Daemon's sight and we need to help Mr. Leadtank calm down. I want to be here when you question him."

Rascal growled and shoved both hands through his hair. "I don't like you being near danger," he admitted in a vulnerable tone.

Wynona let more of her weight rest against his side. "I know," she said. "But at least you're here to protect me."

A strong arm wrapped around her, tucking her in close. She closed her eyes and breathed in his woodsy scent as Rascal kissed the top of her head. Her curls were falling free. So much for hoping the bun would keep it under control. Apparently, being shocked by magic had that effect on her. "Don't you dare touch him again," Rascal warned.

"No worries." Wynona rubbed her fingers together. They were feeling slightly bruised from the shock. "I'll just watch from a safe distance."

"Skymaw will be here in five," Chief Ligurio said from Rascal's other side. His red eyes were pinned on the still fighting dwarf. They darted to Wynona. "I don't know what you did, but I'm not covering it in your pay."

Wynona managed a small grin. She was just grateful Chief Ligurio didn't realize it was her own magic reacting to the spell on Mr. Leadtank. Hopefully, he didn't question why his officers were touching the dwarf with no problem.

Rascal's chest was still rumbling in discontent and his arms tightened. Wynona let him hold her, knowing it would calm the beast within, but she was grateful he wasn't trying to get her out of the room anymore. She was in too deep at this point. Rascal's protection was wonderful, but she needed to see this through. The clues only seemed to be getting weirder, but along the way she was also starting to learn things about herself and in the end...they might prove to be the most useful of all.

CHAPTER 18

The minutes that ticked by until Daemon arrived seemed to stretch forever, though Wynona knew it hadn't been long.

"Skymaw," Chief Ligurio snarled. "About time."

"Sorry, Chief. I was eating," Daemon said, his cheeks turning slightly pink.

Wynona normally would have been fighting a smile at the large man's embarrassment, but right now things were too tense to see the humor.

Chief Ligurio turned his red eyes toward her. "Ms. Le Doux?"

Wynona nodded and faced Daemon. "I believe Mr. Lead-tank...or whatever his name is...is being held by a spell and that something has gone wrong with it." She frowned. "He's too volatile for it to be normal."

Daemon squinted his eyes at the still fighting dwarf. Slowly, he nodded. "Yeah...I can see it." He walked forward, his head tilted to the side as he studied the situation. "It's sparking like it's about to detonate."

Wynona walked up to his side, making sure she didn't touch anything. One shock was enough for a day, thank you very much. "Sparking?"

He nodded, his black eyes turning down to hers. "It's unstable. And the edges are fraying."

"Can you null it?" Rascal asked.

Daemon scowled. "I'm not sure. I can keep magic from being enacted, but this spell was already cast. I don't know if I can..." His voice trailed off and his eyes grew larger. "EVERYBODY DOWN!" he bellowed.

Wynona hadn't had the time to process his command before a large body took her to the floor. She hit with a thud, though Rascal's hand cradled her head so she didn't hit it. Before she could even breathe, a blast burst through the room, dissipating almost as quickly as it started.

A stillness enveloped the room in direct opposition to the chaos that had been happening for the last twenty minutes. Slowly, Wynona opened her eyes. Papers from Chief Ligurio's desk had scattered everywhere, looking like a hurricane had swirled through the space.

She twisted in order to see Daemon's large shape standing above her head. His arms were wide, his forehead slick with sweat, and his chest heaved with heavy breaths. Wynona coughed, shaking Rascal, who was lying on top of her. She always enjoyed having his strong arms around her, but man...he was one heavy wolf.

"Are you okay?" Rascal asked, his voice strained.

Wynona nodded. "I think so. Thank you." Panic hit her in the gut. "Violet!"

I'm here. Chittering came from under Chief Ligurio's desk, just a few inches to her right.

Wynona sighed with relief. "Thank you," she said again to Rascal.

He nodded, his face stoic. Jumping to his feet, he helped her up.

"What just happened?" Chief Ligurio's muffled voice was as sharp as his teeth. He pushed up from the other side of the desk, brushing debris off as he stood. Wynona was particularly grateful that her glare wasn't directed at her.

Mr. Leadtank was lying in his chair, completely limp.

Wynona swallowed. "Is he dead?" she asked softly. Violet scrambled up her leg and arm until she reached Wynona's neck, curling in in a comforting manner.

Daemon shook his head, wiping his forehead with his sleeve. "No. Just unconscious."

Wynona kept her eyes on the dwarf's chest. After a moment, she realized it was slowly moving, which allowed her own breath to relax. She didn't want to see another dead body.

"I'm still waiting for an explanation," Chief said, his voice lower this time.

Daemon nodded. "Sorry, Chief. The spell...well, for lack of a better word...exploded."

"Why would it do that?" Wynona murmured, voicing her thoughts out loud. She had a pretty decent textbook education. Since her family wanted so little to do with her and her time hadn't been spent practicing actual magic, Wynona had spent a lot of time in the library learning all about the ins and outs of magic on a scientific and academic level. But she couldn't remember anything in her studies talking about spells exploding. At least, not ones that had been in place for a while.

Daemon shook his head. "I'm not sure. I told you it looked unstable." He blew out a breath. "I don't think I could suck the spell out of him, but when the energy broke, I was able to absorb it before it blasted everyone else to pieces."

Wynona put her hand on Daemon's arm. His muscles were still tense. "Thank you," she whispered.

Rascal clapped his officer's shoulder.

Daemon nodded and shrugged. "Just doing my job."

Chief Ligurio cleared his throat. "And the dwarf? Will he regain consciousness?"

Daemon's eyes went fully black again as he studied the creature. "I don't see anything that should keep him from recovering, but I have to admit this is my first time stopping a broken spell."

Wynona walked to Mr. Leadtank and hovered over his arm. The buzzing from earlier was gone. Dare she try touching him again?

"Careful, Wy," Rascal warned. "You've already taken two hits today. Third time isn't always a charm."

She nodded. "I know, but..." Warily, she rested her fingertips on the dwarf's sleeves. When nothing happened, she let out a breath. Straightening, she headed to a seat on the opposite side of the office. "I think we can safely assume Daemon's right. The spell is gone." She frowned. "But why did it break? And was that why he was acting so crazy?"

Chief Ligurio righted his office chair and sat down with less ease than usual. He was grumbling under his breath, but Wynona couldn't understand what he was saying. When Rascal tried to hide a snort, however, she knew that the paranormals in the room with superior hearing knew exactly what was being said.

Another, louder snort caught her ear and Wynona turned back to see Mr. Leadtank stirring. She jerked to Rascal, who nodded that he also saw it. With a tip of his chin, the two guards who had been standing in shock closed in to either side of the creature, ready to grab him in case he acted out again.

The dwarf, however, barely moved. He blinked and shifted in his seat. Once his eyes were fully open, they widened to the size of dinner plates. Jerking upright, he leaned back as far as he could go. "What's going on?" he croaked.

All heads turned to Chief Ligurio, who slowly stood from his seat and walked across the room until he stood in front of the suspect. "I'm Chief Ligurio," he stated bluntly. "You don't remember being brought into the precinct?"

Mr. Leadtank put his fingers to his temple and shook his head hard. "Last thing I remember is..." He trailed off, his red face slowly growing pale.

"What do you remember?" Chief Ligurio snapped.

Wynona couldn't help it. It was obvious the dwarf was in distress and she stepped forward, drawing his attention. "Mr. Leadtank, you were working for Alavara Theramin as a janitor at her tea shop. Do you remember that?"

"Alavara?" he growled. "I was doing *janitorial* work!"

Wynona nodded. "She built and opened a tea shop that copied mine, using my business model and nearly copying my name. You were part of that, as a substitute for the brownie working for me."

The dwarf huffed and folded his arms over his chest. "I've never mopped a floor in my life. And I would never work for Alavara."

Rascal growled right back while Daemon backed off, letting the more predatory officer take over.

"What's your name?" Chief Ligurio demanded.

One bushy eyebrow rose high. "I thought you knew."

Red eyes began to glow and the chief smiled in a way that looked the exact opposite of friendly. "I have two names for you," he said tightly, his incisors flashing in the light. "The one you gave me when we first spoke after Ms. Theramin's death and the one I found when we dug into your past."

Mr. Leadtank swallowed hard. "Alavara's dead?"

"Would you care to tell me which one is correct?"

Thick, stubby fingers ran over his nearly bald head. "Alefoot," he finally said hoarsely. "Urnoki Alefoot."

Chief Ligurio nodded and reached back for the folder he had shown Rascal earlier. He flipped through it casually, making Mr. Alefoot sweat along his forehead. "It looks like you've had quite the past, Mr. Alefoot." Chief Ligurio's red eyes darted to the suspect and back to the papers before he tossed them back on the desk. "Now...why don't you tell us what you know."

They only had to wait a few moments before the dwarf caved. He squinted up at the chief. "Where am I?"

"Hex Haven," Rascal offered.

Mr. Alefoot nodded and blew out a breath. "Alavara mentioned that to me before she..." He cleared his throat. "I live in Cauldron Cove. I was a..." He eyed the police on either side of him. "I was in acquisitions."

Wynona pursed her lips as Violet scoffed. The man was clearly a criminal, but she couldn't blame him for not wanting to say that to the police.

"Alavara had hired me to find her items and when the job was done, she asked me to stay and chat." Mr. Alefoot shrugged. "I had nothing better to do and I'm always happy for a good drink or two."

"Get to the point," Chief Ligurio said curtly.

Mr. Alefoot shifted uncomfortably. "She said she had another job for me, but it would require me to move to Hex Haven." The dwarf shook his head. "I don't know why she thought I'd want to move that far for a measly job, but I turned her down." He rubbed the top of his head. "I took a drink, and then I woke up here."

The room was quiet. "That's it?" Rascal asked. He put his hands on his hips. "You don't remember a thing between the offer and waking up from that spell?"

"SPELL!" Mr. Alefoot bellowed. He jumped to his feet. "That *elf* put a spell on me? But how?"

"Sit down, Mr. Alefoot," Chief Ligurio said calmly. "Unless you want me to study this record of yours a little closer."

Face still red, Mr. Alefoot did as asked. "What spell are you talking about?" he asked.

Rascal looked at Wynona and she shrugged. She had no idea what type of spell it had been, though obviously the dwarf hadn't been in his right mind.

"When did Alavara die?" Mr. Alefoot asked suspiciously.

"A few days ago," Rascal replied. "And you don't remember a thing?"

The dwarf rubbed a hand over his face. "No, though that explains a little. It had to have been pretty strong for it to last that long past her death."

"What do you mean?" The words were out of Wynona's mouth before she thought better of it. Usually listening was the best thing she could do during an investigation, but his words caught her attention.

"The spell," Mr. Alefoot said slowly, as if speaking to a small child. "Obviously, Alavara cursed me to follow her here and do that stupid...janitor job you were talking about." He growled. "But when she died, it would have broken the spell. The longer it takes to break, the stronger it was to begin with."

Wynona's heart began to beat hard against her chest. "Spells end with the death of the caster?" she clarified.

The dwarf nodded. "Every magic user knows that," he sneered.

Except they hadn't. Wynona had never had magic before. Rascal was a shifter, Daemon was a black hole and Chief Ligurio was a vampire. None of those creatures had inherent magic of their own.

Did you know that? Wynona asked Violet.

Violet shook her head. *No. But my aspect in this is instinctual. I don't have any regular knowledge of magic except what comes as we work together.*

Wynona blew out a long breath. She looked at Chief Ligurio and gave him a slight head shake. This creature couldn't be their murderer. There was no way for him to have faked that episode. Despite how wild he was at the end, the spell didn't start to unravel until after Alavara's death, which meant he couldn't have gone crazy and accidentally killed her while under the influence.

Chief Ligurio grumbled, obviously frustrated before telling his men to take Mr. Alefoot back to his cell.

"You can't hold me here," the dwarf shouted. "On what charges?"

"On suspicion of illegal activities," Chief Ligurio said with a tired wave.

"That's not a thing!" Mr. Alefoot cried out as he was pulled from the room. The space grew quiet once more as the two officers and their prisoner left, the door shutting firmly behind them.

Chief Ligurio sank back into his chair. "Please tell me you have another lead since you just put an end to the only one I knew of."

Wynona shook her head. "I'm sorry, but no."

"You're sure he's not guilty?" Rascal pressed. His eyebrows were pulled together, obvious concern on his face.

Wynona shrugged. "How could he be? If the spell didn't begin to fracture until after her death, he couldn't have gone crazy in order to kill her." She turned to Daemon. "You're sure about what you saw?"

The black hole scratched the back of his head. "Yes. The magic looked...frayed. As if the weaving of a blanket were coming undone." He lifted his shoulders. "I have no other way to describe it."

Chief Ligurio cursed and leaned back in his seat. "So where does this put us?"

"I don't know," Wynona admitted. She walked to a chair and sat down. "Though I'm thinking we should track Alavara's life before she came here."

"We tried that," Chief Ligurio said. "And got nowhere."

"Yes, but we also didn't realize Mr. Leadtank was really Mr. Alefoot at first either."

Red eyes tried to melt her into the floor, but Wynona was used to it by now. She didn't gloat, simply stayed calm until he dropped eye contact. Pressing a button on his phone, he barked, "Nightshade!"

"Yes, Chief?"

"Have Heskell dig into Ms. Theramin's history. I want every cauldron turned over and every cobble moved. No matter how small, I want to know about it. Got it?"

"On it, Chief."

He leaned back. "We probably won't hear anything until tomorrow."

Wynona nodded. "Thank you for looking into it," she said. Turning her face up to Rascal, she asked, "Can we go back to visit the baker and Officer Montego? If we still come away with nothing, we'll try

Mr. Vrebs again." She frowned. "I just can't help but feel like we're missing something, though I have no idea what it could be."

Rascal took his keys out of his pocket and twirled them around his finger. "At your service," he said with a wink.

The wink did more to calm Wynona than his smile, since it was a move he'd been making since they first met. It was nice to see that some of the happy-go-lucky shifter she had fallen for was still in there somewhere. When this murder situation was over, it was probably time for them to sit down and have a nice long chat. But until then...they had to stay on the hunt.

CHAPTER 19

I n no time at all, they were pulling up to the bakery again. Wynona studied the cutesy shop as they entered. A tiny bell rang, announcing their entrance, but this time, they weren't the only ones in the waiting area.

Ms. Soulton stood behind the counter, smiling widely at a young family of fairies who were picking out treats together.

"Oh, you'll love the lemon bread," Ms. Soulton gushed. She kept talking even as she bent down to open the case and extract a couple of slices. She wrapped them up in wax paper. "Lemon was always my favorite as a child." She passed the slices over the counter with another smile. "Enjoy."

The family said their goodbyes and worked their way past Wynona and Rascal. Violet was peeking from the pocket on Rascal's shirt and her nose twitched.

Smells good.

Wynona hummed her agreement. If she didn't have such good bakers already, she might consider working with Ms. Soulton. *Provided she's not involved in the murder.* Though Wynona struggled to see the kind woman doing anything to hurt another being, but Wynona had seen it all before. She knew better than to count anyone out.

"Ms. Le Doux," the baker said, her voice a little tighter than before. Her eyes flickered to Rascal. "Deputy Chief."

Rascal nodded. "Ms. Soulton."

Wynona stepped forward. "If you have a moment, we'd like to speak to you."

"Again?"

Wynona nodded. "Yes. There have been some...developments."

Ms. Soulton frowned. "Okay." She glanced at the wall clock. "I haven't taken a break today. Hang on." With a twirl of her finger, she turned the "Open" sign to "Closed".

A familiar pang of envy went through Wynona, but she pushed it away. She didn't like giving into it before she had her magic and she wasn't going to be upset now. Someday she would be able to work magic just as easily. It would simply take time.

"Thank you," Wynona said with a soothing smile as they walked into the backroom.

If the front smelled sweet, the back was like walking into an actual baked good. The space was warm and heavy with spices and sugar.

Rascal took in a deep breath, his eyes flashing, obviously enjoying the smells.

Wynona laughed softly and he gave her a sheepish glance.

Violet made a slight squeak before climbing out of his pocket and scurrying to the floor while Ms. Soulton's back was turned. *I'm just gonna look around.*

Be careful, Wynona thought and Violet let out a small noise before disappearing.

"Ms. Le Doux?"

Wynona jerked her eyes up from the floor, hoping Ms. Soulton hadn't noticed a rodent running through the kitchen. "Hm?"

The baking witch held up a tea kettle. "Would you like a drink?"

Wynona shook her head. "No thank you, but I appreciate the offer." She pointed to a chair next to a small table. "Do you mind if we sit?"

"Please." Ms. Soulton's eyes kept darting between her work in pouring herself a cup and her visitors now waiting at the table. "You said there had been developments?" she asked. "Does that mean you've found the murderer?"

Wynona shook her head as the witch came closer. "Not yet, but we're narrowing our suspects."

"Oh?" Ms. Soulton sat down with an elegance that Wynona envied. The baker's willowy build was lovely and a far cry from Wynona's prominent curves.

Warm fingers brushed Wynona's shoulder and she relaxed slightly. Rascal made no qualms about her figure. It was stupid of her to worry about what she didn't have, rather than focusing on Alavara's murder.

"Yes, um...were you familiar with Mr. Alefoot...I mean Leadtank?" Wynona asked.

Ms. Soulton frowned over her cup before setting it down. "Are you referring to the janitor?"

Wynona nodded. "Yes."

Ms. Soulton shrugged. "I had seen him a couple of times. It was impossible not to when I dropped food off every couple of days."

"And did you ever talk to him?" Wynona pressed.

Ms. Soulton shrugged. "I don't know. If I did, it was nothing memorable. More than likely simple pleasantries."

Wynona nodded. "And Ms. Theramin's boyfriend? Officer Montego?"

Ms. Soulton's cup rattled against the saucer. She let go of the cup and folded her arms in her lap. "Sorry. I'm a little nervous."

Wynona frowned. "I'm not trying to frighten you. We simply want to ask you questions."

Ms. Soulton nodded. "I know, but I've never been involved in an investigation before." Her eyes shifted quickly to Rascal, then back to Wynona. "It's nerve wracking."

"Understandable." Wynona took a deep breath. "Tell me about your business," she said, hoping to put the woman at ease.

Ms. Soulton looked around and Wynona followed her gaze. Bright silver pots and several large stainless steel counters and ovens dominated the space. Bright spots of color popped out as tea towels and aprons were scattered everywhere. It appeared that Ms. Soulton liked color and was decidedly messy.

"Well..." Ms. Soulton wrung her hands together, the knuckles turning white. "I'm a kitchen witch." She smiled softly. "I've always loved to bake and it runs in my family."

"How wonderful," Wynona gushed, hoping it would put the woman at ease. "Did you start this place on your own? Or was it a family business?"

Ms. Soulton shook her head. "On my own. My mother and grandmother baked for family and neighbors, but by the time they were my age..." She trailed off and shrugged, making a face. "They were married, so neither wanted to run a business." Her cheekbones were bright pink and Wynona cleared her throat.

She hadn't meant to bring up an uncomfortable subject, but even worse was the fact that Wynona knew she was older than the woman sitting across the table from her.

"I think it's wonderful that you're using your talents to make a living," Wynona said, trying to ignore the ping in her heart. She decidedly did *not* look at Rascal. She knew she loved him, but they weren't to the point of marriage...at least Wynona didn't think so. She knew she was growing more and more dependent on him, but the problem was...she wasn't sure he felt the same. He obviously had feelings for her, but he had never mentioned the "L" word.

"Tell that to my grandmother," Ms. Soulton muttered, rolling her eyes.

Wynona grinned. "Grandmothers can be pretty pushy when they think they know what's right for you." The memories that statement brought back were almost too much to bear, but they still made Wynona smile. She missed Granny Saffron like a man in the desert missed water.

Rascal coughed, trying to cover a laugh, then winked at Wynona when she glanced his way.

Wynona's smile grew before she turned back to the baker. "Can you please tell us again your relationship with Ms. Theramin?"

Ms. Soulton's eyes went back and forth between Rascal and Wynona. "Are you two...together?"

Wynona laughed lightly. "I suppose you could say that."

"Huh." Ms. Soulton leaned back in her chair, folding her arms over her chest. "And you don't think that's a conflict of interest?"

Wynona stiffened. "No, Ms. Soulton, I do not," she said firmly. Who was this woman to make that judgment call? Wynona worked *better* with Rascal at her side than alone.

Ms. Soulton's eyes dropped and her face fell. "Sorry. I didn't think..." She sighed. "I once knew an officer," she said softly, then jerked in her chair. "But that was a long time ago."

Wynona's righteous anger dissipated. The man must have left Ms. Soulton heartbroken if her reaction was anything to go by. Wynona cleared her throat. "Ms. Soulton? Your contract?"

The kitchen witch blinked a few times, as if coming out of a stupor before nodding. "Right. Sorry." She took in a deep breath, straightening in her seat. "I mentioned before that I barely knew her. Ms. Theramin came by, looking to try a sample and take my estimate, and we eventually wrote a contract. I brought her pastries every two days for her shop, delivered through the back door."

"Who delivered them?" Wynona asked.

"I did," Ms. Soulton said, sticking her chin in the air. "There's nothing wrong with that. Small stores can't always afford delivery services."

"Of course not," Wynona assured her quickly. "But if you were in the tea shop, that changes our questions."

Ms. Soulton frowned and looked suspicious. "It does?"

Wynona nodded, but before she could do anything else, the ringing of the front door caught their attention.

"I have to go," Ms. Soulton said, jumping to her feet and pressing out the wrinkles in her apron. Today's fashion was pink with white daisies bundled all over it. Very springy and just right for the upcoming season.

Wynona stood as well. "When can we come back?" she asked.

Ms. Soulton stumbled slightly and looked over her shoulder with wide eyes. "You have more questions?"

Wynona nodded. "Yes. I'd really like to talk to you about Mr. Leadtank, the janitor. We..." Her eyes went to Rascal and back. "We have reason to believe there was dark magic involved in his employment."

Ms. Soulton gasped, her delicate hand covering her mouth. "No..."

"Hello?" a voice called out. "I have a package for Mardella Soulton?"

"Excuse me," Ms. Soulton said, slipping out the door without another word.

Wynona grumbled and stomped her foot. "Why can't she give me a straight answer?"

Rascal's warm hand landed on her back. "I think I scare her," he said, amusement lacing his voice.

Wynona rolled her eyes. "It's not like you growled at her. She had no reason to be afraid of you."

Rascal shrugged. "Maybe not, but she did say she knew an officer once." One thick eyebrow rose high. "Maybe he wasn't a shining example of a policeman?"

Wynona deflated a little and nodded. "True. That could be it." She pushed out a long breath. "Come on. Let's go out through the back. We can study the alley as we go." She stopped. "Violet?"

Scampering feet on tile became audible before Violet rushed over and climbed Rascal's leg. He helped her settle into his pocket, chittering with contentment.

"Find anything?" Wynona whispered as they stepped through the messy kitchen.

Besides the fact that the witch has an obsession with aprons? Not so much.

Wynona scrunched her nose at the smell in the back alley. "I think maybe they need to collect the garbage," she muttered. The air stunk of past due herbs and rotting eggs, mixed with animal feces. It made Wynona pick up her pace just to be away from it all.

Rascal's face was turning red as he nodded and Wynona realized he was holding his breath.

She almost broke out in a giggle, but it really shouldn't have been funny. His sense of smell was much stronger than hers, so it made sense that the alley would offend him more. Still...the large officer holding his breath like a young boy was slightly amusing.

She kept her eyes peeled for anything out of the ordinary, but nothing stood out to her. There were bags of trash scattered everywhere and Wynona had to tiptoe through the alley to keep from stepping in something unsavory. That was all she needed...to cover her shoe in something that would keep Rascal away for the rest of the day.

"Now what?" he asked as they reached the truck.

Wynona buckled up and waited until he was in his seat before answering. "Let's head to Officer Montego's," she said.

Before backing out, Rascal stared at the bakery. "Do you think she was involved?"

Wynona pursed her lips. "Personally? No. But am I ready to rule her out? Also no." She twisted on her hip to look at Rascal. "The problem here is, I don't have a real suspect. No one stands out."

"Which means everyone is still a suspect," Rascal finished for her.

"Exactly."

Once on the road, he reached out and rested his hand on her leg. "If he's still drunk, I'm not sticking around," Rascal growled under his breath. "He was a threat to you and I won't tolerate that."

Wynona nodded. "Thank you," she said, gripping his hand. "And thank you so much for coming along with me. I wouldn't be nearly as brave to do all this if you weren't here."

Rascal squeezed her hand, glancing her way with his signature wink and a roguish grin. "Always."

CHAPTER 20

The lights were off at Office Montego's home and Wynona worried her bottom lip. "Maybe he's not home?"

"According to Amaris, he's not on the roster yet," Rascal said easily as he put the truck in park. "If he's not here, he's probably just picking up groceries or something. We can wait for a while and see if he arrives within a reasonable time."

Wynona nodded and hopped out of the truck, walking around to take Rascal's hand. His warmth, as usual, spread up her arm and all through her chest. She was becoming addicted to that sensation and found herself craving it when he wasn't around.

Rascal knocked firmly on the door. "Montego? It's Deputy Chief Stronclaw. Ms. Le Doux and I need to ask you a few questions."

Wynona waited, the house seemingly empty when the door finally opened, a burst of air hitting her in the face. She blinked against her dry eyes and shook her head. "Officer Montego?"

The man still looked like he hadn't slept, though his clothes were clean and his hair was washed since the last time they'd seen him. "Have you figured out who killed her?" he croaked.

Wynona looked to Rascal, who appeared uncomfortable as he rubbed the back of his neck. "Um, no, we haven't," she answered. "I'm sorry."

The officer groaned and rested his forehead against the doorframe. "Why is this taking so long?" he moaned.

"Officer Montego, we're following some leads and would like to ask you a few questions," Wynona said. "Can we come in?"

Tired, red eyes met hers and he nodded reluctantly. "Might as well," he grumbled, stepping back and waving an arm toward the inside of the house.

"Thank you," Wynona said softly, stepping past him. The place had been sort of cleaned since their last visit. The pop cans and beer bottles were gone, though garbage in every shape and color still littered the space. A wide, red pizza box from the Weeping Widow sat next to a pink striped box half full of cookies. Apparently, the stress of his girlfriend's death had the vampire eating enough for the entire neighborhood.

Wynona wanted to be disgusted with this man's eating habits, but being a vampire meant none of it stayed in his system anyway. Most vampires didn't bother to continue eating once turned, but a few hung onto human habits or simply ate in group settings to blend in better. Instead of giving into jealousy, however, Wynona eyed the couch, wondering if there was a way to sit down without offending him and cleaning it all off.

"Sorry," he muttered, grabbing a couple of wadded up takeout bags from the cushions. He walked across the room to stuff them in the garbage. He pushed down as if to force the bag to accept more than it wanted to.

"It's alright," Wynona answered with a tight smile. She forced herself to walk around and sit down, though she was far from relaxed. The wave of smells was overwhelming, though none were distinctly unpleasant. Simply different savory aromas from the food. She was beginning to think he was a stress eater with how much food was lying around.

"You said you had a couple of leads?" he asked, plopping in the same easy chair he'd occupied last time.

Rascal kept his place as well, standing sentinel behind Wynona. She was sure he wanted to be prepared in case Officer Montego got angry again. Wynona withheld a shiver at the thought. Vampires could be very scary when they wanted to be. A distraught one was downright terrifying.

"Yes." Wynona smoothed out her pants. "Are you familiar with Mr. Leadtank?"

Officer Montego's face pinched. "You mean the janitor?"

Wynona nodded. "Yes."

The policeman paused to think, then shrugged. "Not really. I only know that he was terrible at cleaning."

Wynona tilted her head to the side. "Why do you say that? Why would Alavara hire him if he didn't do his job well?"

Officer Montego shrugged, his eyes on his knee. He picked at an invisible piece of lint. "I don't know. Maybe she had a soft spot for him?"

Wynona pinched her lips together. "Were you aware his real name is Urnoke Alefoot?"

Officer Montego's head jerked up. "What?"

"And that he was working for Alavara under some kind of spell?"

His red eyes grew brighter. "Are you suggesting that Alavara coerced that...*dwarf*...to work for her? That she somehow forced him?" His lip curled and he sneered. "She was an elf, Ms Le Doux. Her magic wouldn't have been strong enough for something like that. It would have drained her to hold onto a spell that long."

"True," Wynona said, slowly nodding in agreement. "But people hire out spells all the time."

His growl grew louder, cutting off only when Rascal growled back. Undead or not, long, sharp claws and canines weren't something anyone was willing to mess with. "Alavara wouldn't have done that to him," Officer Montego said through clenched teeth. "Look somewhere else."

"And where would you suggest?" Wynona asked curtly. "Alavara seemed to keep her friends close. In fact, you're the only *friend* that we know of. Everyone else seems to have only tolerated her." The words were harsh, but Wynona was desperately trying to get a reaction. She didn't want him to attack her jugular, but she did want him to give her more information than his surly attitude was willing to.

Someone had to know more. They'd been cut off from Ms. Soulton because of customers, though the timid woman didn't have a very strong connection to Alavara anyway. Their janitor had been spelled and more than likely had been completely under control during the murder. And the boyfriend was so distraught, he seemed to be barely surviving. Other than patrons, they were the only people that had any connections, no matter how small, to Alavara. One of them had to be holding something back and Wynona figured the boyfriend was the most likely.

The growling was back, and Officer Montego's hands gripped the arms of his chair so hard, Wynona was waiting for them to break. "Not everyone has a lot of friends," he said tightly. "There's no crime in that."

"I understand that," Wynona said calmly. "But Officer Montego, someone murdered Alavara. Someone who was close enough to her that they didn't need to break into the tea shop. She had already proven herself as someone who was willing to bend the law when she created a copycat of my own shop and the odds of this being her first foray into law breaking is slim." Wynona pushed on, despite the warning flash in the vampire's eyes. "I'm begging you to help us give her peace. Tell us about the people around her. Did she have enemies? Had she targeted other businesses? Who would she have hired to cast that spell?"

Sharp fangs began to protrude from Officer Montego's lips, cutting one in the process.

Wynona had to work to keep from following the tiny bead of blood down his chin. It was grotesquely fascinating, but churned her stomach at the same time. She might have a knack for solving crimes, but that didn't mean she liked gore.

A squeaking noise broke the silence and Wynona turned to see Violet rush down Rascal's chest, leaping to the couch and then onto her own arm.

"What in Hex Haven is that?" Officer Montego demanded.

"This is my..." Wynona swallowed. "My pet." She had almost said familiar, which would have given away her ability to use magic. The time for hiding it was quickly coming to an end, but she just wasn't quite ready yet.

"You have a purple mouse as a pet?" the vampire said in disgust. "Do you have any idea what kind of germs those rodents carry?"

Wynona raised her eyebrows, keeping her eyes trained on him, rather than pointedly looking at the filth around her. Talk about the pot calling the kettle black. Wynona pushed a long breath out her nose. "Officer Montego. I'm not trying to fight." Violet nuzzled Wynona's neck and a trickle of magic worked its way up her spine. Wynona stiffened. Violet didn't usually start the magic, she helped filter it.

Another nuzzle brought another tingle.

What in the world are you doing? Wynona asked mentally.

Use your powers, Violet encouraged. *This guy is hiding something. We can all see it. Use your powers to figure it out.*

"What?" Wynona gasped, out loud.

Officer Montego's eyebrows furrowed further. "What?"

Wynona shook her head, realizing her blunder. "Nothing. Sorry. Just thinking out loud." She pinched her lips together. She couldn't use her magic on him! Not only was Wynona not skilled enough to cast the right kind of spell, but she had a habit of throwing too much magic at something. With her luck, she'd kill Officer Montego, and then she'd be the one they were investigating!

A heavy hand landed on her shoulder. "This isn't over, Montego, but we need to go."

Wynona stood, grateful for Rascal's interruption. She had almost given herself away and once again her Wolf in Shining Armor had come to her rescue. "Yes, we do. We have a meeting with the Chief. Thank you for your time."

She nearly fell to the side as a blast of air swooped past her. Officer Montego was now standing at the door with a sardonic smile on his face. "I'd say thanks for coming, but..." He let the words trail off, letting Wynona know exactly what he thought of her.

Holding her head high and confident in Rascal's ability to keep her safe, Wynona marched out. The door slammed behind them and Wynona let herself sag. "I do not like that man," she muttered under her breath.

"I used to," Rascal responded as he opened her door. "But he's not helping me keep that feeling."

Prickles went across Wynona's neck and she paused again. "Violet, stop that. Using magic on him would be completely unethical."

Violet scoffed. *I'm not doing anything.*

"What?" Wynona paused, studying the feeling on her skin. The fine hairs on her neck were standing on end. It was very similar to how she felt when magic was touching her, but...slightly different.

Rascal's ears twitched. "We're being watched," he said under his breath.

"What?"

Is that all you can say? Violet demanded.

Wynona ignored her. "What do you mean, we're being watched?"

Rascal's ears continued to shift, growing elongated as he concentrated. Slowly, he spun, his eyes moving around the neighborhood before finally standing down. "They're gone."

Wynona shivered even as her neck went back to normal. "Who was it, do you think?"

Rascal shook his head. "Don't know. It could have been anyone. Even just a nosy neighbor."

She snorted. "This case seems to be full of them." A light breeze blew her hair back from her face as she began to climb into the truck and Wynona paused.

"Wy?" Rascal asked, his eyebrows raised. "Something wrong?"

"Violet," Wynona whispered.

The mouse stuck her nose in the air, waiting for her to continue.

"Can you slip into Officer Montego's kitchen and have a look around?" Wynona whispered. She sent a mental picture to her familiar of an item Wynona thought might be hanging around.

Rascal's eyebrows shot up, but he waited patiently.

Violet's nose quivered before she nodded.

Rascal reached to Wynona's shoulder, lifted the purple rodent off and let her down.

"Let's wait in the truck," Wynona said, glancing around. "We don't need an audience."

Rascal nodded again and helped her inside. "Anything in particular she's looking for?" he asked once settled in his own seat.

Wynona pinched her lips together. "Yes. But I'm not certain about it yet." Her mind was churning like a bubbling cauldron. Pieces coming together that could mean nothing, but could mean everything. If Wynona's suspicions were correct, a big piece of the puzzle was about to fall into place.

"Does this mean I have to wait?" he whined, giving her wide puppy dog eyes.

Wynona couldn't help but smile and laugh softly. She put a hand to his cheek. "I'm sure you can think of something to do in the meantime," she teased.

He growled playfully and pulled her across the front bench. "Never tempt a predator," he whispered in a husky tone.

"What if I *want* to tempt the predator?" Wynona responded, her heart picking up speed for reasons much different than danger.

Rascal dropped his head and kissed along her jawline. "Then prepare to be caught."

Wynona closed her eyes, enjoying his attention, though it could only last a few moments. "That's the best part," she said breathlessly.

His answering rumble was enough to send electric pulses through her chest and she found herself wriggling closer, the truck was not a conducive spot to enjoy a short break in.

Open the door!

Wynona jumped back, her heart spiking for another reason. "Umm..." She blinked to clear her thoughts, which were a muddled mess after Rascal's kisses. "Violet's back." Purple ribbons floated through the air, dissipating as she and Rascal pulled apart.

Rascal blew out a breath, his eyes glowing brightly. Grumbling, he opened his door and jumped out, crouching to pick up the mouse.

Meanwhile, Wynona tried to straighten her hair and scooted back to her side of the bench. This was just another example of how she needed to get her magic contained. How was it that after almost a year of dating, he could still sweep her off her feet within only a few seconds and have her losing control? His ability to distract her seemed to get stronger with every moment they spent together, rather than fading.

Violet sniffed from his pocket. *Don't tell me...I have no desire to know.*

Wynona kept from rolling her eyes, but only barely. "Did you see anything?"

A smile spread across the rodent's face. *Oh yeah.*

Wynona returned the emotion. "Okay, my handsome wolf. You were right. We need to report to Chief Ligurio."

He started the truck and pulled out within moments. "I'm gonna have you say that again," he said, casting a teasing look her way. "So I can record it for posterity."

Wynona laughed. She was suddenly feeling much better than she had that morning. This case had seemed to be going in circles, but now she had a break and a sweet kiss from her favorite shifter. Hopefully this bit of information was enough to start them toward the finish line.

CHAPTER 21

"Chief?" Rascal poked his head in the police chief's office. "You free?"

"What do you need, Strongclaw?"

"We've got a development."

Chief Ligurio huffed and Rascal pushed open the door, letting Wynona go in before him.

"Hello, Chief Ligurio," she said politely.

Red eyes glared at her. "You cracked the case already?" he snapped. "I'm impressed."

Wynona gave him a winning smile. "I'm afraid not, but I do think I've got a portion of it figured out."

He snorted and waved her to a seat.

Wynona shook her head. "We don't have time to sit down. I need you to get together a team."

"A team?" His eyes narrowed. "What are you talking about?"

Wynona pinched her lips together. This was going to be tricky. Chief Ligurio wasn't going to like what she had to say next. "You need to arrest Officer Montego."

"What!" Chief Ligurio jumped to his feet, his eyes flashing.

Wynona backed up without thinking about it and ran straight into a rumbling chest. Fear slithered down her spine and she felt her fingers begin to tingle.

Keep it together, Wynona!

Violet was right. Now was not the time to lose control of her magic, but with an angry vampire in front and a terrifying shifter behind her, Wynona had little control of her emotions at the moment.

She knew that Rascal would never hurt her, but that didn't mean he couldn't get upset.

Forcing her shaking knees into movement, she shifted to the side, but strong arms banded around her and Wynona squeaked in surprise.

"Stand down, Chief." Rascal's voice was almost unrecognizable.

The rough tone only stoked the fear licking up her spine and the electricity of her magic trying to protect her grew stronger. She could feel the magic tickling the tips of her fingers and purple sparks were in her peripheral vision. Wynona clenched her hands into fists, trying to control the magic, and closed her eyes, focusing on the fact that Rascal was protecting her. She wasn't helpless. If it came down to it, even her crazy powers could save her from a vampire, but Wynona wasn't ready for Chief Ligurio to know. Once the cat was out of the bag, there would be nothing keeping her family from figuring out that her curse was gone and Wynona wasn't sure how to avoid them pulling her back home just yet.

She knew she couldn't keep it all a secret forever, but she wanted to be in better control before she faced Hex Haven's most powerful magical family.

"You're accusing one of my men of murder?" Chief Ligurio said through his elongated fangs.

Wynona had never seen him quite so far gone to his creature.

"I said, *stand down!*" Rascal ground out. His arms pushed her behind him.

Wynona let out a relieved breath when she was cut off from being pinned by that red gaze. She gripped the back of Rascal's shirt, noting that it was tighter than normal. His muscles were taut and larger than normal as he also fought the creature inside. There was barely any give in his shirt for her to hold onto, but touching him seemed to help calm her flaring magic.

"Chief, I know you're upset," Wynona said carefully. "But I promise I'm not doing this out of anything but concern for the case."

Chief Ligurio growled, then cut it off and pressed fingers into his eyes. Slowly, Wynona watched his fangs retract and he carefully sat back down. He was stiff, but his creature had receded, for which she was grateful. "You truly think he's involved?"

Wynona nodded. "I'm sorry."

"Why didn't you say something before?" Rascal asked over his shoulder. He also had calmed, but he didn't move from standing in front of Wynona.

She gave him a sympathetic look. "Because it was just us. I was afraid if I explained it all, you'd try to take him on by yourself."

Rascal snorted, but didn't argue the point. "You realize I can take on a vamp?"

Chief Ligurio growled again and Rascal put his hands in the air.

"Sorry, Chief, but Montego isn't anywhere near as strong as you are."

Chief Ligurio nodded. "True." He pushed a hand through his hair, making it less than pristine, which was unusual for him. "I never would have guessed," he muttered. "How did I not see it?"

"No one likes to know there's a traitor in their midst," Wynona assured him. "No one blames you for not seeing it. The closer we are to the case, the less we tend to see."

His eyes darted up to hers. "You had better be right about this, Ms. Le Doux. I've learned to listen to what you have to say, but in this case...it's not the time to start making mistakes."

Wynona nodded sadly. "I know," she said softly. "I don't want to do this any more than you do."

He nodded, paused, then nodded again. "Fine." The vampire stood. "Deputy Chief...take five officers. Let's bring him in."

Wynona waited in the office, keeping her breathing as calm as possible. She knew this wasn't going to be pretty. The other officers were going to be just as upset as Chief Ligurio was and that anger would all be directed at her. She couldn't blame them, but she also couldn't ignore the mounting evidence.

Officer Montego was involved and Wynona could prove it.

It took another half hour for them to all be ready to drive to Officer Montego's house and Wynona spent the whole time in the office trying to contain her anxiety. Violet was on her shoulder, rubbing under her ear soothingly, but even her familiar wasn't enough. Wynona had never been involved when an officer had been arrested and she wasn't looking forward to it now.

"We're here," Rascal said in a low tone as he put the truck in park. Three other cars pulled up around him, lights flashing as they blocked the street and the front of the house. "Do you want to wait here?" he asked, looking at Wynona with concern.

She hesitated, then shook her head. "No, I need to show Chief Ligurio what's going on."

Rascal nodded. "Right." He leaned over, leaving a sweet kiss on her cheek and sending purple sparks into the air. His usual smug grin was missing as he said, "Let's go."

They both climbed out of the truck and Wynona hung back as the officers pounded on the door.

Wynona looked around, noting several curtains twitching as the police continued calling for Officer Montego. They were garnering a lot of attention and it would mean the end of Officer Montego's ability to live in this neighborhood.

Quit doubting yourself and focus, Violet scolded.

Wynona nodded. "I know," she agreed. "I just hate that someone who's supposed to uphold the law is the one breaking it."

Violet chittered an agreement and wrapped her tail around the back of Wynona's neck.

The fine hairs stood up and Wynona shifted. "Are you doing that?"

Violet pulled her tail back. *No. I was just trying to help.* She sniffed.

"Usually it does," Wynona murmured. She rubbed the skin, but the feeling wouldn't go away. "We're being watched again."

Violet snorted. *Of course we are. The whole neighborhood is watching.*

"No...that's not it." Wynona kept looking around. There was something they were missing. She could feel it.

"He's not here," Rascal said tightly, coming back to Wynona's side. He pushed a hand through his hair. "Do you think he figured out you were on to him?"

Wynon's brows pinched together as she replayed their interview. "No...I don't think so. I didn't even catch on until we were outside." She paused, more pieces falling into place. Maybe he had panicked, thinking Wynona knew more than she did. If that was the case... "I know where he is." She raced to the truck. "Come on! I know where he is!"

The other officers looked to their chief, who growled, but waved toward the cars. "Let's go!"

Wynona clambered into her seat in a far less ladylike fashion than she preferred, but it worked. Breathing heavily, she buckled her seat belt. "Head to Ms. Soulton's bakery," she said to Rascal.

He gave her an incredulous look, then whistled low. "Okay..."

Speeding with their lights on, it only took five minutes for them to arrive and surround the bakery the same way they had surrounded Officer Montego's house. A couple on the sidewalk startled, then turned and ran the other way as the police filled the street.

"Chief!" Wynona yelled as she jumped down.

Watch it! Violet cried out, gripping Wynona's neck hard enough to pinch.

"Sorry," Wynona whispered.

"What?" Chief Ligurio shouted.

"Can you catch someone moving at vampire speed?"

He stared at her, then shook his head in disbelief. "Yes."

"Go around back," Wynona directed. "To the kitchens."

Chief Ligurio began barking orders. He sent two through the front and everyone else, including Rascal and Wynona, went to the alley.

Wynona scrambled after the men, knowing that if they didn't hurry, they would miss him.

They paused only a second at the back door before bursting in and rushing into the kitchen. Screams came from the front of the shop and Wynona winced, knowing that Ms. Soulton or her customers were terrified by the intrusion. She would have been too, but if they didn't catch everyone by surprise, Officer Montego would get away again.

"Stop!" one of the front officers shouted.

"Montego!" Chief Ligurio called out. "Don't make this harder than it has to be. Come with us peacefully."

Wynona was standing at the door threshold, her eyes and ears on full alert as she looked around the kitchen. At first glance, nothing seemed out of the ordinary, but she knew he was there. "He has to be," she murmured to herself.

Rascal frowned and looked over his shoulder just as a wind burst the pantry door open.

"You're under arrest!" Chief Ligurio shouted.

Wynona cried out as the wind pushed her into the frame, sending a sharp pain through her shoulder. "He's in the alley!" she called. Bodies rushed past her, knocking Wynona around, but finally arms that she knew better than her own gripped her and tugged her into a broad chest.

"Are you alright?" Rascal whispered into her hair.

Wynona nodded, her face crushed into his sternum. "Yeah. Just a bit bruised." She raised her head. "But we have to find him. If he gets away, he'll disappear."

Rascal raised his chin toward the alley. "They got him. Montego's fast, but Chief is faster."

Wynona looked over her shoulder and slumped in relief. Officer Montego was pinned under two officers, one of them tying the Old Hag's thread around his wrists while Chief Ligurio read him his rights.

"Would someone please tell me what's going on?" a femnine voice screeched.

Wynona jumped and looked over to see Ms. Soulton entering the back room with two officers hot on her heels. "Ms. Soulton," Wynona said, straightening from Rascal's embrace. Oh, how she wished she could simply burrow in his arms forever.

Patience, Violet reminded her. *Let's save the shop first.*

Wynona nodded an acknowledgment of her familiar's words, but kept the conversation on track. "We're going to need you to come with us."

Rascal turned, fully acknowledging the woman now that Wynona had stated their intentions. "Oozog. Take her in your car."

"What?" Ms. Soulton cried, pulling against Officer Oozog's hold. Her arm wrenched free and she spun on Wynona. "Where are you taking me, and why?"

A scuffle from outside caught their attention. Wynona glanced back to see Officer Montego being dragged toward the front of the building. His legs were limp and he had a bloody nose, but it was the look of utter defeat on his face that hurt the most. Wynona knew the policemen hadn't hurt him badly, it was his emotional turmoil that had him collapsing.

"What are they doing to him?" Ms. Soulton shouted, walking toward the door.

Officer Oozog once again took her arm, his hold firm but gentle. "Ms. Soulton, we need you to come with us," he said, repeating Wynona's words.

"I will not," she said, pulling against him again. "Not without an explanation."

Wynona sighed. "We need to question you...fully this time...about why you lied."

Ms. Soulton stiffened. "What do you mean? Lied about what?"

"About the fact that you're having an affair with Office Montego." After dropping that bombshell, Wynona headed inside. "Deputy Chief, if my hunch is correct, there's something we need in here for evidence."

CHAPTER 22

"Where did they put Ms. Soulton?" Wynona whispered as she and Rascal stood just outside the interrogation room. Office Montego had been put inside and Chief Ligurio was grabbing his briefcase and laptop. He had said they would take care of Montego first.

"She's in room B," Rascal said, his eyes skittering down the hall. "We'll talk to her once we've figured out everything from Montego."

Wynona nodded. "Here we go." She glanced to make sure Violet was still safely attached to her shoulder, then headed inside.

Officer Montego's eyes were so narrowed it was a wonder he could see. The Old Hag's thread kept him from accessing his magic, which meant his fangs were gone and his eyes weren't glowing, but the malice streaming from his body was enough to make anyone think twice before speaking to him.

Wynona swallowed hard and began to walk to her usual spot in the back corner, but a voice stopped her.

"Ms. Le Doux," Chief Ligurio said firmly.

Wynona spun around.

"Up here, please." He waved at a chair next to his behind the interrogation table.

Violet grumbled slightly, but Wynona nodded and walked up. She felt as if she were the one in the hot seat instead of Office Montego, but she also understood that the officer was here under her accusations. Chief Ligurio would need Wynona to lead the conversation.

Her back was stiff, but Wynona was finally able to take a full breath when Rascal's heat came up behind her. She was so grateful

for his support. He hadn't liked arresting an officer any more than
the rest of the precinct, but Wynona never doubted that her shifter
had her back.

Chief Ligurio let Officer Montego sweat for a few moments
while he set up his computer and opened his laptop. Wynona kept
quiet. She knew the vampire chief was only trying to unsettle the officer.

Officer Montego must have known it as well, since he rolled his
eyes and slumped in his chair. "Why am I here, Chief?"

A single eyebrow rose on Chief Ligurio's pale face. "I was hoping
you could tell me why you were at Ms. Soulton's bakery."

Montego huffed. "Is it a crime to buy cookies?"

"No..." Chief Ligurio said easily. "But most customers don't find
their way to the pantry, let alone the back of a place of business." He
folded his long fingers together and leaned his elbows onto the desk.
"Want to tell me what that was all about?"

Officer Montego shrugged, his eyes on the floor. "She needed
help with some heavy supplies. I was lifting them for her."

Rascal let out a snort, then sort of tried to cover it with a cough.

Officer Montego glared up at his superior. "Something funny,
Deputy Chief Strongclaw?"

Wynona glanced over her shoulder to see Rascal's eyes glowing
gold and a sarcastic smile on his face. "I fail to see how aprons could
be so heavy," he said tightly, then shrugged. "But maybe the baker really is that weak."

"Don't call her that," Officer Montego snarled.

"Ahh...and here we get to the real crux of the problem," Chief
Ligurio said calmly. He turned his head to Wynona, giving her the
go ahead.

Wynona took a deep breath and blew it out slowly, trying to
calm her racing heartbeat. Finding and following clues was intrigu-
ing. Dealing with the criminals still scared her to death. She much

prefered her little seat in the back where she could observe but not be involved. "How long have you and Ms. Soulton been seeing each other?"

Officer Montego jerked back. "What are you talking about?"

Typical, Violet grumbled.

"Officer Montego," Wynona said in her best soothing voice. "I'm sure you're a very intelligent man, and you did a good job of covering your steps in this case, but in the end, like all creatures, you made several mistakes and there's no reason for you to deny it now. Not when all the evidence points otherwise."

The vampire's jaw clenched and his eyes narrowed, but he didn't speak.

Sighing, Wynona decided it was best to show him what she knew. "On your coffee table was a box of cookies." She raised her eyebrows. "A pink striped box of cookies. Can you tell me what bakery they came from?"

"Lots of people go to that bakery."

Wynona nodded. "I'm sure they do. But it would beg the question... If you already had a box of cookies at home, why were you picking up more this afternoon? And why would a vampire have enough food in his house for more than one person, when he rarely ate at all?"

Officer Montego's pale face paled even further and some of the hostility drained from his eyes. "How do you know how much I eat?" he asked weakly.

Wynona sighed. "Vampires who regularly indulge in human food tend to be sickly, since it doesn't agree with their systems in large amounts. If you had been consuming as many calories as you have around the house, you would be in the hospital." She pinched her lips together. "I also noticed that the garbage strewn around your apartment this morning wasn't quite right." Wynona gave him a sympathetic grin. "Truth was, your house was already clean, wasn't it?

You had put on a good show when we'd first come to visit you, but when we came a second time, you needed to still look like you were mourning, so before you opened the door, you rushed around throwing garbage onto the floor and couch. The plastic bags had already been scrunched, like you did when you pushed them back into the can." She leaned in. "You used your vampire speed, that's why we were hit with a burst of air when the door opened. The same burst I felt when the button disappeared from Alavara's office." Wynona glanced at the chief, who looked resigned, as if recognizing where her evidence was heading.

Officer Montego's nostrils began to flare and Wynona could feel the other officers in the room stiffening. The air was thick with tension and she was struggling to breathe properly again. But when purple squiggles danced in the periphery of her vision, Wynona knew she needed to keep going and get this over with.

"I know you didn't kill her," Wynona said breathlessly. "But you were trying to protect the person you thought did...weren't you?"

Officer Montego was coiled so tight, Wynona was afraid he would shatter, but he must have hit his breaking point because his body collapsed and he buried his face in his hands, groaning. "It wasn't supposed to be like this," he said in a muffled tone. He looked up, his face stricken and desperate. "I love her."

Wynona nodded. "Why don't you tell us what really happened?"

His baritone voice choked on a sob, but he nodded, slumping in his seat as if completely defeated. "Alavara and I had been together for years," he said softly. His red eyes met Wynona's. "She used to live here when she was younger, did you know that?"

Wynona shook her head.

"We grew up together." Officer Montego sighed. "High School sweethearts and all that. Began dating in earnest once we graduated, but life separated us for a while. We caught up to each other in Cauldron Cove when I went on a weekend trip and..." He splayed his hands out as best he could with them connected by the thread. "It just was so easy...but..." He closed his eyes and hung his head. "I didn't feel the same about her as I did before and then, after Alavara moved here, Mardella showed up." A small smile tugged at his lips. "Where Alavara had become jaded and harsh over the years, Mardella was sweet and soft." He jerked upright, leaning forward as if desperate to gain their approval. "I wanted to break up with Alavara, but we just...had so much history together." He pushed his hands through his hair, the movement awkward, but he must not have noticed in his agitation.

"I fell hard and fast for Mardella, but was struggling to break free from Alavara." He shook his head. "She was unstable. I was afraid if I broke up with her, she'd do something drastic."

Wynona frowned. "She was suicidal?"

He made a face and looked away. "Maybe overly dramatic is a better word for it, but she had threatened to hurt herself before, so..."

Wynona tucked that piece of information away for another time. "What about Mr. Leadtank, or better yet, Mr. Alefoot. How did he fit into all this?"

Officer Montego shrugged. "I honestly had no idea he was under a spell. The dwarf was her janitor. He wasn't exactly someone I spent a lot of time with." He let out a long sigh, leaning onto his elbow and putting his hands on his head. "But Alavara had always been one to flirt with the line of...propriety?"

"So, this button," Chief Ligurio said, clearing his throat. It was obvious he wanted Wynona to explain.

Still watching Officer Montego, Wynona answered the chief. "Ms. Soulton must have been in the office at the tea shop at some point. I've noticed she has a thing for aprons." She turned to the chief. "The button came from one of those aprons. During the murder investigation, you told me you had sent Officer Montego home, but after discovering the button, I stepped out into the hall. A breeze blew past me and when we went back in only moments later, the button was gone."

"I'm guessing he didn't go home," Chief Ligurio said tightly.

"No. He stayed close, watching for clues, and I discovered one for him." She turned back to the broken creature. "He used his vampire speed to steal it, worried that Ms. Soulton would be implicated in the murder."

Wynona looked over her shoulder at Rascal. "If someone would please bring the apron I took from the bakery, I'll show it to you."

Rascal sent a look to the officer at the door, who quietly slipped out. It only took moments before the article of clothing was passed inside. Rascal took it and handed it to the chief.

Chief Ligurio searched the apron. It looked like a nutcracker with a bright red front, blue bottom half and gold buttons running down the front. He frowned. "All the buttons are on here," he said, handing it to Wynona.

Wynona nodded. "That's because he sewed it back on."

Chief Ligurio frowned. "How can you tell?"

Wynona pointed to a button. "See how the thread is all neat and it matches?" She pushed aside the last button. "But this one..."

"The thread is different," Chief Ligurio muttered.

"And the direction is wrong," Rascal added as he leaned over Wynona's shoulder.

"Right. He was at the bakery putting it back, which is why Ms. Soulton didn't know he was there. She hadn't known that he'd taken the apron in the first place and he was trying to keep its return from her as well." Wynona handed it back to the Chief. "You might want to hang onto that."

He handed it to an officer with instructions for bagging it as evidence. "So you thought your mistress had murdered your girlfriend." It was a statement, not a question.

Officer Montego shook his head. "No...Mardella could never do that, but I couldn't let her be accused. Don't you see?" he pleaded. "She's innocent in all this," Officer Montego said. "I was trying to save her from being framed. We were together the night that Alavara was killed, which is why I didn't tell you before." He huffed. "I wouldn't have put it past Alavara to discover our affair and kill herself just to frame Mardella."

The room was quiet for several heartbeats before Wynona spoke up. "Chief, I think we've gotten everything we can here," she said softly. "He didn't kill Ms. Theramin. But he did make some really stupid choices."

The chief studied his officer, pity flashing in his eyes for a split second before it disappeared. "Take his badge and get this vamp out of my sight," he said in a low tone.

Wynona felt bad as she watched the disgraced officer be dragged from the room. He might have been trying to save those he loved, but he'd gone about it all wrong and now an investigation was thrown on its head because of his idiocy. It was difficult to justify any of his decisions, since he'd spent so much time lying and deceiving everyone around him, but Wynona was positive that he'd hidden evidence, but he hadn't killed Alavara. He'd made things harder, but he hadn't done the deed.

"Are you going to tell me what else tipped you off?" Chief Ligurio asked, his voice still low and tightly controlled. "It couldn't have only been a box of cookies and a breeze."

Wynona shook her head. "No. There were several things that I didn't see until afterwards." She glanced up at Rascal. "The first time we visited he was pretending to be drunk."

Rascal frowned. "I could smell the alcohol."

"I know. But it takes a lot to get a vampire drunk and one bottle of beer won't do it."

"But..." Rascal's eyes widened. "The six pack was only missing one bottle. The others were still full."

"Right," Wynona confirmed. "There were soda cans and blood bags everywhere, but no more alcohol bottles. No one can get drunk on soda, he was simply setting a scene. He needed to appear upset and getting drunk was a natural reaction if you lost someone close to you."

Rascal scrubbed his face and muttered a word Wynona didn't ask him to repeat. "He's been playing us this whole time."

"And you still don't think he murdered her?"

Wynona shook her head. "No. Everything he's done has been off the cuff and frantic. That's why there were so many mistakes. His skills and experience as an officer gave him some ideas, but once we looked past the surface, it was easy to see where it all went wrong. Whoever killed Alavara had planned it all out. She was alone, she was at the shop, they used a non-magical weapon in order to not leave any clues." Wynona took in a deep breath. "If he had murdered her, he would have had the after-acting all planned out. Instead he was making it up as he went along, keeping one step ahead, but not for very long."

"What about Ms. Soulton?" Chief Ligurio asked. "Was she involved?"

Wynona pinched her lips together. "I don't think she had anything to do with Officer Montego's part."

"Mr. Montego," Chief Ligurio snapped. "He's not an officer anymore."

Wynona gave him a sad smile. "Right. Mr. Montego. I can't rule her out of the murder, but other than the button, I have nothing to pin on her either. And with her propensity for aprons, that button could have been dropped at any time. Multiple people have said Mr. Alefoot wasn't a good janitor. Who knows when he last vacuumed?"

"The witch is still waiting for us in the other room," Rascal said. "Should we go ask some questions?"

Wynona waited for the chief to agree and they all stood up. Chief Ligurio led the way and the group headed down the hall.

Right before they reached the door, Rascal took Wynona's hand and gave it a squeeze. "You're brilliant," he whispered against her head, leaving a kiss.

Wynona melted at his praise and wished they had a few more moments alone before she had to do this again. At some point, her life had to calm down. Someday she wouldn't be hiding her magic, she wouldn't be constantly trying to save her business and she wouldn't be afraid of her family.

She was determined that someday, she would find her happy ever after, and it would definitely include the handsome wolf at her side. There was no other option.

CHAPTER 23

"Hello, Ms. Soulton," Wynona said pleasantly as they entered the interrogation room. They had all agreed in the hallway that the questions coming from a woman might help to loosen Ms. Soulton's tongue, especially since none of them were quite sure what they were getting into.

Ms. Soulton could be an unfortunate pawn in this game, or she could have been involved from the beginning. They would have to see how her interview stood up against Officer Montego's.

"Hello," Ms. Soulton said coolly. She looked wary and unsure, which was consistent with what Wynona had learned about her thus far, but the coldness in her tone was new.

Easy, Violet warned. *She's in a police station and her cheating boyfriend was just interrogated. Don't jump to conclusions.*

Wynona gave a subtle nod. Violet was right. Wynona just wanted this case over and done with so badly that she was rushing things. Putting an innocent creature behind bars would be far worse than spending another couple of days on the case. She took a deep, cleansing breath and sent Rascal a small smile when he rubbed her lower back.

"What happened to Haar?" Ms. Soulton asked, her eyes darting from one person to the next.

"He's being processed," Chief Ligurio said as easily as if they were talking about the weather.

"What!" she screeched. "What for?"

"Tampering with evidence, removing evidence from the scene of a crime, lying to the police." Chief Ligurio raised an eyebrow. "It's a long list. Did you want me to name everything?"

Ms. Soulton pressed her lips together, the thin white line ruining the usual softness of her face.

"Ms. Soulton." Wynona leaned forward in her seat. "When did you and Officer Montego first get together?"

At first, the witch glared, but after a moment she slumped in her seat. "You have to understand," she said softly. "Alavara was...unwell."

Wynona frowned. Officer Montego had said as much. But there was no one else to back it up. Maybe they needed to talk to the neighbor again. His blunt opinion might help them know if she was emotionally struggling or simply a hard woman.

"Haar was such a handsome man," Ms. Soulton said wistfully. Her eyes were unfocused, as if she were looking at something beyond them. "But so sad." A frown marred the witch's face. "And that...elf," Ms. Soulton spat, "treated him as if he were useless. Disposable." She suddenly focused her blue eyes on Wynona, straightening in her seat. "She didn't deserve someone so warm and sweet." Tears misted Ms. Soulton's eyes. "But Haar was worried. He said if he left her, she would do something drastic." She sniffed. "Maybe even kill herself."

Wynona watched carefully, seeking for any sign that there was deception going on. She believed Ms. Soulton really did love Officer Montego. But was she really willing to sit back and play second fiddle? Most women would struggle with that. "What was your plan then?" Wynona asked. "Or were you planning to remain the mistress forever?"

Blue eyes flashed and Chief Ligurio's stiffening told Wynona he noticed it too. "I wasn't the mistress," Ms. Soulton said tightly.

Wynona lifted her eyebrows. "I'm sorry. What did you prefer to be called?"

The witch sniffed and ran her hands down her apron, straightening wrinkles. "I was the love of his life. It was Alavara who was in the way."

She's speaking in circles, Violet grumbled.

Wynona reached up to pet her familiar. Somehow, Ms. Soulton was avoiding answering any real questions. Time to pin her down. "Where were you the night Ms. Theramin was killed?"

The sad, resigned witch was back. "I was with Haar. He spent the night at my house." She glanced up. "He was there from just after dinner until we both left for work the next morning."

Wynona's eyes widened. "And you weren't worried about Alavara finding you? That's a long time."

The baker sniffed and shrugged. "Alavara often worked late. She had already told Haar she would be unavailable for the night." She picked at a loose thread on her apron. "We don't get to plan our time together in advance, so there was no way we were passing up an opportunity like this."

"And what was Alavara doing so late at the shop?" Wynona pressed. "Was she meeting with someone?"

Ms. Soulton shook her head. "I have no idea. I never asked." A sheepish smile crossed her face. "As you can imagine, the two of us weren't close friends." Her eyes widened. "I wouldn't have put it past her to have been having a rendezvous of her own, though. Alvara cared nothing for other people's feelings. She might very well have been cheating on Haar."

Oh, good grief, Violet whined.

"How about your button?" Wynona asked. "Can you tell us how it ended up at the crime scene?"

Ms. Soulton nodded, her shoulders slumping slightly. "I had been wearing that apron when I delivered the pastries that morning. We went into her office to discuss an amendment to our contract. It must have fallen off during our chat."

"Were you unhappy with the arrangement?"

Ms. Soulton shrugged. "It stated that I had to bring the food by seven every morning. At first I hadn't worried about it. As a baker I'm up early anyway, so I thought it would be fine." She blew out a breath, shifting hair that was hanging around her face. "I'm guessing it fell off when we were in her office discussing things."

"And how did that discussion go?" Chief Ligurio inserted.

Ms. Soulton huffed. "As well as you can imagine. She told me I'd signed the contract and needed to fulfill it or she would take it up with a lawyer."

"When did you become aware the button was missing?" Wynona asked.

Ms. Soulton shook her head. "When you took it from the bakery." She shrugged. "If you hadn't noticed, I have a lot of aprons. One going missing didn't even register."

Alavara's list of attributes just gets longer and longer, Violet said sarcastically.

Wynona tapped her fingers on her knee. "What do you know of Mr. Leadtank?" Wynona asked. "Were you aware he was under a compulsion spell?"

Ms. Soulton blinked. "What?"

"The dwarf," Rascal snapped.

Wynona jumped. He had been so quiet she had almost forgotten he was there. It was apparent, however, that despite his silence, he wasn't impressed with what was going on.

"The janitor?" Ms. Soulton asked.

Wynona nodded. "Yes. His real name is Urnoke Alefoot." She tilted her head, studying the witch's reaction. "Ms. Theramin cast a spell on him and compelled him to work for her, changing his name and bringing him from Cauldron Cove, where she moved."

Ms. Soulton's mouth formed a perfect O. "I had no idea," she said breathlessly. Her eyes slowly hardened and she pointed at Wynona. "I told you that woman cared nothing for others. Something was wrong with her." She shook her head. "Normal people don't treat others that way."

Wynona leaned back in her seat, her mind churning. "Thank you for your time," she said politely.

Ms. Soulton straightened. "I can go?"

Wynona looked at the Chief, who raised a questioning eyebrow at her. Wynona nodded. Chief Ligurio turned to the waiting witch. "Thank you for your cooperation, Ms. Soulton. If we have any further questions, we'll let you know."

She nodded, her countenance still depressed. "Will...will Haar be released any time soon?"

Chief Ligurio sighed. "Ms. Soulton, he will more than likely be held until the hearing. After that, it will be up to the judge."

Her bottom lip trembled and she nodded. "I understand. Thank you." Bringing a hand to her mouth as if to hold back a sob, she walked out. The officer at the door followed her, presumably to lead her to the front of the precinct.

Rascal waited until the door had closed before growling. "I don't like her."

Wynona looked over her shoulder, giving him an understanding smile.

"Ms. Le Doux?" Chief Ligurio snapped, catching her attention. "What are your thoughts?"

Wynona sighed. "I'm with Rascal. Something about her just isn't...genuine."

The vampire rolled his eyes. "It isn't against the law to sneak around with a committed man behind someone's back."

Wynona nodded. "I know, but I just..." She held her hands out. "I think she did it."

Black eyebrows furrowed together. "Are you talking about the murder?"

Wynona nodded. "Yes. I think she killed Alavara."

Chief Ligurio's long, pale fingers tapped against the table. "She has an alibi."

"One that's been backed up by her boyfriend," Rascal added. He walked around the desk and sat in the newly vacated chair so he was facing Wynona and the chief.

"I understand that," Wynona said. "But I still think she did it." She held up a hand to stop their arguments. "I don't know *how* she did it. But she did it."

Chief Ligurio narrowed his eyes. "So what will you do next? I need something solid before I can charge her."

Wynona squished her lips to the side. "I'm not sure. Maybe I'll go back and talk to the neighbor." She sighed. "Although, I'm not sure how that's going to help. Odds are he never saw Alavara and Ms. Soulton together."

"Doesn't hurt to ask, I suppose." Rascal slapped his knees and stood up. "But first we need to grab something to eat. I'm starving."

Wynona laughed softly. "I'd say you're always hungry, but I could use some food myself." She looked over. "Chief? Can we have something brought to you?"

"A fresh mug would be nice, thank you."

Wynona worked hard to keep her shock from showing. It was a rare day that the chief treated her so amiably. "I'll tell Amaris to send it back as we leave."

"Thank you." The vampire stood and Wynona followed. "Let me know what you two figure out." With those parting words, he left.

Wynona started at the door, then turned and let Rascal see her shock. "Did we truly just have a civil conversation with your boss?"

Rascal chuckled and walked over to take her hand. "Kind of makes you feel like anything's possible, doesn't it?"

Wynona nodded. "I didn't know he was capable of saying please and thank you."

Rascal laughed loudly, drawing the attention of several officers in the hallway. He ignored them and guided Wynona to the front doors. "Nightshade, send Chief a hot one." He winked at Wynona. "Please?"

"On it, Deputy Chief," Officer Nightshade said easily. "See you later, Wynona."

"Bye!" Wynona waved. She took in a cleansing breath as they arrived outside. The cool breeze felt wonderful after sitting in stuffy interrogation rooms for several hours. "Where would you like to grab dinner?" she asked. Normally, she would cook for Rascal, but she just wasn't feeling it this afternoon. She was starving, her mind was spinning and she didn't want the stress of extra work right now.

"Want to grab some pizza from the Weeping Widow and take it back to my place?" Rascal opened the passenger door.

Wynona smiled in thanks and began climbing into the truck. "That sounds perfect."

Violet chittered her agreement and they settled into the truck.

It took another half hour for them to arrive at his apartment and the smells coming from the pizza box were making Wynona's stomach growl.

Rascal smirked. "And you complain about my appetite."

Wynona laughed. "Sorry. I told you I was hungry. Maybe it was worse than I thought."

Rascal closed his door and came around to help her. He opened the door, took the box and leaned in for a quick kiss. "It's my greatest honor to make sure your needs are taken care of," he whispered.

A pleasurable shiver ran down her spin and Wynona wasn't sure her legs would hold her well enough to walk. "How did a wolf get to be so smooth?" she asked breathlessly.

Rascal winked as he held out one hand to help her down. "I could probably offer a little too much evidence to the contrary, but I'm not exactly upset that you think that, so...I think I'll let it go."

Wynona put her arm through his and sighed in contentment. "We need to figure out how to nail that woman. I'm ready for us to have some non-sleuthing time together."

A playful growl rumbled through Rascal's chest. "Don't tempt me. I might just take you and run off into the wilderness in order to get it." His eyes flashed. "I do have a wild side, you know."

Wynona leaned her head on his shoulders, her smile refusing to budge. The end of this case couldn't come fast enough.

CHAPTER 24

"Mmm..." Wynona moaned as she took a bite of the pizza. Who would have ever guessed that a banshee would find her calling making pizza? The Weeping Widow had the best pizza in all of Hex Haven, at least Wynona thought so. At the rate Rascal was eating, he must have similar feelings. She smiled and handed him a napkin.

Grinning sheepishly, he took the napkin and wiped his face. "Better?"

She nodded. "Better." She raised an eyebrow. "You were just showing me how good your manners were. Are you saying that doesn't extend to table manners?"

"Not when I'm starving," he said through a full mouth.

Wynona rolled her eyes, knowing he was teasing her on purpose. He didn't usually eat like the wild animal lurking inside of him. "So...what were your thoughts about Ms. Soulton?"

Rascal chewed and his eyes went up as he thought. "I'm on the same page as you. I don't have a good piece of evidence, but my gut says she's lying." He took another big bite. "And I always listen to my gut."

"Which is why you're always eating," Wynona said with a grin.

He growled at her, then grinned. "It hasn't steered me wrong yet."

She nodded. "In all seriousness, though, something is just off. She and Officer Montego have the same alibi, but did they plan it ahead of time? Or is it true?" Wynona tilted her head consideringly. "It seems weird that they would have planned their alibis when she didn't seem to know that he'd taken the button."

"Right." Rascal set down his glass of soda. "Why make sure your stories matched if you didn't know you needed a story to begin with?"

Wynona nodded.

Violet made a noise and Wynona looked down to realize her familiar was snoring.

"Niiice," Wynona said softly. "Some help she is."

"It's been a long day," Rascal said through a chuckle. "I think we've all earned a rest. Unfortunately, you and I are on the clock."

"Oh, to be a mouse," Wynona mused. She tapped her fingers on the tabletop. "There has to be something we're missing."

"But what?" Rascal challenged. "We've been over the shop, the house, the bakery and Haar's. What's left?" His growl wasn't the playful one from before. "I can't stand the thought of a murderer getting away because we can't find the right evidence."

"Well, if the DA would simply listen to your gut, we'd have it all solved."

Rascal gave her a look and shook his head. "Funny."

"I thought so."

Before their banter could continue, a knock interrupted them. Rising to his feet, Rascal put on hand at this back where Wynona knew he held his stun gun. The idea of him needing to use it frightened her, but she stayed still. Rascal would keep her safe if someone had followed them.

He stopped at the door and sniffed, then relaxed and gave Wynona a look. Opening the door, he said, "Mama Reyna. How nice to see you."

"You have the girl here?"

Wynona closed her eyes and prayed for patience. She hadn't spoken to Mrs. Reyna since she had kicked her and Rascal out. The older shifter was keeping things from her about her grandmother and Wynona wasn't sure how to handle it. In fact, she hadn't even consid-

ered trying to handle it until the case was taken care of. She could only handle so many things at a time and a revelation about her grandmother might be more than Wynona was ready to take on at the moment.

Rascal folded his arms over his chest. Normally, Wynona would
be enjoying the view, but today there were too many emotions running through her system. "I don't think that's a good idea right now,"
he said tightly.

"I have things she needs to hear," Mrs. Reyna said in a low voice.

Rascal's stance changed. His legs spread and his muscles coiled.
"It will need to wait," he said more firmly.

"Stand aside, wolf. I'm not here to hurt your mate."

Wynona stiffened. "Mate?" she whispered. She and Rascal were
definitely dating, but the term *mate* was a whole different story. Soulmates were rare and only the lucky few got to experience the bliss of
that type of relationship. Most creatures didn't bother holding out
for one, though Wynona was sure that almost every young female
paranormal had dreamed of it at one point or another. The same way
human children dreamed of being a pretty, pretty, princess.

But the chances were so low that it was rarely even spoken about,
let alone hoped for. *But is my relationship like that with Rascal? Is
there any possibility—*

"Wy?"

Wynona blinked and came out of her thoughts. She hadn't heard
what Rascal had said in response to Mrs. Reyna's challenge and she
wished she had. She needed to know what he was thinking. Did he
think they were mates? Or was he as surprised as she was?

"Do you want to talk to her?" he asked softly, studying her with
concern.

Were his ears red? Wynona narrowed her gaze, trying to see better. Why would he be embarrassed?

"Wy?" Rascal asked again.

Wynona shook her head. "Sorry," she rasped. She blew out a breath. "Might as well let her in. She won't let up until you do."

Rascal raised his eyebrows, silently asking if she was sure.

Wynona nodded and stood. "Hello, Mrs. Reyna," she said as the woman marched inside. She kept her face serene, though the wolf was glowering at her.

"I'm old. Not deaf."

Wynona nodded. "Understood."

"Hmph." Mrs. Reyna stormed to the couch and sat down.

Wynona slowly followed, but sat in a recliner across the room. She didn't trust Rascal's neighbor currently. Folding one knee over the other, Wynona rested her entwined fingers on top. "You have something you wanted to tell me?"

A warm presence stood just to her side. He was always there, supporting at times, leading at others. Wynona's chest warmed as she realized just how much Rascal was a part of her life. She wouldn't have half of what she did if they hadn't stumbled into each other's paths when a man had been murdered in her office.

Mrs. Reyna's face didn't shift, but her eyes darted between Wynona and Rascal. "I still think it's too soon, but Saffy says otherwise."

Wynona's lung collapsed. "Says? You..." She rasped. "You spoke to my grandmother?" The smug look on the elder woman's face was almost enough to have Wynona snapping. She clenched her fists and tried to keep her emotions under control. She could do this. She had spent thirty years holding her emotions at bay when she was under the thumb of her family. One tiny old woman wouldn't be the one to break her.

Mrs. Reyna shrugged. "It's been necessary."

"What's been necessary?" Wynona asked, not being able to stop the edge to her voice. "Lying to me? Or talking to my dead grandmother behind my back?"

Mrs. Reyna's eyebrows shot up. "There might be a bit of Saffy in you yet."

Wynona pinched her lips together. "Please say what you wanted to say, Mrs. Reyna. We're very busy with a case and have leads to look into."

Mrs. Reyna looked unimpressed. "Too busy to hear what your grandmother wanted to tell you?"

Wynona didn't budge. Mrs. Reyna was purposefully baiting her and she didn't like it one bit.

Mrs. Reyna sighed and slumped into the couch cushions. "How strong are your powers?" she asked.

Wynona's eyes widened as Rascal coughed so hard she was sure he would lose a lung. "Excuse me?" she choked out.

The wolf shifter rolled her eyes. "Not all of us are so blind, missy. But we need to know just how far things have developed."

Wynona looked up at Rascal, at a loss for words. "Did you?" she whispered.

He shook his head adamantly. "Not a word."

Mrs. Reyna snapped her fingers. "Now you just told me you were in a hurry, but you're speaking around me and not following the conversation." She shook her head and stood up. "I told Saffy it was too soon." She stomped toward the door. "You get that case cleared up, and then come back and we'll talk."

The door rattled with the force of her slam and Wynona was sure the whole hallway had heard the noise.

"Wy." Rascal kneeled in front of her. "Breathe, sweetheart. Breathe."

Wynona's lungs unfroze and she sucked in a shaky breath. "How did she know about my magic?" she rasped.

A scurrying of feet brought Violet from the kitchen table. She rushed up Wynona's leg and onto her shoulder. *Cranky old biddy,* Violet grumbled. She nuzzled Wynona's neck. *She's just trying to mess with your head.*

"For what purpose?" Wynona asked, swallowing hard. Her mouth felt dry and her heart was racing. Sweat was beading at her hairline as if she'd been running through the Forbidden Forest instead of sitting in a recliner at her boyfriend's house.

Rascal rubbed her hands, bringing warmth back to the cold digits. "I'm not sure," he said carefully. "She always did seem to know more than she should." His golden eyes flashed to the door and glowed slightly. "I have half a mind to force her to finish what she was going to say."

Wynona used her free hand to rub her clammy forehead. "I shouldn't have been so sharp with her, I suppose," she said softly, guilt mixing with the shock. "But I was so caught off guard and she seemed to be trying to say as little as possible." Wynona sighed. "I suppose I allowed her to make me angry."

Rascal growled. "This isn't your fault," he assured her. "Mama Reyna has always been difficult." His lip curled. "Although, to be honest, I've never seen her be quite so bad as this. I had no idea she had been friends with your grandma and to know that the two of them are plotting even after death..." He shook his head. "I'm not even sure what to think about that."

"But the magic," Wynona pressed. "How in the world did she know about the magic? Granny Saffron didn't even know about it. I didn't start to get my powers until she was gone."

Her headache was becoming legendary. She could barely think straight, while her stomach churned and her heart ached. She wanted to call Mrs. Reyna back. She wanted to beg forgiveness and find out what Granny Saffron wanted her to know. There were so many questions running through her head that Wynona didn't even know where to begin.

She turned her teary eyes to Rascal. "What do I do?" she asked. "Should I go ask forgiveness? Maybe she'll talk to me if I grovel."

Rascal shook his head, wiping her tears with his thumbs. "No, sweetheart. As frustrating as Mama Reyna is, she was right. We need to solve this case. We're close. I can feel it. Your plate is too full. Let's get this gone, I know you too well to think you'll be happy just walking away. Catch the killer, and then we'll focus on Mrs. Reyna and your grandmother." He tilted his head down so his eyes looked more intently at her. "Together. I promise not to let Mama Reyna get away without spilling all of it." He snorted. "She owes you that at least for being so rude."

Wynona pinched her lips together. "And will you spill it all too?"

Rascal frowned. "What?"

She reached out and let her fingers trail over his stubbly cheeks and chin. "I don't only have questions for my grandmother." Her heart fluttered at the sensation against her fingertips. She was well and truly in love with this wolf. She hoped that pushing him a little wouldn't change his mind about her. "How do you always seem to know when I'm in trouble?" she asked softly. "How do you always understand my feelings?" She leaned in. "Why can you understand my familiar at times?"

Rascal opened his mouth, then snapped it shut.

"And why did Mrs. Reyna call us mates?" Her voice dropped off at the end and Wynona found herself holding her breath again.

Rascal closed his eyes and hung his head. "I've wanted to tell you," he said softly. He brought his eyes up to meet hers. They were glowing ever so lightly. "But you always had so many things on your mind." He gave a weary smile. "There was always another case. Or another problem. Or another crisis." He shrugged. "I didn't want you to feel any pressure and I didn't want to add to your stress."

Wynona's breathing went from still to practically panting. "So, it's true." She swallowed. "We're soulmates?"

Ever so slowly, he nodded.

"How do you know?" Her voice was much higher than it should have been. "I'm not a wolf. I thought it mostly happened between shifters."

Rascal rubbed the back of his neck. "It's less common between different species, but not completely unheard of." He cleared his throat. "I realized it when I came to help you take down Roderick." His eyes darted between hers. "My wolf knew it. I've been able to sense you and feel you since the moment your life was threatened by that dirty wizard."

Despite the fact that the little voice in the back of her mind was going ballistic, Wynona felt more calm than she would have expected. There was something...right...about what he was telling her, though she wanted to shout that she wasn't ready for this. Her heart seemed to know more than she did because it didn't even flinch, but her brain was spinning in circles.

She traced his eyebrows and down his cheekbones. "I think that means we need to talk," she said softly.

He nodded, never losing eye contact.

"But can we do it when this is over? I agree that my plate is a little full at the moment. I need to save my business and reputation, and then I'll have enough energy to figure this out, plus whatever's going on with your crazy neighbor and my granny."

Rascal blew out a breath. "I think that sounds perfect."

Wynona leaned down and left a lingering kiss on his mouth. "Then let's go talk to Vrebs and get this settled once and for all."

CHAPTER 25

Vrebs was outside, sweeping his driveway as they arrived in the truck. Wynona's head was still spinning from all the revelations she'd received in the last half hour. Rascal was her *mate*. Her actual *soulmate*. Those were so rare, Wynona had never met another creature with the blessing.

But HOW does he know?

The thought kept running through her mind, but Wynona had no answer. She knew she had fallen hard and fast, she knew she didn't feel complete until he was around and she knew she would do anything for him, but did that really mean they were soulmates? Or was she just a woman in love?

Rascal chuckled, pulling her out of her reverie. "I don't think he's happy to see us."

Wynona looked at the goblin, glaring at them from his house. "I think you're correct," she said. "But...I'm afraid it really doesn't matter."

"Right." Rascal hopped out of the truck and walked around. He was always so considerate of Wynona, making sure she was taken care of.

Is it because he's my soulmate? Or because he's a gentleman?

She shook her head and shoved the thoughts aside. Why was she making such a big deal out of this? It was something she should be excited about, instead of suspicious of. She loved Rascal. Being his soulmate should be a wonderful thing.

Maybe so, but you've spent your life being manipulated by others, Violet inserted. *It's natural for you to be cautious, even of the people you trust.*

207

Wynona scratched Violet's head. "Thank you," she said softly.

Rascal's shoulders rounded, obviously having heard Violet's bit of the conversation.

Wynona squeezed his hand. "Please, understand...It's a lot," she reminded him. "But don't worry. I'm not going anywhere."

He gave her a small smile, but it was a far cry from his usual playful smirk. "One thing at a time," he said softly.

Wynona nodded and together they walked over to the goblin. "Hello, Vrebs," Wynona said politely. "I don't know if you remember, but I'm Wynona Le Doux and this if Deputy Chief Strongclaw."

Violet flicked Wynona's neck with her tail.

"Excuse me," Wynona said by way of apology. "And this is Violet."

The goblin's eyes were pinched at the corners. "I remember," he said shortly. "Though I don't know why you'd bring a purple mouse around." He sneered. "Nasty vermin."

Violet screeched in outrage and Wynona took her off her shoulder, cuddling her close to calm the creature down. "I have a friend who loves being as clean as you do," Wynona said, tilting her head and ignoring the insult. "I think you and Lusgu would get along very well."

The goblin paused. "You know Lusgu Roich?"

Wynona's eyes widened. "Yes. He works for me."

A snort escaped Vreb's lips, once...twice...before a full belly laugh broke free. The small man-like creature bent over at the waist, laughing hysterically for a couple of minutes before finally getting himself under control.

"I'm sorry," Wynona said carefully. "I don't understand what's so funny."

Vrebs waved a dismissive hand through the air. "Lusgu doesn't work for anybody." He chortled.

Wynona frowned. Lusgu absolutely did work for people. He had been sent over by the Hex Haven Career Resource Center for Paranormals, or HHCRCP, but Wynona didn't feel like it would be a good idea to bring that up. He was definitely a unique character with his bow ties, fedora and suspenders, all while wearing no shoes and looking like he hadn't washed his feet in ten years.

He appeared to be a walking contradiction, but he was also the best janitor Wynona had ever known. Her family castle had been cleaned daily by a multitude of servants and it had never been as clean as Wynona's tea shop.

Rascal's hand landed on her lower back and Wynona decided a change of subject was in order. She had been trying to find common ground with the goblin, but apparently it had only led to being off topic. "Mr. Vrebs," she said over his laughter. "I wonder if we could ask you a few additional questions?"

The neighbor slowly brought himself back under control and he leaned on his broom handle. "I haven't laughed like that in ages," he admitted. "What can I do for you?"

Rascal hmphed.

Wynona wasn't about to look a gift horse in the mouth. Vrebs had been a terror before, she would take any advantage she could get now. "Have you ever seen a woman come over who has long brown hair? She likes to wear aprons and sometimes her hair is pulled up in a bun." She used her hand to show what the hair might look like. It had been Ms. Soulton's standard attire at the shop, but that didn't mean it was what the witch liked once out of the kitchen.

Vreb's scowled. "I told you she rarely had visitors. I saw that boyfriend a few times, but that's about it." He snorted. "It's hard to miss a cop stalking around at night."

Wynona could practically hear Rascal's eyeroll. "But no one else? Ever? Are you sure?" She really hoped their trip out here hadn't been a waste of time. They had wasted too much of it already. It seemed that at every turn they were running into dead ends. The break with Officer Montego had been lucky, but wasn't enough to put the killer behind bars.

If she wasn't here, then we won't find anything to tie her to the murder, Violet grumbled.

Wynona didn't respond. She didn't want to give away that she could talk to her familiar. The goblin would definitely notice.

"I told you before a woman visited, but she never wore aprons." Vrebs growled.

"Are you sure?" Wynona pressed. Who else could have visited Alavara? Who were they missing?

"Do I look like a goblin who misses things?"

Wynona gave him a placid smile. "You're right. Thank you, again, for your time." She turned and headed up to the house.

"You still want to go inside?" Rascal asked, catching up to her. "Why, if Ms. Soulton wasn't here?" He worked with the lock until the door swung open.

"Because, despite his arguments, even the most nosy neighbors miss things," Wynona stated as she walked inside. "Plus, now we have part of the mystery solved, so we know to look for different things." She studied the small entryway. Nothing was out of order since the last time they were there.

"True enough," Rascal murmured, looking around himself. He made a point of sniffing a few times. His nose was one of his best tools and Wynona reminded herself she should have him use it more often.

"Anything?"

He shrugged. "Nothing out of the ordinary. Something in the fridge is going bad and the house definitely needs a good cleaning, but otherwise, it's all pretty normal stuff."

Slightly discouraged, Wynona continued on into the family room. The place was just as they'd left it and still, nothing looked like it had anything to do with her murder.

"You still think the witch did it? Even after talking with Vrebs?" Rascal asked from across the room. He fingered a couple of nick-nacks. "I'm assuming the motive would have to do with Haar? And who is this mystery visitor? If she didn't wear aprons, I'm guessing it wasn't Ms. Soulton."

Wynona pursed her lips and put her hands on her hips. "She could have left her aprons at the shop, and I definitely think it had to do with Officer Montego."

"Not an officer," Rascal growled.

Wynona nodded. "Alright. Mr. Montego. I think she was trying to get rid of the one person who stood in her way of having him all to herself."

"A valid motive, but she's a witch." Rascal read a book cover. "Why use a non-magical method? And how could she do it if she was at home with company?"

Wynona grit her teeth. "I don't know," she said. "I just don't know. But there was something about her interview that set me on edge." She looked at Rascal's smirk. "Don't tell me you didn't feel it? She was about as genuine as my mother."

Rascal chuckled. "And that's saying something."

Violet chittered her agreement and scrambled to the ground.

"Let me know if you find something," Wynona called after her.

Yeah, yeah, Violet said through their connection.

"I'm going to head to the bedroom," Wynona announced, walking toward the hallway. She passed two small guest rooms and a bathroom before finally opening the door to the master. A large bed took up most of the space, covered in a dark red, silky bedspread.

The room itself was quite dark with matching curtains on the window, blocking any afternoon sun that might have dared peek into the space.

"I thought elves preferred light things," Rascal muttered from behind her.

"Me too," Wynona said. She picked at a shirt hanging off the back of a chair. "But Alavara wasn't exactly a...light type of person. I suppose every species has its range of eccentricities." A pink box caught her eye and Wynona walked over. "Rascal."

His warm breath hit the back of her neck. "That's from Ms. Soulton's place?"

Wynona nodded. She carefully lifted the lid. "Apparently, whatever it was was enjoyed." Nothing but crumbs remained in the bottom of the box.

Rascal snorted and moved on. "Ms. Theramin could have brought that home, or even Haar could have brought it with him."

"There is something so wrong about that," Wynona muttered. "Why do people have to cheat? If you don't want to be with a person, break it off."

"Even if that person might hurt him or herself?" he challenged.

"Yes," Wynona snapped. "If they're in a place where they're suicidal, then they need help, not a significant other."

He raised an eyebrow, causing Wynona to notice how she was talking.

"Sorry," she said in a softer tone. "I just..." She blew out a breath. "I should be more compassionate, but it's hard when they purposefully hurt those they're supposed to love." Her family hadn't cheated on her, but Wynona certainly knew what it was like to have those who were supposed to have her back, betray her instead. She didn't wish it on anybody, criminal or not.

Rascal's warm hand landed on her neck, massaging gently. "I get it," he said. "Wolves mate for life, so cheating makes no sense to me either."

Wynona glanced at him sideways. "So you're saying you're stuck with me?"

He smirked. "I think it's the other way around." He gave one last comforting squeeze before moving toward the attached en suite. "She liked lavender."

"Interesting choice," Wynona said, following him. She blew out a breath, standing in the doorway. "I don't think Officer...excuse me, Mr. Montego, spent much time here."

Rascal nodded. "There's no men's stuff in here." He studied the counter. "No razor, no aftershave, no combs."

Wynona pursed her lips. "This isn't working. There's nothing for us to find."

"The murder happened at the shop and Ms. Soulton works and lives elsewhere. I suppose it makes sense."

"I know, but I was still hoping that there would be a clue that Ms. Soulton was lying. Something we could do to shake her up a bit." Wynona huffed and walked back to the gathering area.

Wynona!

"Violet?" Rascal's heavy steps could be heard behind her as Wynona rushed to the kitchen.

Violet was on the counter, studying a leather bound book.

"What is it?" Wynona asked. She frowned. "It looks like a journal. Violet, where did you find it?"

Violet pointed toward a row of cookbooks. *It was in the middle. I think that's why the police missed it.* She tapped her snout. *But I could smell the leather. Who makes leather cookbooks?*

"That's my girl," Rascal said, giving Violet a good rub behind the ears.

Violet chittered and smoothed her fur.

"This says Alavara had an appointment the night she died," Wynona murmured. She flipped the page back and forth. It held very little, but the fact that their murder victim had an appointment opened up a new slew of questions.

"BK," Rascal mused. "Who is BK?"

Wynona shook her head. "Either BK was a nickname for Mardella Soulton that we don't know about...or there's a whole other suspect we have somehow missed." Wynona rubbed her forehead. "It could be the woman who didn't wear aprons that Vrebs had mentioned."

Violet groaned and Rascal growled lightly. "Every clue just seems to bring more questions," he said tightly, flipping through the book some more.

Wynona nodded. "I know. And somehow we need to piece it all together and get that killer behind bars." Her eyes misted over slightly. "I miss my shop and I haven't practiced my magic in days." She could see purple sparkles at the periphery of her vision as her emotions got the best of her. "It's getting antsy and needs an outlet."

"Ah, Wy." Rascal groaned, pulling her into his chest. "Don't worry. We'll get this figured out." He rubbed her back soothingly and the purple sparks began to calm down. "Let's take the book to the station and see if anyone else can get something from it." He pulled back to look her in the eye. "And we can take the time to reset. Okay?"

She nodded, feeling so weary that she wanted to crawl into bed and never come back out. "Right. Next steps. That's all we can do."

They headed to the door and Wynona waited on the porch while Rascal locked the bolt. The tiny hairs on her neck began to rise again and Wynona stilled. "Rascal? Can you smell anything?" she asked softly.

He paused, then sniffed. His eyes flashed in response. "Someone's here."

CHAPTER 26

R ascal spun in a slow circle and growled under his breath.
Wynona frowned. The feeling was eerie, but not malevolent. She simply felt as if she were being watched.

Use your sight, Violet snapped.

Wynona's eyebrows shot up. "Do you think that's it?"

Violet sighed and began cleaning her face.

Wynona took a deep breath. Violet was right. She should have thought of this before. Was it all just a ghost reporter causing the hubbub? It would explain a lot. She blew out a slow breath, centering herself. Slowly, her vision grew slightly blurry, then cleared into a lovely lilac color.

"Whoa," Rascal said. "Your eyes..."

Wynona nodded. "I know, but it's what happens when I look for..." She cut off as her eyes caught on exactly what she had been looking for. "There." She pointed to the edge of the house. "Ghost reporter."

Rascal straightened and put his hand on his stun gun. "Corporeal. Now," he barked.

A man's voice began to grumble as the floating body disappeared from Wynona's vision. She blinked, pulling back her magic until she could see the slightly transparent man.

His head was bald and his frame light. A camera hung over his neck and his nose was twitching.

Cat, Violet said in disgust.

"He's a shifter?" Wynona whispered.

Violet hmphed.

"That's what he smells like now that he's mostly solid," Rascal confirmed. He glanced down at her. "Cats are notoriously curious."

"As in a house cat?" Wynona pinched her lips together. "I actually didn't know that was a thing. I thought it was only wild cats."

The man sniffed. "Not all of us eat raw meat on our days off." He glared at Rascal.

Wynona realized she had a wolf, a cat and a mouse in close proximity to each other. No wonder Violet and Rascal were so on edge.

Speak for yourself, Violet snapped. *Cats are disgusting. And they think they're better than everyone else.*

Wynona chose not to comment on the fact that Violet seemed pretty confident in her own superiority. "Why are you following us?" she asked, though she figured she knew the answer.

The man rolled his eyes. "Really?" Rascal growled and the reporter jumped before hissing back. "Back off, *dog.* I'm not doing anything illegal."

"You're following a deputy chief," Rascal said tightly. Wynona was positive the "dog" comment had gotten to him. "There are rules against invisibility at a crime scene."

The man fumbled with his camera, his eyes down. He wasn't quite as confident now that he knew he was following someone a little higher on the food chain than a regular officer. "I needed the story, alright?" He glanced up from under short lashes. "My editor said if I didn't turn something in ASAP, I was gone."

Wynona tilted her head. She was honestly curious about the ghost reporters. They were annoying and relentless, but in order to stay on this plane as a ghost, they had to have tenacity. It made her wonder what had been so important in their lives that they chose to stick around. "What does a ghost do if they aren't a reporter?"

The man made a face. "I don't mean I'd be jobless, I mean I'd be cast out. Pushed through the golden light?" He made a face at her. "Ring a bell?"

"They can do that?" Wynona gasped. "Your editor can force you to cross over?"

He hissed again and put his hands on his hips. "Are we done here? I'm not really interested in sharing the whole history of ghost reporters."

Wynona made a mental note to get a book on the creatures. It sounded like there was so much more to them than what the media and her own experience portrayed. "How long have you been following us?" she asked, folding her arms over her chest. She needed to appear strong if she was going to get answers from this guy. He didn't seem like a natural do-gooder, who would simply respond to her questions easily.

The cat scoffed. "Do I look like a newbie to you?"

"Your name, cat," Rascal growled, stepping forward.

The man grew jumpy again. Apparently, only Rascal was going to be able to get answers out of this guy. "Koto," he wheezed. "Koto Hesa."

Wynona stepped back slightly, allowing Rascal the lead. Now was the time to listen.

"Answer the lady," Rascal continued. "How long, Mr. Hesa?"

The shifter's shoulders slumped. "Any time I can find you." He shrugged. "I've only found you a couple times. You're always driving away and I can't keep up."

Wynona raised her eyebrows. A slow ghost? Huh. Another new fact to add to her growing library.

"And what have you seen?"

Mr. Hesa's lips pinched into a line whiter than the outline of his body. "Nothing," he spat. "As far as I can tell, you two have run around finding nothing."

Wynona relaxed a little. He didn't know about the break this morning. That was in their favor, she supposed. "Have you followed anyone else?"

When he didn't answer, Rascal stepped up again, another growl rumbling out of his throat.

The reporter began to tremble slightly and Violet snickered in Wynona's mind. Wynona didn't like the fact that they had to scare the man to get answers, but she needed to know what he knew. What if he'd seen something?

"How badly do you want to stay on this plane?" Wynona asked, pulling attention to herself once again.

Mr. Hesa scowled. "Why do you ask?"

"Because at the rate you're going, you're going to get kicked out." She smiled softly. "We're trying to bring a murderer to justice, Mr. Hesa, and you want a story. If you have information that might help us, that would put you in a pretty decent spot for a headline."

The cat shifter stilled and studied her. Wynona could just imagine his tail twitching back and forth. "I want exclusive rights."

"I can't promise you that," Rascal said easily. "But if you have something helpful, I can promise to be slow in announcing it to others."

"Good enough." The man stuck out his hand and Rascal shook it.

Wynona wondered if it was cold or felt odd. He didn't look quite solid, but there must have been something to touch, or they wouldn't have been able to shake.

A scraping sound caught their attention and everyone looked to see Vrebs cutting his already immaculate shrub, his beady eyes watching them steadily from over the row of bushes.

"Oh, good heavens," Wynona whispered.

"Mr. Hesa," Rascal said, stepping back. "Come inside with us, please." He unlocked the door again and they all marched inside.

It occurred to Wynona that she didn't have that same feeling on the back of her neck when the reporter was in this form. It was only in his ghostly form. Another tidbit to tuck away for later examination.

Wynona and Rascal sat on the couch while Mr. Hesa took a spot in a chair across from them.

"Okay," Mr. Hesa said, leaning in. "I've watched that officer guy. The one who dated the tea shop owner." He looked at Wynona. "Your business partner. The dead one."

Has no one taught this man any manners? Wynona thought in shock. His bluntness and lack of finesse were to the point of offensive. "We weren't business partners," she said automatically. She sighed. She needed to just let it go. It really didn't matter at this point.

Mr. Hesa's jaw dropped. "What do you mean, you weren't partners? Didn't she open a satellite shop for you?" His eyes glowed green. Apparently, even in death shifters animals came to the surface.

Wynona slumped back. "She was a copycat, Mr. Hesa. I was just about to bring in a lawsuit when she was killed."

"Ah..." He nodded slowly. "So you're a suspect then?" He waved his arms. "I thought you were helping the police, but you must be trying to clear your name."

Rascal growled again.

Mr. Hesa cringed.

"I'm sorry, but no," Wynona said, putting a hand on Rascal's arm. He immediately relaxed a bit, for which she was grateful. All this testosterone was starting to choke her. "I'm not a suspect," she clarified. "I was with Deputy Chief Strongclaw when the murder occurred. And I am working with the police as an independent consultant." She folded her hands in her lap. "I've helped them on a few cases now and Chief Ligurio thought I might be of service."

She knew that description was stretching her relationship with the chief a bit, but it was the politically correct one and she was under no delusion that what she was saying wouldn't eventually end up printed somewhere.

"Is that because you're the president's daughter?" he pressed.

"Mr. Hesa." It was time to put her foot down. "We brought you in so you could tell us what you've seen as you've been following the case. Not so you could examine my motives or lack thereof."

Mr. Hesa grumbled and Wynona chose to ignore some of his more colorful words. "The cop guy has a chick on the side," Mr. Hesa said. He smirked. "Been spending a lot of time at her house." When Wynona and Rascal didn't react, he huffed. "Already knew?"

Wynona waved him on.

"That's it," he said, throwing his hands in the air. "There was a murder and a cheating couple. What more do you want?"

"What we want is the killer," Wynona said easily. "But if you already had all that, why haven't I seen it in the news?"

The cat shifter grumbled again. "Editor says it's not enough. Plus I don't have proof."

Wynona frowned. "Why not? Didn't you take pictures?"

Mr. Hesa looked down at his camera. "It's broken," he said in a soft voice.

"Then how were you...?" Wynona shook her head and rubbed her forehead. This was ridiculous. How had this man ever made it as a reporter?

Violet tapped her neck. *He could be an ally.*

Wynona looked at her shoulder. "What do you mean?" she whispered.

He's invisible. Get him a new camera and place him at the witch's. We need evidence. He needs a story. Win, win.

Wynona gave her familiar a scratch. That was brilliant...actually.

Violet made a smug face. *I know.*

Wynona laughed softly before turning back to the reporter. He was eyeing her curiously and she straightened. She didn't mind helping him get a story, but she didn't want it to be about her hidden magic. "I have a proposal," she said clearly. "A...bargain."

His thin eyebrows pulled down. "I'm listening."

"We have a suspect that we would like someone to keep eyes on," Wynona said carefully. "We're curious about her habits and behaviors, but have yet to be able to find anything helpful."

He nodded. "Okay..."

"You promise to follow her, and I'll get you a new camera." She leaned in. "But your first pictures need to be to finish this case."

The cat shifter stayed still for a moment before his hand burst forward. "You've got yourself a deal, Ms. Le Doux."

Wynona's curiosity was satisfied when her hand gripped a cold, but very solid appendage.

Once done, the reporter stood and faced Rascal. "I'm holding you to that head start."

Rascal stood and the reporter stepped back a few paces. Deal or no, the two weren't going to be besties.

Wynona hid a smile behind her hand. "Follow us to the store and we'll get that camera."

The reporter tugged on his collar and nodded.

Rascal took Wynona's hand and led her outside, waiting long enough for Mr. Hesa to leave before locking it tight. "Smart move," he whispered in her ear as they got in the truck.

"It was Violet's idea," Wynona admitted. "The genius was all hers."

Rascal grinned and reached over to pet the mouse. "That's my girl."

Violet preened the whole way to the store.

CHAPTER 27

Much to her surprise, Wynona heard from Mr. Hesa the next morning. She had expected it to take a little more time before he found anything worth reporting, but she wasn't going to be upset about moving faster.

"Hey, Wynona!" Officer Nightshade said with a sharp smile as Wynona walked into the police station.

Wynona waved and paused at the desk.

"You drive yourself today?" Officer Nightshade teased.

Wynona grinned. "I'm getting used to his massive truck. Makes my Vespa feel like a toy."

Amaris laughed. "I can see that. Does it make you want to buy something bigger?"

"No way," Wynona responded. "I can't imagine trying to park that thing. My little scooter fits everywhere."

Amaris pointed a red nail at Wynona. "Very good point." She grinned again. "But as an officer, we tend to park wherever we want, so..."

Wynona laughed softly. "I've seen that. Rascal has blocked entire streets before."

"Eh." Amaris shrugged. "If it needs to be done, it needs to be done."

Still laughing, Wynona began to walk toward the hallway. "I'm assuming he's in his office?"

Amaris shook her head. "Interrogation room number one."

"Oh. Thanks." Wynona turned direction and headed to the other hallway. She had no idea why they would be meeting in an interrogation room, but it wasn't like it really mattered. She'd gotten really comfortable in her boyfriend's office, but perhaps it was good to shake things up a bit.

She knocked and waited for a response before opening the door.

"Wy," Rascal said in a serious tone.

Mr. Hesa was already seated in the room and he grinned wildly, his slightly sharpened canines glinting in the fluorescent lighting. It was amazing how solid he appeared, especially with his ability to turn full ghost on command. The whole phenomenon was one Wynona wanted to research.

Later, she reminded herself.

She sat down next to Rascal. "Nice to see you again, Mr. Hesa," she said with a welcoming smile. "I hear you've already got something for us."

The cat shifter nodded eagerly. "Yeah. Look." He thrust his camera at her.

Wynona took it and studied the small screen. She frowned and looked at it again. "I..." She turned to Rascal. "She's throwing away an apron."

Her favorite wolf leaned over her shoulder. "Huh." He took the camera and expanded that particular part of the shot.

Wynona gasped. Despite the fact that the picture was taken at night, there was no mistaking the garment. "It's the one with the gold button."

Rascal nodded and set the camera in his lap. "But why? Why is she throwing it away? We already figured out Haar's connection to it."

Wynona pinched her lips together and glanced at her shoulder, raising her eyebrows. She wasn't always comfortable speaking in her mind and she didn't want to talk out loud in front of Mr. Hesa.

Violet shook her head and held out her hands. She didn't have any ideas either.

"What's the significance of the apron?"

Both Wynona and Rascal turned back to the reporter. She wasn't sure how much they could tell him, so Wynona waited for Rascal to respond.

"You want the story, you have to wait until it breaks," he said in a low tone.

Mr. Hesa only hesitated for a moment before nodding firmly. "It'll be better to have it all at once anyway."

Rascal told the ghost about Haar's illegal activities in retrieving the button and resewing it on the apron in order to save his mistress from being accused of murder.

"Do you think there was something we missed on that apron?" Wynona asked. "Or perhaps it was the fact that the button had been covered in blood." She scrunched her nose. "Maybe Ms. Soulton didn't want to wear it anymore after discovering that."

Rascal nodded. "That's a fair point. She does work with food after all." His long fingers tapped against his knee. "What I can't figure out is why she even had it. It should have been down in the evidence locker."

Wynona stilled. "It wasn't given back to her?"

"Why would it have been?" Rascal asked. "The case is still open and both Haar and Ms. Soulton are involved."

Wynona blew out a breath. "Can we talk to the officer in charge down there? At least, I'm assuming someone is in charge."

Rascal stood and held out his hand for her. "Yeah. There's always someone on duty."

Once standing, Rascal walked her toward the door and a scrambling sound came from behind them.

"Better ghost up," Rascal said over his shoulder. "It's probably best if no one else knows you're there."

Wynona looked back just in time to see the man disappear. She held back the desire to pull up her magic as the hairs on her neck stood on end. Now that she knew it was just Mr. Hesa, she should be feeling easier, but the sensation was still slightly unpleasant.

Rascal led her through a section of the precinct she had never seen before, before opening a door to a set of stairs.

"Oh," she breathed. She grinned at Rascal. "Kinda spooky."

He chuckled and guided her downstairs into a concrete basement. At the bottom there was a small waiting area, then a wall with a service window. Metal was fitted over the window and it took Wynona a moment to realize it was the Old Hag's thread they used for handcuffs. It was supposed to negate any and all magic, which should go a long way in helping keep the evidence safe.

"Zallah!" Rascal barked.

A shuffling sound, followed by heavy footsteps, could be heard long before the troll appeared at the window. "Deputy Chief," the troll drawled with a wide smile. "I haven't seen you down in here forever." His eyes flitted to Wynona. "And with a woman!" His grin grew. "Why, if I didn't know any better—"

"Yetu," Rascal scolded. He gave the older creature a look. "We're at work."

The troll laughed heartily. "We're always at work."

Rascal rubbed his forehead, obviously slightly embarrassed.

The troll waved Wynona forward. "Come here, pretty thing, and introduce yourself to me."

Wynona couldn't help but smile. The man was acting exactly like a grandfather in a fairy tale. It made Wynona long for her own grandparents. "Wynona Le Doux," she said, reaching through the bars to shake his hand.

His massive stone paw gripped her surprisingly gently. "Yetu Zallah," he said with an incline of his head. "Or Officer Zallah if you want to be formal." He winked. "But I don't hold by that around here. Not enough visitors, you know."

Wynona laughed. "You're a charmer, Yetu. I can see that now."

Rascal pulled her back, making Yetu chuckle. "We have a question about some evidence."

Yetu straightened. "Then you came to the right man. I've been on duty down here for fifty years."

Wynona's eyes widened. "Don't you ever go home?"

The older gentleman chuckled again. "This is my home." He waved around. "It's as good as any mountain or cave that you find my kind in." He leaned in. "And it's got better reception."

"Wow," Wynona responded. "I had no idea."

The troll shrugged. "Most don't. And I'm just fine with that." Leaning onto his elbows, he continued studying her. "But now that you know I'm here, you won't mind visiting once in a while, will you? Old boulder like me can get awfully lonesome."

Wynona smiled back and leaned into Rascal's side. "I'm sure that can be arranged, Yetu. I have a feeling a visit with you would be absolutely delightful."

Rascal cleared his throat. "I do have business,Yetu."

The troll slapped the counter, shaking the wall. "Right. What evidence did you need?"

"We have reason to believe something that should be down here is gone," Rascal stated in a low tone.

The smile on the troll faltered. "You can't be serious."

Rascal nodded. "Can you look for piece Theramin-A3?"

Frowning severely, Yetu disappeared and Wynona could hear the sound of his feet, followed by slamming drawers and doors. But when a loud roar rocked the room, she ducked into Rascal's side, afraid for the first time since they'd arrived.

Yetu lumbered back up to the front. "It's gone." He growled. "I don't know how. But it's gone."

Rascal nodded and pushed a hand through his hair. "That's what I thought."

"Fifty years," the troll thundered. "Fifty years I've worked down here and never lost an artifact."

Wynona turned to Rascal. "Get Daemon," she suggested.

Rascal's eyebrows shot up. "Good idea." The troll continued his tirade in the background as Rascal turned. "Be right back." In a rush, he ran up the stairs and disappeared through the door.

Wynona bounced on her heels, dodging falling bits of rock and dust. "If you take any pictures, I'll break that camera myself," she whispered. "Not to mention our deal will be off."

A groan filtered through the air and she knew Mr. Hesa had understood. He was getting plenty for his story out of this. Hurting a kindly, old troll wasn't going to be part of the plan.

Footsteps thundered down the steps and Rascal came into sight, Daemon on his heels.

"Yetu?" Wynona called. It took her a minute to catch the troll's attention. She smiled sweetly at him. "Would you be so kind as to allow us back there? I'd like my friend Officer Skymaw to look at the place where the evidence was kept."

Gone was the kind grandfather and in his place was an angry mountain of a creature.

Wynona held her ground, but if her insides were quivering slightly, no one could blame her. She was grateful when Rascal put his hand on her back, helping steady her nerves. Someday, she would be skilled enough with her magic to feel safe in a situation like this, but today was not that day.

Yetu hesitated, then nodded. "Only for you, pretty lady. For the first time in fifty years, I have failed." He sighed and his massive shoulders slumped. He looked so sad when he unlocked the door that Wynona was tempted to throw herself at him for a hug.

She settled for patting his arm. "I think you're doing a wonderful job, Yetu. Whatever happened here wasn't your fault."

The troll smiled slightly. "Pretty words from a pretty lady." He glanced at Rascal. "Don't mess it up."

Rascal nodded as if he understood the strange comment. "Where was it kept?"

Yetu guided them through several rows of metal lockers, then stopped and pointed. "Theramin-A3. Blue, nutcracker apron."

Wynona turned to Daemon. "Well? What do you see?"

His black eyes expanded. "Magic," he said softly. "It's a light, baby yellow." He shook his head, his eyes coming out of their trance. "I don't recognize it, though."

Wynona huffed and put her hands on her hips. "It's a start, I suppose."

"No one is supposed to be able to do magic back here," Yetu grumbled. "The Old Hag's thread takes care of that."

Wynona pinched her lips. "Have you let anyone else back here recently? It would have been sometime in the last twenty four hours."

Yetu shook his head. "Only you three."

Violet slapped Wynona's neck with her tail. *The garbage.*

"Ow," Wynona murmured. There had to be easier ways to get her attention. "Excuse me, Yetu." She pointed around him. "May I look at your garbage?"

The huge troll frowned. "My garbage?"

Wynona leaned sideways. A pink box lay in the can. "I see you like dessert."

Yetu followed her gaze and nodded. "Yes. A friend brought me cupcakes." He grinned sheepishly. "They were delicious."

"I'll bet they were." She turned. "Daemon? Can you look at the box?"

He nodded. "I see where this is going."

Wynona sighed. "Or at least where we're trying to get it to go." She still felt as if Ms. Soulton was more involved than she admitted.

If they could find evidence of her deceit, it would be much better than searching for an entirely new suspect.

Daemon walked around Yetu and peered into the box. "The same yellow magic." He carefully picked it up. "Deputy Chief?"

Rascal walked over and took a deep sniff. His nose twitched. "It's an herb of some kind. But I'm not sure what."

"May I?" Wynona asked.

Rascal brought the box to her.

She sniffed inside. He was right, there was something there. Closing her eyes, Wynona let her tea gift drift, hoping something would..."Valerian root!" she shouted triumphantly, then winced. "Sorry." She faced Yetu. "Valerian root is meant to put people to sleep."

Large, gray eyes widened. "I was drugged? Me? A troll?"

"I'm sure that's why I can smell it," Wynona mused. "She would have had to use a large amount."

"So she drugged him and got inside," Rascal said. "Once in, doing magic wasn't a big deal."

"Who gave you the cupcakes?" Wynona asked.

"Officer Montego," Yetu said. "Brings them from his girlfriend. Said she made this batch especially for me."

Wynona stepped forward and patted his chest. "Thank you, Yetu. We'll get out of your hair now."

The troll rubbed his rocky head. "Not much there to speak of," he said with a sad chuckle. "I'll have to bring this to the chief."

Wynona shook her head. "We're headed to talk to him," Wynona assured him. "Don't worry. Everything's going to be fine."

She followed the men upstairs, her mind churning. They were onto something. Right now they only had evidence that the witch was involved in stealing her apron back, not murder. But with the right steps forward, Wynona was sure that they were about to put Alavara's case to bed permanently.

CHAPTER 28

The group burst into the chief's office, everyone shouting at once. Chief Ligurio's black eyebrows shot up. He slammed his phone down in the cradle and held up his hands. "STOP!" he shouted.

The power of manipulation in his voice rang through the room so hard that Wynona's whole body stopped. She teetered, slightly out of balance, but the strength of the vampire's magic held her in place.

Slowly, the chief put his hands down. "I'm going to let you lose, but you better have a good reason for barging in here like a pack of wild shifters," he said in a low growl. With a snap of his fingers, the room came back to life.

Wynona stumbled, barely catching herself from falling over. Rascal growled, obviously upset at having been manipulated, and Daemon stood with wide eyes. He must not have been using his black hole powers, which would have stopped the vampire from treating them like misbehaving children.

You were being children. Violet sniffed.

Wynona wanted to roll her eyes, but refrained. Nothing like adding fuel to the fire. "I'm sorry, Chief," she said sincerely. "I think we were just all too worked up with what we found downstairs."

Chief Ligurio didn't even grace her with a look. Those red eyes were pinned on Rascal. "Do we have a problem here, Strongclaw?"

Wynona swallowed. Rascal was an alpha, and was not one to be pushed around. He hadn't become deputy chief for nothing. But it was clear that Chief Ligurio also had gifts that made him a dangerous foe. His role as chief had been earned, and rightly so by Wynona's judgment. She hadn't felt that outmaneuvered in a long time.

Rascal's teeth were clenching so hard, Wynona was afraid he would break something, but the wolf shifter finally nodded. "No problem, Chief."

"Good." The wolf was dismissed as if he were no more than a flea. Those two might grapple for power at times, but Wynona chose to believe that Chief Ligurio's dismissal was based on trust. He knew Rascal would hold to his word.

Violet snorted.

"Ms. Le Doux," Chief Ligurio said firmly, finally turning his dark gaze her way. "You were saying?"

Wynona looked at Rascal, making sure he was alright before addressing the chief. "We hired a ghost reporter to keep an eye on Ms. Soulton," she started.

"What?" Chief Ligurio snapped. "How was I not aware of this?"

Wynona winced. "It happened last night. We caught him following us and ended up making a deal with him."

Chief Ligurio pinched the bridge of his nose. Wynona knew it was his go to move when he was stressed or had a headache coming on.

She immediately stood and headed to his small kitchenette area. Eyeing him carefully, she picked out a couple of herbs he had on hand to make a tea. "Chief, can you please call for a warm cup of blood?" That, combined with her herbs, would be the best thing for him. Truthfully, with all they had to share, he might need something stronger by the time their chat was over.

He glared, but followed her orders.

"On it," Amaris said from the other line.

Wynona knew it would only take her friend a few minutes to have the drink in the office. She waited patiently, while the men shifted their weights back and forth, anxious to get going. A happy vampire, however, would make their situation a lot better. It wouldn't do to start things off on the wrong foot.

"Here you go." Officer Nightshade came in with a steaming cup. She winked at Wynona as she was leaving, snickering as the door closed. The sheer amount of testosterone in the room was enough to tip off any supernatural that things were rough in here.

Wynona fixed the tea and set it in front of the chief. "Give it three minutes, and then you'll be good to go."

He softened just slightly as he watched her sit back down. "Go on."

"We promised him a head start when the story broke." Wynona waved her hand toward Rascal. "Your deputy chief was smart enough to say it couldn't be exclusive, but he could have it first." That feeling hit the back of her neck. Apparently, Mr. Hesa had decided to join them now that the noise was calming down. "Please show yourself," she said to the room.

Chief Ligurio's eyes widened, then widened even more when Mr. Hesa appeared near the door. He glared at Wynona. "How did you know?"

Shoot, she thought. *That was careless.*

A frantic look at Rascal brought him to her rescue. "He's been following us through the precinct this morning," Rascal said.

Chief Ligurio thought about it, then nodded, accepting the explanation. "Fine." He turned the glare on the small ghost. "What did you find?"

The man walked forward, looking ready to bolt at any moment, holding out his camera.

Chief Ligurio took it and studied the picture. He cursed. "How did she get the apron?" he shouted.

Wynona took a slow breath. "That's why we went down to the basement," she said carefully. "We talked to Yetu and discovered the empty locker, and that." She pointed to the box that Rascal was close to crushing.

Rascal tossed it on the desk.

"Is this from the witch's bakery?" Chief Ligurio growled.

Wynona nodded. "Mr. Montego brought it." She held up a hand. "But I don't think he knew that Ms. Soulton had added Valerian root to the cupcakes." She pinched her lips together. "Yetu had no chance to stay awake with that in his system."

The chief rubbed his forehead.

"Take a drink," Wynona ordered. "Please," she added when he shot her a glare.

He picked up his mug and took a long pull. His expression hadn't eased much when it landed on his desk with a thunk.

"That's why we called Daemon, uh, Officer Skymaw in," Wynona explained. "We had him do a residual magic scan." She sighed. "He found yellow magic on the empty locker and the pastry box."

The chief leaned back. "So where do you plan to go from here?" He indicated the evidence with his hand. "None of this links her to the murder. Just other petty crimes."

"Right." Wynona leaned forward. "We need a warrant. One for her house."

"And just what do you hope to find?" the chief asked.

"A link to the murder," Wynona responded.

A single black eyebrow rose up. "Ms. Theramin was killed with a kitchen knife. One from her own kitchen. There wasn't any magic involved."

"I understand," Wynona said. "But the biggest reason we can't do more to take down Ms. Soulton is her alibi. One which her boyfriend backs up."

A light went on behind the red of the chief's eyes. "You want to see if she used magic to get out of the house."

Wynona nodded. "Yes. If she can put a troll to sleep, why not a vampire? If we can find evidence that she spelled him to sleep so she could go to that meeting with Alavara..." She shrugged, letting the chief figure out the rest.

He reached for the phone. "This might be the best five dollars I've ever spent," he grumbled, punching in a couple of numbers.

Rascal came to Wynona's side and rubbed her shoulder before squeezing lightly. His own eyes were glowing brightly. "You did it," he whispered.

Wynona shook her head. "No. This definitely took all of us." She made sure Daemon understood he was part of that group by giving him a wide smile. "And it's not over yet. We still have to find the evidence."

"It's there," Rascal said with assurance. "It has to be."

"No criminal is perfect," Daemon said tightly. "There's a mistake somewhere. And we're going to find it."

Chief Ligurio set down the phone. "The message has been sent to the judge." He picked up his mug. "Now we wait."

Wynona grimaced, but knew there was nothing she could do about it. Warrants always took a little time. At least the judge was in the office. Tracking one down was often the longest part of the wait.

Wynona absent-mindedly pet Violet while they all stood around. She knew everyone else felt the same as her. They didn't want to leave on the off chance the warrant would arrive quickly. The entire room was eager to see this case put to rest.

Thoughts floated through her mind, everything from the beginning of the case until this moment. Was there anything they had missed? Could they have solved this before now? Did they actually need the warrant?

Her mind stuttered on a picture. "Alefoot," she breathed.

Rascal frowned. "What?"

Wynona straightened. "Chief. Can we see Mr. Alefoot again?" She waved her hands in the air. "Wait. Daemon."

The black hole raised his eyebrows.

"What color was the magic around Mr. Alefoot? The spell you saw breaking apart?"

Daemon's eyebrows pulled together and his eyes dropped to the ground in thought. "It...was..." His eyes widened. "It was flashing multiple colors."

Wynona leaned forward. "Are you sure?"

Daemon shrugged. "Yeah. With the spell on the verge of breaking, it was slowly turning black, like it was becoming rotten."

"Would looking again help?" she asked. "Would any residual magic hold the original color?"

Daemon scrunched his face and scratched his head. "I'm not sure. Maybe. I've never seen a spell disrupt like that, so I have no way of gauging the magical fall out."

Wynona turned back to the chief. "Can we bring in Mr. Alefoot? Perhaps a second look would answer a few questions."

The chief nodded and punched the intercom, ordering the dwarf to be brought in. It only took five minutes for the small man to be shuffling through the doorway. His hair was a mess and he was dressed in one of the prison jumpsuits, but otherwise, he appeared fine. He didn't look ill or upset in any way, for which Wynona was grateful. She truly felt like he was a pawn in this game and didn't want to see him mistreated.

"Mr. Alefoot," she said by way of greeting. "Thank you so much for coming to see us."

The dwarf huffed. "Not like I have a choice," he grumbled.

Wynona nodded and folded her hands in her lap. "We just wanted to ask you a couple more questions." Her eyes darted up to Daemon, who was squinting and tilting his head to the side. "Do you have any idea how Alavara put the spell on you?" Wynona asked. "Was it something you ate? Or perhaps drank?"

The dwarf shook his head. "No. I told you the whole thing is a blank."

"Nothing? You didn't eat dinner together, or a dessert?" The last word was simply a hunch. She was starting to understand just how

Ms. Soulton worked and had decided Alavara and Mardella were closer than anyone would admit. They simply kept their relationship a secret.

Ms. Alefoot shifted his weight. "There might have been some cookies at our chat." He wouldn't meet her eye. "There's nothing wrong with liking cookies."

Wynona nodded. "No, there's nothing wrong with liking cookies." She looked at Daemon again. He nodded. "Thank you, Mr. Alefoot. That was a tremendous help."

The dwarf gave her an odd look, then left with an officer.

Once gone, Daemon jumped right in. "It was barely there, but it was yellow." He pursed his lips. "I think it has to do with the strength of the spell. What was left of the spell was even lighter than the locker downstairs." He pushed a hand through his hair. "I think it's the same person. The yellow is very buttery. It has a softness to it that I haven't really seen before."

"This still doesn't tell us she murdered anyone," Chief Ligurio pointed out.

"No," Wynona agreed. "But it does mean that Alavara and Mardella knew each other before Alavara arrived in Hex Haven." She turned to fully face the chief. "I think those two have been in league with each other for a long time, but have kept their work together in the dark. Alavara didn't have much magic of her own, but she had access to a witch. A witch who eventually saw Alavara's boyfriend." Wynona tilted her head consideringly. "It's possible the two women weren't even friends, more like frenemies. But somehow, they used each other to get what they wanted."

"And Ms. Soulton ended up wanting Haar," Rascal finished.

"Right." Wynona leaned back in her seat. "I always wondered why people kept going back to Alavara's tea shop, when I was constantly getting complaints that the tea was horrible."

"You think there was something in the pastries that kept them coming back," Chief Ligurio filled in.

"I do. I think Alavara saw a good business model and had access to the right resources to duplicate it. Her ability to manipulate decor and fashion, and Ms. Soulton's ability to keep customers returning." Wynona's shoulders fell. "It would have eventually put me out of business, since I don't have magical desserts, but everyone would have continued coming to her."

Chief Longurio tapped his fingers on his desk. "It's quite the theory."

"But it makes more sense than before," Rascal added. He sat on the arm of Wynona's chair. "Now we just need that last bit of evidence to pin the murder on her."

The phone rang and every set of eyes in the room jumped to the sound. Chief Ligurio picked it up. "Hello?"

The other three waited in tense silence for the conversation to end.

"Yes, sir. Thank you, sir." Chief Ligurio hung up and looked to Rascal. "Grab the warrant on your way. It'll be signed and waiting."

Wynona jumped to her feet.

"Ms. Le Doux?"

She spun before walking through the door.

Chief Ligurio hardly ever smiled, but one side of his mouth tipped up just the tiniest bit. "Good work, Detective."

Wynona grinned. "I don't want that title, but thank you anyway."

"At the rate you're going, you'll have it whether you want it or not."

Wynona laughed softly. "I prefer tea-maker, but thanks." Still smiling, she walked out, Rascal and Daemon at her side. It was time to catch a murderer.

CHAPTER 29

M s. Soulton's home was not quite what Wynona had expected. She lived in a much different part of town than Alavara had. The home was neat, but worn. It needed a new coat of paint, and the boards on the small front porch squeaked so badly that Wynona worried they would break underneath the boots of the officers with her.

Rascal knocked against the door. The sound was loud and rattled the wooden frame. No one answered.

"I'm sure she's at the shop," Wynona said, looking around. That feeling that she was being watched was strong. She was sorely tempted to use her new magic sight to look for spirits, but she refrained. She didn't want to show the entire neighborhood her glowing purple eyes, and she didn't think it would help her situation to know they weren't alone.

Hopefully, it's only Mr. Hesa, she reassured herself. The reporter had to be frantic to see this case to the end. It would be a huge career boost for him to nab this story before anyone else.

"Probably," Rascal muttered. "But we have to knock anyway." He pounded one more time. "Ms. Soulton! It's the Hex Haven Police Department. We have a warrant to search the premises."

"We're not alone," Daemon said under his breath. His eyes weren't on the house, instead moving up and down the street in that practiced way of a man who knew what danger felt like.

Wynona shivered. Curtains twitched and a cold breeze teased her skin. Even the Grove of Secrets behind her house didn't give her such a feeling. The neighbors weren't just curious, they honestly did not like having the police in their area.

Rascal tried the knob, but it was locked. "Ms. Soulton, this is your last chance to open the door before I break it down." He stepped back, grabbed his stun gun and counted to three. When the door remained closed, he raised his foot and slammed it into the fragile wood.

Wynona cringed as splinters flew around the deck, pinging off her skin. Violet squeaked and tucked herself deeper into Wynona's hair for safety. Wynona wished she could do the same.

On tiptoe, she followed behind Rascal's protective stance.

"Ms. Soulton?" Rascal shouted one more time. "Is anybody here?" He looked back at Daemon, who stood in the same stance and tilted his head toward the hallway. "Wait here," he murmured to Wynona.

She wasn't thrilled with being left behind, but his glowing eyes were fierce and she also didn't want to get in the middle of something if Mardella happened to be home, but was hiding. The seconds ticked by slowly as the two officers moved around the space, disappearing from view, then coming back and going another direction.

"All clear," Rascal finally announced, putting his stun gun back in its holster. He put his hands on his hips and looked around. "Where do you want to start?"

Wynona debated. "I think we need to search the bedroom and kitchen in particular, but I don't know if it matters which one first."

"Bedroom is that way," Daemon said, pointing down the hallway.

Wynona forced her fear aside and led the way. The hallway was dark and cold and Wynona kept feeling as if something was lurking in the shadows. Only Rascal's heated presence behind her kept her moving forward. He would protect her. She knew it as well as she knew her own name. Rascal would do anything within his power to see her safe.

She pushed open the door to the room and stepped inside. A large bed took up most of the room, the sheets and bedspread rumpled. Pillows were everywhere. Mardella might not have been much for decorating the rest of her house, but the bedroom apparently got extra attention.

The blankets looked lush and soft and Wynona was curious as to how it would feel to touch. Her revulsion at the situation kept her curiosity in check. "Daemon?" she asked. "Do you see anything?"

The black hole stood in the doorway, his eyes scanning the space. He shrugged. "There are traces of magic," he said slowly. "But nothing concrete. Magical beings use magic all the time." He pointed toward the bathroom. "Her lotion and make up all have magic in them." He shifted and looked deeper. "As well as the shampoo in her shower." Spinning, he looked at her dresser. "It looks like her glasses also have magic." He shook his head. "None of that appears unusual, though. It's exactly what we would expect of a woman, let alone a witch."

Wynona nodded. "Right. Can we look at the kitchen?"

Rascal held out his arm and guided her back into the hallway. The kitchen was just off to the right. Like the bedroom, it had gotten more of Mardella's time and attention than the rest of the home. Bright, stainless steel pots and pans were hanging from the ceiling in neat order. The stove and oven were abnormally large for the small kitchen and had to have been especially put in for the hearth witch to work with.

Daemon whistled. "This place reeks of it," he murmured. "She puts a lot of effort into whatever she bakes."

"Am I allowed to search the cupboards?" Wynona asked.

Rascal nodded. "Looking for anything in particular?"

"Valerian root," Wynona threw over her shoulder. She began opening cupboards, shifting things around and looking for anything resembling an herb. She could hear Rascal and Daemon doing the same thing behind her. It was the third door she opened that finally brought a smile to her face. "Bingo," she exclaimed.

Rascal came up behind her. "Find it?"

"Not yet." Wynona began pulling jars and containers off the shelves. She arranged them on the counter, looking through each one. "Lavender. Rosemary. Sage..." Wynona frowned. Nothing here was unusual. It was all things she would expect to see in a hearth witch's kitchen. Wynona finished reading the labels, but nothing stood out. She blew out a breath and rested her fists on the counter. "It's not here."

Rascal scratched behind his ear. "Could she have hidden it somewhere else?"

Wynona turned and eyed the rest of the cupboards. "We can finish looking through the cupboards, but for as organized as this place is, it seems weird for her to place herbs somewhere else."

"Doesn't hurt to look," Daemon replied. He went back to his side of the kitchen. It only took another couple minutes for them to finish. "There's nothing here," he announced, closing the last one.

Wynona scowled. "We have to be missing something. There are too many things pointing to her." She put her hands on her hips. "Where are those seventeen cats she talked about? I don't smell or see any of them."

Violet shuddered. *Unnatural.*

Rascal nodded. "I don't know. Maybe what we're looking for is at the shop?"

Wynona shook her head. "That doesn't make sense, though. She was here with Mr. Montego that night." Wynona pushed her hands through her hair. "I suppose she could have baked it at work and brought it back, but I just don't see it. If she was spending the evening with Mr. Montego, why spend extra time at the shop?"

Daemon rubbed the back of his neck. "I see your point, but it doesn't mean it couldn't have happened."

Wynona nodded and slumped against the counter. "I know. You're right." She blew out a breath. "Now what?"

"Now we finish searching the house, seeing if there's anything else helpful, then we call Chief and get a warrant for the shop if necessary." Rascal grinned. "That should actually be pretty easy, since we confiscated the apron from there and it's now missing."

"Right." Wynona began to walk around the rest of the home. The gathering area was small and sparsely decorated. No personal pictures or trinkets adorned the end table or the walls. Unlike the bed, the couch held no extra pillows or throws.

Violet grumbled. *I guess she has her priorities set. Can't blame her for the kitchen though.*

Wynona tapped her finger on the back of the couch, an idea coming to her. "Daemon?"

He poked his head in from the hall. "Yeah?"

"Are you still using your sight?"

He shook his head. "No. Do I need to? It's hard to maintain, so I've only pulled it out when we thought we would find something."

Wynona swirled her finger around the room. "Can you tell me what you see in here?"

"Sure." He emerged fully from the hallway and his eyes went completely black. "Whoa..." He nodded. "Lots of residual magic." He frowned. "None of it yellow." He turned to Wynona. "What does that mean?"

"Just a second. Can you do the same to the hallway and the front entry?"

Daemon walked around. "It's all covered in the same grey magic." His eyebrows remained pulled together. "But I don't know whose it is."

"I'm guessing we would find a bunch of it at the tea house, wouldn't we?" Rascal asked from behind Wynona.

She looked over her shoulder. "Bingo."

"You're kidding," Daemon huffed. "So, the witch wanted the real thing in the kitchen and bedroom, but the rest of the house was under a glamor." He folded his arms over his chest. "I guess that's how it all worked, huh? They used their magic to help each other."

"Or at least to pay each other," Wynona pointed out. "I'm still not convinced they were friends."

"We're still lacking evidence of the murder," Rascal said softly. "I know this is good and interesting, but it doesn't tell us who murdered Alavara."

Wynona sighed. "I know. But we're getting closer. We have to be." She wandered back to the kitchen. "Has anyone checked the garage?" she asked.

"Nope." Rascal followed her. "I'll come with you."

Wynona pulled it open and gasped. The smell of herbs was enough to knock her off her feet. She worked with herbs all day every day and she loved the fresh and bitter fragrances that tickled her nose. But this...this was something else. Ash, brimstone and feline were mixed with the familiar smells, turning the herbs into something far more toxic than Wynona had ever experienced before.

She pulled her shirt over her nose and reached inside with fumbling fingers to turn on the light. "What?" she cried, dropping her shirt when the room illuminated. The space was clean. Empty and clean. A shelving unit sat on the far wall, with just enough room for a small sedan in between it and Wynona.

Rascal coughed, the sound several feet behind her.

"Oh." Wynona turned. His nose probably wasn't having an easy time of it.

"What's there?" Rascal wheezed.

"Nothing!" Wynona threw up her arms. "It's completely empty!"

Violet tapped Wynona's neck. *Remember the glamor?*

"The glamor is gone," Wynona pointed out. "It died when Alavara died. That's why we can see the old sofa and such."

Violet hummed in consternation.

Wynona's eyes widened. "Daemon?"

He walked over briskly. "Need another look?"

She nodded and stepped back, watching his face closely. There had to be something there. The smell was too strong to be anything but a laboratory, and not the kind of laboratory Wynona would want anything to do with. Whatever had been cooked up in this place was for evil intent.

"Oh yeah," Daemon said. He held a hand over his nose. "She's hiding the room, but apparently she can't hide the smell."

"How do we get through it?" Wynona asked breathlessly. This was it. She was sure of it. The evidence they needed was behind that wall.

"You don't."

The feminine voice was anything but welcoming and Wynona spun with a gasp. Mardella was standing in the kitchen and before Wynona could ask how she'd gotten in without Rascal hearing, she realized her boyfriend was on the ground...his face was red, but it wasn't anger this time. It only took a moment for Wynona to realize the witch was strangling the wolf.

CHAPTER 30

"What did you do?" Wynona shouted, her body lunging forward, only to stop midair.

"Uh, uh, uh," Mardella said coolly. Her glasses were on top of her head, just in front of her messy bun. Tendrils drifted along her face in a soft caress that was deceptive of the cruelty that lurked inside the woman.

Wynona couldn't move. She couldn't get to Rascal, who was starting to look purple. *VIOLET!* She screamed.

The tiny creature scrambled down Wynona's stiff body and scurried across the floor.

Wynona lost sight of her, but sent a hope to the universe for her familiar's safety.

"Did you really think you could just show up at my house and everything would be fine?"

Mardella was out of Wynona's view, but she could hear the witch getting closer. Her feet padded against the shiny tiles until they were just in Wynona's line of sight. A hand landed on her hair, petting Wynona as if she were an animal.

"It's too bad you were cursed," Mardella said softly. "We could have been great friends, you and I. Your family holds so much *power.*" The way Mardella said the word was enough for anyone to recognize her desires. There's no way that Haar was the only reason the witch killed Alavara.

Anger bubbled inside Wynona. She was sitting in a position she knew all too well. Helpless. Trapped. Impotent. Her family had called her worthless and broken and right now Wynona felt it. She still couldn't hear Rascal breathing, Daemon hadn't come to her rescue, which meant he was trapped the same as her. And Violet had disappeared.

The emotion became so hot that Wynona began to feel actual pain in her stomach. She wanted to scream, to close her eyes and let out everything that had been building for so long. All the stress, the weight, the unknown, the frightening, the chaos...

Purple flickered in the edge of her vision and her ears were unable to hear Mardella's monolog as blood roared through her veins.

Purple! Her magic!

Wynona focused on the sensation. She felt as if she might melt and a bead of sweat ran down the side of her face, hitting the tile floor.

"What?" Mardella bent down. "Are you...sweating? It's not hot in here."

Wynona could see the witch, but she ignored her, instead keeping her focus inside. She needed to build this feeling. She needed it to break her free from whatever spell Mardella had cast.

A gasp caught her attention and Mardella fell on her backside. "Your eyes," she whispered, putting a hand over her lips.

I'm coming! Violet shouted, rushing over.

Mardella paid the mouse no attention.

Don't blow, Wynona! I'm almost there.

NO! Wynona screamed back and her mouse came to a screeching halt. Even in her mind, Wynona's voice was panting. *I need it to...* Stronger, stronger, her heart raced and her shirt was soaked. She couldn't breathe fast enough to keep up. But she didn't want Violet to help her control the blast. Wynona needed it to break free. She knew that if Violet held her back, it wouldn't be enough.

You're going to kill yourself! Violet cried in anguish. The usual snark in her tone was nowhere to be found. Fear and worry coated each word that came through their bond.

I need to save him, Wynona called back. Rascal had been suffocating too long. Even a supernatural eventually gave in. The lava in her core built until she felt as if the very skin was melting off her bones. Her eyes no longer saw clearly, purple shades coated everything within view as objects blurred together until she thought she was losing her mind.

Mardella scrambled to her feet, making enough noise to wake the dead. "I'll just have to do this the old fashioned way," she said hoarsely.

The words barely registered in Wynona's frantic mind, but once the meaning hit, it was the exact motivation she needed to end it all.

For a split second, the world went silent right before Wynona lost it.

She understood the phrase "calm before the storm" as she never had before. Complete and utter destruction burst from her body in a great purple wave. Wynona's body came back to life, but not in time to stop from hitting face first on the tile. Her body hit so hard, her breath was gone and it felt as if a great weight was sitting on her back.

Moans and groans filled the air around her, but Wynona didn't have the strength to move in order to save herself or her friends. She heard stomping boots, followed by curses and shouts.

"She was cursed! How could she do that?"

"Shut up!" a masculine voice sounded.

"Get off me! Why won't my magic work? Don't touch me!" the woman screamed again.

Wynona?

A soft voice infiltrated Wynona's mind. She wanted to answer it. It seemed so worried. But how could she comfort the voice when she was dying herself? Her eyelids fluttered closed, though Wynona hadn't realized they were open.

"You have the right to remain silent..." The masculine voice disappeared, growing too faint to capture her attention.

Something twitched inside of Wynona. She was barely holding onto consciousness, but couldn't interact with anything around her. There was something she needed to do...to check...a person...someone who was hurt...

Wynona! Answer me!

Tiny paws tapped her cheek, but Wynona couldn't speak. The paws were comforting, though they were hitting a little hard, as if trying to get a reaction. Something wet slid down her chin, the tile was cold against her cheek and her lungs began to burn from lack of air. She tried to tell her body to move. To check her injuries. To see what exactly had happened, but nothing responded. She was frozen in time, a feeling she was positive she had felt before.

But when...?

Darkness beckoned in her mind. There was something there...waiting in the shadows... It felt so peaceful...so quiet compared to the shouts going on around her. The floor bounced and rumbled, the sounds almost overpowering the weight still sitting on her chest. Great cries and orders bounced around the room and Wynona felt herself being touched and handled, though it wasn't enough to pull her back to the present. The darkness was so inviting. The voices were giving her a headache and she was overwhelmingly tired. Surely sleeping would rid her of the panic and pain surging through her system at the moment.

Don't you dare! That small voice cried again. *Turn around right now, Wynona! Come back!*

"She's flatlining!" a voice cried.

Wynona felt the voice begin to slip away as she grew closer and closer to the shadows. Yes...this was much nicer... The shadows would soothe and she wouldn't have any more pain. A low sound caught her attention, stopping Wynona just before she took the first step into the dark.

She turned, wincing at the movement. Her body was being jostled and people were still screaming, but there was something there...something she needed to hear.

The sound grew and she finally recognized it as a growl. Wynona frowned. Why was someone growling at her? Who would be growling?

"Wy," a harsh, masculine voice rasped. "Wy, come back to me, sweetheart."

Wynona glanced at the dark, so sweet and inviting, then turned back again. There was something about that voice...

Something touched her hand and a jolt went up her arm. She jumped and looked down at her fingers. In her mental state, they looked perfectly whole, but something had happened. Something that outweighed the pain her physical presence was experiencing.

The touch went to her cheek, down her neck and along the collar of her shirt. Electricity followed, building in momentum and strength. The touch stopped on her sternum, staying there while the jolting sensation built up under the spot.

In her mind's eye, Wynona covered her eyes as a blinding light landed in front of her.

"Wy...I love..." the gravelly voice cooed, "...soulmate..."

The light burst and Wynona felt her mental presence sucked into the blast like an object too close to a vacuum. She gasped and her lungs moved for the first time in several minutes. The sounds and destruction around her came rushing back into her ears, splitting her head with the weight of it, but her chest was free. Her lungs pushed air in and out and she registered a warm brush of air across her cheek.

"I love you," the voice whispered. "Thank you for coming back."

The past hour came rushing back to Wynona, bringing her headache to nearly unmanageable levels. Her fingers twitched and she sent commands to her jaw and lips. "Rascal?" she asked. Her voice was raspy and hoarse. It felt unused and dry, as if she had been ill for weeks, rather than a few moments.

"I'm here." His voice also sounded off, and Wynona realized it had been from the strangling.

She forced her eyes open, groaning when the light hit them. "She tried to kill you," Wynona said, her voice barely audible even to her own ears. Her shaking fingers went to his neck, but there were no marks to indicate the strangling.

Rascal sighed at her touch, his wolf whimpering. "She tried to kill us all." He touched her chin. "That's going to need stitches."

The sting on her chin flared to life at the reminder. "I'm..." She squeezed her eyes shut. "I'm struggling to put it all together."

Rascal shook his head. "Don't," he advised. "You just let them take you to the hospital and when everything's calmed down, we'll talk it out. Okay?"

"But you?" Wynona had a flare of panic. She didn't want him out of her sight.

Rascal reached into his pocket and pulled Violet up. "Don't worry. We're right behind you." He tapped his neck. "And I'll be fine in a couple minutes." He winked. "Shifter healing is a gift."

Wynona allowed herself to relax, then looked at Violet. "I heard you..."

Violet sniffed, but it lacked its usual superiority. *Well, you sure didn't listen.*

"Excuse me, Deputy Chief," a medical worker interrupted their chat. "Now that you got her back, we need to finish taking care of her injuries."

Rascal nodded and climbed to his feet, towering over Wynona, who was still laying on the floor. "I'll follow."

The worker nodded at the officer, then at someone Wynona couldn't see. Finally, he turned his bright blue eyes in her direction. "Hang tight, Ms. Le Doux. We'll get you taken care of in no time."

Wynona tried to respond, but fatigue was quickly taking over and instead, she allowed her eyes to close again. Whatever she was lying on was lifted and moved. A wheel squeaked and she felt the sunshine caress her face before being shut in a vehicle. The engine roared and a siren screamed just as she gave herself over to a healing sleep.

CHAPTER 31

Wynona had no idea how long had passed before she opened her eyes again. Bright lights shone over her head, but when she turned away from their harshness, she was hit by sunshine instead.

She moaned and squeezed her eyes shut. Her head couldn't quite handle the piercing pain in her head. Her entire body ached, which should have alarmed her, but it was the fact that she couldn't remember what had happened that had her heart pounding an erratic pattern.

"Wy?"

Wynona's eyes popped back open. "Rascal?" she croaked, then coughed. Her throat was so dry.

"Hold on."

She turned her head, to see the back of his police uniform as he fumbled at a table before turning back to her with a cup. "Can I help you sit up?" he asked softly.

Wynona nodded, never taking her eyes off his face. She had thought she'd lost him. When she'd been frozen and could only hear his choking, she had been sure that he would die before anyone saved them. That hearth witch had caught them all off guard, though Wynona's memory was a little fuzzy as to how it all ended.

She remembered Rascal's red face, she remembered her vision going purple, she remembered Violet screaming and she remembered something about being killed the old fashioned way.

How the pieces all flowed and how it all ended was beyond her.

Rascal smiled softly and chuckled as Wynona continued to stare. She knew she should feel embarrassed by her teenage-like reaction, but she couldn't look away. Something had...changed...between them. She didn't quite know what it was, but it was there. She could *feel* him. His amusement that she was staring. His protective streak about her safety and the despair floating directly behind it that he had failed to keep her safe. His concern for the future, mixed with a little helping of hope.

But most importantly, she felt his love.

He loved everything about her. Her dark hair, her pale skin, her nearly black eyes. He loved her tenacity and curiosity and how she fought so hard to be the opposite of her selfish family. He loved that she befriended those who needed it most and that she was determined to do the right things no matter what it cost her.

The feeling had her breathless and her head swimming and yet, she still couldn't look away.

Rascal's smile grew and he set the cup aside, which she hadn't even realized she had emptied. His calloused fingers caressed the edge of her face. "You feel it, don't you?"

Wynona nodded, then winced. The movement brought the headache back to the front. "What is it?" she asked through the pain. She closed her eyes as his fingers continued their ministrations. They felt so good against her skin. The tiny pulses of electricity seemed to calm the pain and her entire body relaxed.

"The soulmate bond," he said softly.

Her eyes popped back open. "What?" Her mouth gaped open, but she snapped it shut. She could feel his sincerity. He was telling her the truth. "Why?" She didn't even know how to finish the question. He had told her they were soulmates, but she hadn't been quite positive he was right. She loved him. That was easy enough, but love didn't constitute the power of soulmates and they'd never been able to have the conversation about how Rascal was so sure.

Or how Mrs. Grumpy Faced Reyna knew, Violet interrupted.

Wynona gasped and glanced around. "Where are you?" she whispered.

Violet's nose peeked out of Rascal's pocket. It was the mouse's second favorite spot to linger.

Rascal pulled her out and carefully set her on Wynona's lap. "Mama Reyna wasn't always so grumpy," he said carefully. He tilted his head to the side. "Something's definitely going on with her."

Violet huffed, then turned up to look at Wynona. Her tiny face seemed to soften. *Are you alright? You had me worried.*

Wynona pet her familiar comfortingly. "Sore," she said. "But okay." She rubbed her forehead. "I'm actually not quite sure what all happened. I only remember bits and pieces." She shot a look at Rascal. "And it sounds like there were a few big events."

Violet rolled her eyes. *You could say that.*

"Before we get into all that," Rascal interrupted, "I need to let the chief know you're awake." He squeezed Wynona's hand. "Then we'll go through the story all together."

Wynona frowned. "You seem to be understanding Violet better. You told me before you couldn't always hear her."

The tip of Rascal's ears turned red, a sure sign he was slightly embarrassed. "Another soulmate perk," he murmured. He watched her closely and it occurred to Wynona he was watching for how much she could handle. He didn't want to overwhelm her.

Before she could ask more questions, a healer bustled in through the hospital door. "Hello, dearie," the elderly woman said. She wore long white robes and her hair pulled into a tight bun on top of her head. Despite her hair color, her skin was wrinkle free, announcing to everyone that magic was at play. She smiled and waited until Rascal had backed up before waving her hand over Wynona's body. "You've still got a ways to go before your stores are replenished, but it appears that you're well on your way."

Wynona blinked. "My stores?"

The healer smiled. "Your magic. You nearly killed yourself, expending as much as you did."

Wynona's eyes widened. There was no way to deny it as the heat and explosion from the confrontation played back through her mind. She could feel the temperature that had nearly burned her alive as it ate its way through Mardella's spell. The hearth witch had been surprisingly strong, for someone who spent most of her magic in the kitchen.

The healer chuckled, then turned to Rascal. "If you can promise to keep your mate quiet and keep her plied with food and regular naps, I'm pretty sure we can send her home. It's mostly time at this point."

Rascal nodded. "Consider it done."

The woman smiled again, patting Wynona's hand. "Let me finish the paperwork. I'm sure you'll sleep much better in your own bed."

Wynona nodded, still dumbfounded. Once the woman was gone, she turned to Rascal. "Should we have asked her not to tell anyone about the magic?" she whispered.

Rascal bit his lips between his teeth. "I don't think that'll help at this point."

Wynona groaned and pushed a hand through her hair. "That doesn't sound good."

"Let's just say, Chief Ligurio will have lots to say and not all of it about the case," Rascal muttered.

Wynona's head hung. She wasn't ready for all this. A warm, electric hand slid into hers, pulling it away from her face.

"Shhh..." Rascal crooned. He kissed her fingers and kept them sandwiched between his own. "We'll work this out." His eyes flashed. "Together."

Wynona could feel his determination, even the hint of worry that sat in the back. He was trying to hide it, but Wynona realized there really wasn't anything he could hide from her. If she wanted to know, all she had to do was look.

She jolted. "You can feel me too, can't you?" she asked hoarsely, as the truth hit her.

Rascal nodded, his lips twitching.

"How long?"

His amusement faded. "Before you," he finally responded.

Wynona sighed. "This is going to take some getting used to."

He squeezed her hand, kissing it again. "I know. But in the end, it'll be worth it. I promise."

Wynona nodded and leaned back in the bed. She was exhausted again. This talk had been emotionally taxing and she was feeling it. The healer was right. She was drained. She jerked upright as another thought hit her. "Is the soulmate thing why you've been so..." She cut off. How did she ask this nicely, without hurting his feelings? She needed to know, but didn't want to start them off on the wrong foot.

"On edge?" Rascal filled in for her, amusement twinkling in his golden eyes. "Grumpy? Possessive? Temperamental?"

Wynona winced but nodded. "Yeah."

He blew out a breath and pushed a hand through his hair. "Yeah." His boyish face was adorable. "Most soulmates, especially among wolves, know right away and finish the bond quickly."

Wynona sucked in a quiet gasp. "But we didn't," she whispered. "You waited, so I could have time to adjust."

Rascal nodded. "And my wolf was getting...antsy, is probably the right word. He was getting harder to control." His ears turned pink. "I'm sorry if I scared you."

Wynona shook her head and lay back in the pillows. "It's all forgotten. I just needed to understand."

He nodded. "Sleep," Rascal whispered. "I'll take care of the paperwork."

Wynona closed her eyes, trusting the wolf to take care of her. With her new abilities to feel him, she knew without a doubt that nothing would ever get to her without first going through Rascal ever again.

Several hours later, Wynona was just running a brush through her hair when there was a knock on her front door. Rascal had gotten her home and she had managed a long, luxurious shower before they had told her friends and the station that they could come over.

"Got it!" Rascal hollered.

Wynona mentally thanked him and finished getting ready before walking out to the front room.

"Nona!" Prim had already arrived and had brought offerings since the whole gathering area was full of flowers. The currently human-sized fairy rushed over to hug Wynona.

"They're beautiful," Wynona whispered in her friend's ear. "Thank you."

"They've been imbued with healing powers," Prim said, her voice thick with emotion. She pulled back just enough to look in Wynona's face. "Though they have their own powers as well." She pointedly looked at a vase. "Lavender, roses and calendula all aid with healing." She squeezed Wynona's hands. "The sage and ginseng are for energy."

Wynona pulled her best friend into another hug. "I feel better already."

Prim laughed and pulled back, walking them both to the couch. "I think that has more to do with your mate than anything else."

"You know too?" Wynona gasped. "How?"

Prim folded her arms and looked smug. "Everyone can feel it now."

"Feel it?" Wynona looked back and forth between Prim and Rascal, who was standing in the doorway with several officers behind him. "I..." She snapped her mouth shut. She wasn't sure she wanted to talk about it with a huge audience.

Rascal shook his head. "It's alright. It's not a secret anymore." He gave her a hopeful smile. "There's an energy between us. Any supernatural should be able to feel it." He rubbed the back of his neck. "It formed when you completed your side of the bond."

Chief Ligurio walked the rest of the way in and took a chair across from Wynona. Daemon slapped Rascal on the back, his grin wide. "Congrats," he said to his superior, then nodded the same to Wynona. The black hole glanced at Prim, then looked at the ground, his cheeks growing slightly pink.

Prim sniffed next to Wynona, but Wynona was too tired to worry about whatever was going on there. As far as she knew, the two barely knew each other. But maybe she had missed something.

"Thanks," Wynona said softly in response to Daemon's greeting. Would the hits ever stop coming? She had read so many books during her growing up and yet somehow, she had missed all of these things. Either her parents' library simply didn't have anything on the subject of soulmates, or nothing had been written about it. At least nothing quite as extensive as she needed.

Rascal walked to her side and sat on the arm of the couch. "I know it's a lot," he said softly. "But we'll get through it."

"Together," she finished for him, smiling gratefully. She had a feeling that word would encompass a lot of her future. Truthfully, she didn't mind. She had already found herself craving more of his company and this simply fast forwarded the inevitable. She turned back to the rest of the officers. "I'm afraid my memory is a bit fuzzy," she said to Chief Ligurio. "Can we go over what happened at the house?"

He steepled his long, thin fingers together and stared at her. "Tell me what you remember."

Wynona swallowed hard. Rascal had hinted that the chief knew she had her magic back, but she hadn't spoken about it in the open yet and it was hard to break that habit now. "We couldn't find anything in the house," she forced out. "I thought the kitchen or the bedroom would be the most obvious places, but nothing seemed out of the ordinary." She cleared her throat and Rascal darted away. "We finally opened the door to the garage and although it looked normal, we could all smell the herbs and cats and Daemon could see there was a large amount of magic in the space."

Rascal handed her a glass of water.

"Thank you," she said gratefully, taking a long sip.

"After that?" Chief Ligurio tilted his head sideways. "Do you remember anything?"

"I remember Mardella coming up behind us." Wynona's voice shook and she set the glass on her lap. "When I turned around, Rascal was choking." She took in a shuddering breath, still remembering the look on his face as he was struggling for air. "I tried to go help, but Mardella froze me." Another sip of water helped her keep going. "I couldn't hear anything from Daemon, so I assumed she had caught him off guard as well." Wynona closed her eyes, welcoming Rascal's hand on her neck. His touch centered her and calmed her racing heart. "Mardella stepped up to me, admitted to the murder, then bragged about how she was going to get away with it. I sent Violet to help Rascal, knowing that he couldn't last much longer. I could still breathe, I just couldn't move. But while Mardella was talking, I noticed that my body was heating up. My vision went purple." She looked to the chief. "It's what happens when my magic surges."

He nodded, no emotion showing.

"I realized that even though I was frozen, I could access my magic." She could feel her cheeks heat up at her next admission. "I'm not very good with my magic yet, since it's new to me, so I wasn't able to break her spell right away. I wasn't sure how to do it at all, but I kept feeding the feeling and eventually I..." She winced. "When Mardella saw that I was building magic, it must have scared her because she said she was going to kill us the old fashioned way and gathered a knife. At that point, I kind of exploded, I think."

Chief Ligurio snorted.

Daemon covered a laugh with a cough and tried to bring a stoic look back to his face, but he was failing miserably.

She looked up at Rascal. "How bad was it?" she asked.

Rascal was solemn as he responded. "All of Hex Haven felt the impact."

"What?" she breathed.

He squeezed her shoulder. "It was as if an earthquake hit the area, but it was magical."

"But no one could tell it was me, could they?" she asked, afraid of the answer.

Rascal's eyes softened. "The masses? No. But your family? Or anyone who has been around you for a decent amount of time?" He nodded. "They'll know."

"My parents know." The words left Wynona's lips, but it didn't quite sink in. "And they haven't come after me yet?" She shivered. That worried her almost more than if they'd made a move.

"They won't come from the front," Chief Ligurio said. His voice was still firm, but it held a touch of sympathy. Having dated Wynona's sister, he obviously knew exactly what her family was capable of. "They'll wait until no one is watching and your guard is down." He narrowed his gaze. "I recommend you get control of it and you get control of it now." He relaxed his glare. "It will be the only weapon you have."

Wynona leaned into Rascal's side and rubbed her forehead. "How did my life get so complicated?" She looked back to the chief. "Mardella. What happened?"

Chief Ligurio straightened. "She's in custody. Her garage held a glamor to hide her activities. Her lab was full of herbs and her feline familiars." He shrugged. "Vampires can't sense magic, so Haar had no idea what was going on." He shook his head. "Poor idiot."

"We have a witch on the force who pulled it down," Rascal inserted. "All the evidence we would ever need was right there. The Valerian root and many other herbs that were being used to manipulate the people around her. The seventeen cats were used to aid in the spells before creating her baked goods." He scrunched his nose. "I'm glad I don't frequent that place. Who knows if there was any cat hair in the cookies."

Chief Ligurio gave his second officer a look. "She's confessed to the murder, admitted that although she wanted Haar, she mostly wanted away from Alavara's demanding attitude." Chief Ligurio raised an eyebrow. "You were right that they were...what was the word? Frenemies?" One side of his mouth pulled up. "They worked together in the shadows, but secretly hated each other. Haar's cheating simply gave Ms. Soulton the excuse she needed to rid herself of the chains once and for all."

"And the apron?" Wynona asked. "Why did she steal it?"

"There were traces of the herbs in the pockets," Rascal said. He made a face. "Apparently, our investigative team hadn't bothered to swab them, so we didn't know it, but Ms. Soulton couldn't take the chance."

Chief Ligurio stood up. "All in all, your instincts were right on, Ms. Le Doux, which you have proven time and time again." He nodded to her. "Thank you for your help. Your paycheck will be processed and sent through the mail."

Wynona grinned. She was going to frame that dollar bill.

The vampire paused at the threshold. "This case was messy, but you handled it well and put together pieces we didn't see." His eyes darted to Rascal, then back to her. "But we will be discussing your new...abilities...before I ever think about hiring you again. Oh, and we figured out the spell with Mr. Alefoot."

Wynona waited.

"Ms. Theramin used the witch's goods to keep him under control. His instinct to eat cake came from the need to keep him plied with the magical herbs."

Wynona shook her head. "The poor man. I wonder why she chose him, of all people."

Rascal shrugged. "He fit the bill size-wise and was easy to control under the spell. Why not him?"

Wynona sighed.

"Very soon, Ms. Le Doux, we need to have another talk," Chief Ligurio said, his tone unusually soft. "I believe another story time is in order, but this time, I won't be the one speaking."

Wynona hesitated only slightly before nodding. She owed it to the vampire to tell him everything. Despite being grumpy and difficult, he had supported her and listened to her when others didn't. She owed him that much.

Without another word, Chief Ligurio disappeared. When the front door closed, the whole room seemed to sigh in relief. He was a good vampire, but definitely intense.

"Finally," Prim muttered. "Now we can actually talk."

"I need tea," Wynona immediately stated, standing up.

"Any chance you have a few leftover pastries?" Daemon called out, settling himself further into his recliner.

"The shop's been closed," Wynona reminded him. She smiled when the black hole grumbled under his breath.

Rascal stepped up to her side and helped her get water on to boil and get down the loose tinctures she kept in the cupboard.

"Where's Violet?" Wynona realized her familiar had been absent during their little chat with the police.

"Napping." Rascal got out a tray. "She said to leave her alone for the next couple of days."

Wynona grinned just as someone knocked. She paused. "Who now?" She closed her eyes. "Please don't let it be a reporter."

Rascal frowned. "We dealt with Mr. Hesa while you were sleeping." He wiped his hands on his pants. "I got it." He disappeared to the front door. "Mama Reyna. What are you doing here?"

Wynona froze. What was the old wolf shifter doing here? And how did she even know where Wynona lived?

"It's time."

The two words should have been simple enough, but they sent a punch through Wynona's system. She only hoped she would still be breathing when she got to the other side.

CHAPTER 32

Wynona's hands were shaking and her tea was dangerously close to sloshing over the edge, but she forced herself to take a sip. She desperately needed its healing powers at the moment. The chamomile was smooth on her throat, but nothing was going to stop the racing of her heart.

Mrs. Reyna sat across from her, looking as grumpy as ever, but the surprise guest was Lusgu, who had followed her inside.

As far as Wynona knew, the brownie had never left the tea shop since the day he'd been hired. While Mrs. Reyna was glaring at Wynona, Lusgu was giving the same stink eye to Rascal. Daemon and Prim were sitting off to the side, two feet of space between them, while they looked back and forth between the other parties, unsure of what was going on.

Wynona set her tea down, doing her best to quell her nerves when the tea wasn't as helpful as she hoped. "You had something to share with me?" she asked Mrs. Reyna.

The wolf's eyes darted over Wynona's shoulder before coming back. "Your case is over."

It was a statement, not a question, but Wynona nodded anyway. "We caught the murderer, yes."

"And the whole town now knows of your powers."

This time it felt like an accusation.

Wynona shrugged. "That's what I've heard. But it was necessary in order to save Rascal and Daemon." She shouldn't have defended herself, but it was a natural reaction when feeling like someone was disappointed in them.

Again, Mrs. Reyna looked over Wynona's shoulder.

Wynona frowned and turned to follow the gaze. She saw nothing. "Mrs. Reyna," Wynona said, pulling the woman's attention back. "You said my grandmother wished you to share a message?" She raised her eyebrows. "Now that the case is over, why don't we get this settled?"

Mrs. Reyna sighed, looking weary and aged for the first time since Wynona had met her. "Don't you think this would be better coming from you?" she said tartly.

Wynona jerked back. "What?" The back of her neck began to tingle and Wynona automatically turned on her magic vision. Turning, she saw a purple blob. Wynona stiffened. "Mr. Hesa?" she asked, calling out the only ghost she personally knew.

The ghost drew closer and a soft touch ran down Wynona's cheek.

Tears filled Wynona purple eyes. "Granny?" she said hoarsely. Slowly, the purple shape disappeared from view and Wynona turned off her magic.

"Hello, sweet pea," Granny Saffron said with a smile. Her body was transparent around the edges, but Wynona knew from her time with the ghost reporter that if she reached out, she would touch the woman responsible for her raising, her education and her whole purpose in life.

Wynona stood on shaky legs, ignoring Prim's gasp, and lunged forward, wrapping the tiny older woman in a hug. "I can't believe it's you," she whispered through her tears.

"I know," Granny said, patting Wynona's back the same way she had when Wynona was a little girl. Apparently, even in death, her grandmother hadn't changed.

Wynona pulled back and wiped at her face. "Why are you still here?" she asked. "I thought only beings with unfinished business were allowed to stay."

"That's fairly close," Granny responded. "But there's a little more to it than that." She sighed. "To answer your question, however, I'm here because of you."

"You stayed for me?" Wynona shook her head. "Why?" A heated presence behind her had Wynona leaning back, soaking up the support Rascal was offering. His calm demeanor helped her breathe easier, but she could feel his concern as well. He was worried this next revelation would start them on a path she wasn't ready for.

She didn't disagree with him. This wasn't just a family reunion. Granny wasn't the type to stay on this plane for something that trite.

"Because you need help with your powers, now that the curse is fully gone," Granny said simply. She spread her hands to the side. "Violet is helpful, but you need true guidance, or your family will take you back and it'll all have been for naught."

Wynona shook her head. "How do you know the curse is fully gone?" An awful suspicion began to build in the back of her mind. Hadn't she just learned that curses faded when the cursor died? The stronger the curse, the longer it took to fade?

"Because it broke completely with your little show at that kitchen witch's house," Granny said, peering down her nose and raising her eyebrows.

Nausea began to churn in Wynona's stomach and Rascal wrapped his arms around her. "But how do you *know?*" she pressed.

Her mind spun with all the knowledge she had gained on the subject. Mrs. Reyna and Lusgu both knew Granny. They'd both shown up in her life after she'd gained her freedom. Mrs. Reyna had tested Wynona several times on her ability with teas and muttered about things to come.

Lusgu had twice stopped Wynona's emerging magic with a simple Latin word of his own. He lived at the tea shop and had built a portal into the corner, coming and going as he pleased, showing that he had great magical strength and was able to keep Wynona's abilities under control.

Pieces began falling in place, just like when Wynona helped solve one of the police's cases. Little things she didn't see the first time around, but now recognized as significant.

Lusgu not wanting her close to Rascal, whose soulmate status had helped her magic emerge.

Granny teaching Wynona everything she needed to know to survive without magic, yet now Wynona realized that doing that work was actually utilizing magic after all.

The investigation during her young years that never found the culprit of her curse.

Violet's coloring after Celia had tried to kill the rodent and Wynona had panicked.

So many little things, so many memories that had seemed random but now added up to a horrible truth.

Purple.

Her magic was purple. The color of royalty. She hadn't thought about it until now. Daemon said each color signature was unique and declared the strengths or weaknesses of the caster.

"How?" The word slipped out like a plea, but Wynona wasn't ready for the answer.

Granny sighed, looking resigned. "Because I'm the one who cursed you."

Don't Miss Wynona's Next Adventure!
"Murder in the Tea Leaves"

Hurt.

Shocked.

Betrayed...

Wynona finally knows who cursed her, but she wasn't prepared to handle the weight of the knowledge and now her fragile world seems to be unraveling at the seams.

As if that wasn't enough, her family is lurking in the shadows, looking for a way to add her powers to the family coffers. But Wynona is desperate to hold onto the life she's created, and refuses to go quietly, even as the police need her help to solve yet another murder.

With her faithful wolf at her side and Violet muttering snarky comments in her ear, Wynona will have to pull out all the stops if she's going to prove once and for all that she isn't the weak little girl her family raised.

Look for it at your favorite retailer!

CPSIA information can be obtained
at www.ICGtesting.com
Printed in the USA
LVHW080746191122
733589LV00031B/1494